THE SPRING HABIT

DAVID HANSON

ad lib
BOOKS LLC
www.adlibbooks.com

Published by:

ad lib
BOOKS LLC

Ad Lib Books, LLC
217 E. Foxwood Dr.
Raymore, MO 64083
www.adlibbooks.com

ISBN:0-9752976-0-0

Library of Congress Control Number: 2004103892

Books published by Ad Lib Books are available at special quantity discounts for sales promotions, premiums or fund raising. For information, please call or write:
Special Markets Department, Ad Lib Books, LLC, 217 E. Foxwood Dr., Raymore, MO 64083; 816-331-6160

Printed in the United States of America

Prologue

"Sister Mary Bernadette! How many times have I asked you not to wear cleats in the sanctuary?" Father Michael's voice was both kind and firm — very firm — as he slowly rose from the back pew of St. Francis Catholic Church in tiny Wanuga, Nebraska. He was seventy nine, too old really to be a parish priest, but too stubborn to give into retirement.

"I'm sorry, Father Michael," Sister Mary Bernadette answered as she stopped in the middle of the sanctuary. She was a small woman with mousy hair and brilliant blue eyes. At that moment, she wore a tattered baseball uniform, worn black cleats, a nun's habit and an old beat up mitt.

"The place is falling apart as it is. There is no sense tearing up the floors when we have no money to repair them," Father Michael complained out loud.

"I'm sorry, Father, I really am," Sister Mary Bernadette said and bobbed impatiently. "I have to go. I'm late for the game."

Father Michael groaned, "The baseball game, you mean."

Sister Mary Bernadette nodded. "It is Thursday."

"Sister Mary, it's February! It's too cold to play baseball."

Sister Mary smiled back at the old man. "Father Michael, it's never too cold for baseball."

"Baseball, bah!" Father Michael proclaimed. "What you should be doing is staying here and praying with me."

"Maybe if you told me what you were praying for today, I could pray later," Sister Mary answered hopefully.

"I'm praying that we can find the funds to fix St. Francis, or I'm afraid we'll have to close its doors. Is that important enough to delay..."

The screech of tires echoed from outside. Seconds later, a stereo blared out "Turn the Beat Around."

Father Michael jerked his head around and asked, "Now what is that?"

"That," Sister Mary answered with a slight hint of a menace, "is the new guy." With that, she bounded toward the back door.

Outside, Sister Mary pulled a seed corn cap over her short hair and jogged out across the gravel road to Wanuga's dirt ball field. The day was crisp and there was just enough of the morning frost left to shimmer in the early afternoon sunlight. Those sparkles, under just the right light, always made the young woman believe that magic was still a part of this world, even if most people in 1994 didn't believe in magic anymore.

The music ended abruptly as Sister Mary reached the field. She stopped at the third base line. Her father had always told her to only take the field when she was ready. She took a deep breath and marched up to the pitcher's mound.

"How many warm-ups you want?" Gabe Meyers, a local farmer called from his first base position.

"I'm ready," Sister Mary called back, nodding to the rest of the locals who made up her team. "Where's the new guy?"

Gabe didn't answer. He pointed to behind the home dugout. There was the new player.

Matt Danzig was an eighteen-year-old phenom who routinely took high school fastballs for four hundred foot rides into the glorious histories of all the ball fields in Western Nebraska. At six foot three and two hundred and fifteen pounds, he was being aggressively courted by major league scouts. He was a mighty slugger who had met all the challenges Nebraska could offer a baseball player, except for finding out for himself whether the stories old men in bars told about an unhittable pitch were true.

Danzig approached home plate. He knocked the dirt from his cleats with the massive piece of timber he called his bat. He looked up and saw Sister Mary waiting on top of the pitcher's mound. This was probably just a big waste of time. The pitcher was all of five-five maybe, and not one hundred and twenty pounds soaking wet.

As Danzig settled into the box, he glared out at the woman. He thought he might put a little fear of God into her. His glare, however, was met with the stare of deep blue, extremely focused eyes. What he saw was Sister Mary bent forward and waiting for a sign from the catcher. She nodded her head and began her windup.

Danzig immediately noticed that she had no high leg kick, no flailing right arm. The movement was compact and quick. The ball trekked across the infield and headed for home. Not two feet after being thrown, the ball began to dance, and Danzig started to sweat.

The stories of the pitch's movement were no longer tall tales. They were a hard cold fact that now looped toward the plate. Over and over, he told himself to wait, but the pitch lured the idea of crushing it into his consciousness. The ball hung fat in mid-air just off the plate.

Danzig couldn't take it any longer. He stepped with a big left foot and launched his bat through the strike zone. The ball, at that moment, dove outside. Danzig's mighty swing connected. However, all it did was launch the longest foul ball any of the players had ever seen.

It carried the road as it arched toward St. Francis. As the other players gasped, the ball crashed through the top red plate of a stained glass window. Sister Mary sprinted off the mound and ran for the church.

Gabe Meyers strolled up to Danzig. "You didn't think it was going be like that, did you?"

"That was amazing." Danzig took a deep breath, in no hurry to see that pitch again. "I've never seen a woman throw like that. Why isn't she pitching somewhere?"

The first baseman turned and pointed at St. Francis Church, as the pitcher disappeared inside the door.

Sister Mary ran up the sanctuary aisle toward Father Michael, who knelt in the first pew. He had been praying, but now he held the baseball and studied it.

"Are you all right?" Sister Mary asked timidly.

"I'm fine." Father Michael stood and turned to face the broken window.

"I know that this building is crumbling and will probably fall apart. I can't tell you how sorry I am. I'll say a million prayers. It was just a freak play," Sister Mary said.

"It was a miracle. I've been praying for an answer to our

financial problems. Then God answered."

"Really, what did he say?" She smiled at the old Priest.

"He said you were right, Sister Mary Bernadette, February is a good time for baseball."

Chapter 1

"And that's where it came through the window." Father Michael strained a bony finger toward the hole in the stained glass at the front of the sanctuary. Father Michael turned and put a gnarled old hand on the shoulder of Moss Thompson who stood nearby.

"That's quite a story," Moss answered. He shifted his feet nervously. Moss had never felt comfortable in church.

"And of course, it being a baseball, I thought of you, Peter."

Father Michael and Moss's parents were the only people who still called the most famous son of Wanuga by his given name. In Moss's youth, Boy Scout Billy Meyer noticed that he always stood to the North of Mike Dade, his best friend. Since moss grows on the north side of trees, a nickname was born.

The old priest produced the ball and handed it to Moss. He took it and felt the smooth leather with his fingertips. Father Michael's emergency call was now starting to make a little bit of sense. Moss's life was baseball, and baseball had blessed Moss well.

Moss had left Wanuga to pursue a pro baseball career at seventeen. He'd had a big fastball and rose quickly through the minors to the major leagues. In his second season, he'd made his one and only World Series appearance.

He'd pitched twice, game three and game seven. Moss had his greatest performance in that final and decisive game. He'd struck out ten and allowed only one unearned run through eight and two-thirds. After walking a man, Moss had been pulled. It was said you could hear the groans of disappointment from all of Wanuga all the way to Omaha. The local residents all swear that Moss would've gotten that last out. He should've won game seven, but it wasn't meant to be. A reliever named Wally had thrown a fastball right down the middle of the plate and saw it knocked over the farthest fence in centerfield. The lost game seven haunted Moss because he'd missed his only chance at conquering baseball's greatest prize. At least when he came home, he heard how some people still believed he would have won it. It only partly helped.

When his playing career came to an end, Moss fell into a depression. Pitching had defined his life. He was lost. It was Father Michael who suggested coaching and made a call to an old friend to get the ball rolling. The journey kept him in baseball and eventually made him the manager of the Washington Memorials.

Moss finished third in the balloting for major league baseball's manager of the year last year. He'd have won it, if not for the late season slide that cost his team the playoffs. While the sting still hurt, Moss was ready for the upcoming season. He, and the rest of the world, knew that lack of pitching depth had killed the team last year. In fact, Moss believed that the Memorials were one starting pitcher away from being unstoppable this year. Moss felt that he'd find that arm. After all, he was on a lucky streak.

He'd won $500 at a Las Vegas Black Jack table the night before Father Michael's message found him at two thirty in the morning. While the message was short, it was detailed enough for Moss to call the airlines right then and change his flight. According to the old priest, St. Francis needed its favorite and most famous son. Moss was on the five a.m. flight the next morning. By the next afternoon, Moss stood in the tiny church next to the ancient priest and looked up at a cracked stained glass window.

"So you said you had something to show me? Is the window it?" Moss asked.

"No," Father Michael said. "I asked you here to show you a miracle."

"All right, where is it?" Moss sighed more than asked.

Father Michael gently took Moss's arm and led the large man to the back church door. "She's right this way."

Moss Thompson did not have the opportunity to see a miracle every day. He wasn't even a regular in the pew on Sunday in his local parish church. In fact, his first instinct was to shrink from believing that God had reached down and altered the universe on a divine scale right here in this tiny town on the open plains.

Moss knew that it was most likely an errant foul ball from the baseball field across the street, and not a message from on high that Father Michael had caught while praying. He was well aware that people had made far more out of far less in certain religious circles, but he never figured Father Michael for one of those types. It was abundantly clear to Moss, though, that Father Michael really believed he was taking Moss to see a miracle.

As the two men reached the back door and started down the stairs to the basement, Moss's stomach began to tighten. It was the same feeling he'd had when he faced men on the corners with a good bunter up and less than two outs. The options would race through his mind. The outcomes would chase them around his stomach. He'd pop an antacid, make a sign and dream about which sportswriter would question the call if it didn't work.

Father Michael led Moss across the dark back room toward the boiler. Moss noticed the rusty, worn pipes dangling from the ceiling. They didn't look capable of carrying anything. They all needed repair. Moss knew he wouldn't leave without making a small donation to the building fund. That's when it hit him.

The pipe, that is. It was hung low. Moss was taller than Father Michael and hadn't quite made it under the rusty, moist junction of two pipes. He rubbed his head, silently cursing his decision to even visit. The pain cleared his mind. Moss knew instantly what was going on. Father Michael had dragged him down here to show him the problem, so that Moss would come to his aid. There was no miracle, except perhaps that the toilets still worked.

Father Michael reached a back door and waited for Moss to catch up. Moss rubbed his head, trying to figure out how he was going to tell Father Michael that managers don't make enough money to fix up churches.

"Are you ready?" Father Michael asked.

Moss nodded his head. He wished, however, that he was on his field in Florida working with the pitchers and the catchers.

Father Michael turned the knob and threw open the door. The room immediately filled with light, and Moss froze. The light grew in intensity, blinding both men momentarily. Moss instantly regretted every sinful thing he'd ever done, including those he'd enjoyed, fearing that he hadn't prepared to meet his maker. Then the light abruptly dimmed.

Moss rubbed his eyes to clear the spots. When he opened them
again, he saw Father Michael standing next to a slender young
woman with short brown hair, wearing greasy overalls and holding a
pipe wrench in one hand and a flashlight in the other.

"Peter Thompson," Father Michael began. "I'd like you to meet
our miracle."

"I—" Moss felt stupid and underwhelmed and not at all sure
what to say.

"Please forgive Father Michael," the young woman said. "He
tends to exaggerate."

"I do not!" Father Michael said in a tone only obstinate men
over seventy are allowed.

The woman stepped into the room. She looked to be late
twenties, with the rough skin of someone who spent a lot of time
outside. Moss noted both her quiet confidence and her deep, penetrating blue eyes.

"I'm Sister Mary Bernadette." She stuck out an oil-covered
hand, which Moss took and shook.

"Nice to meet you," Moss stammered.

"I've looked forward to meeting you. Although I must admit, I
am a little nervous. But don't worry. I'll get over it." Sister Mary
Bernadette realized she hadn't wiped her hand off before offering it
to Moss. She retracted it quickly, wiping it on the leg of her overalls.
She offered Moss a rag.

"Sorry about that."

"Don't worry about it," Moss mumbled between his teeth, as he
snapped the rag from the woman.

"I'm all packed, and I just finished here. Let me get cleaned up
and I'll meet you out front." The nun exited, before Moss fully heard
the sentence.

"All packed?" The manager asked.

"Well, that's the miracle." Father Michael smiled.

"The nun is the miracle?" Moss's voice rose in confusion and
impatience.

"Of course. She's going to go to spring training with you."

Moss grabbed his head. "Father, it's not that she isn't welcome,
but I have to concentrate on getting the team ready to play. I don't

have time to take care of a spectator."

Father Michael placed a knowing hand on Moss's shoulder. "Peter, she's not going as a spectator. She's going as a pitcher."

Chapter 2

Sister Mary Bernadette wanted to do about a million things as she stood in front of the small cupboard she called a closet in the corner of her room. She couldn't decide whether to scream for joy or breathe deeply for calm. Should she let someone else besides Father Michael know that she was leaving? Most of all, she wanted to take her time, which was impossible.

Her room was a tiny space on the second floor of the church residence. Her bed took up half the space. The rest was divided between a small desk, a chair and the cupboard closet. There was a large window, and she got plenty of sunshine, with a view overlooking the small ball field next door.

The room and its view often reminded her of college and a memory of a dream rarely thought of since graduation. She quickly packed her oversized bag to calm herself long enough to say a prayer of thanks for Father Michael.

Sister Mary had never doubted that Father Michael actually knew Moss Thompson. The local legend of small town boy made good was the spice of life in this tiny town of Wanuga. Moss stood with Bull Laskey, a pro football player of the '50s, as absent town treasures. The nun had figured her only sighting of the major league manager would be if someone decided to name a ball field after him.

She had nodded politely when Father Michael had first explained his "miracle" to her. She admitted only in her private moments that she doubted the priest. It wasn't that she didn't believe in signs. She just didn't want to get her hopes up. She couldn't fathom having baseball yanked from her life again.

The few clothes she had were neatly packed in the bag. That left one last item. A well-used mitt sat on the top shelf of the closet. She took it down slowly and gingerly. The light brown leather was nicked and scratched from hours of hard use. It was a gift from the Wanuga little league team she coached. A group of young boys who took it to heart when they learned there was no money at the church for their coach to buy a glove. They saved allowances, detasseled corn and rougued soybeans until they amassed enough to buy this old, used glove for Sister Mary.

It wasn't autographed by a star or former star, or made of the highest quality of leather. It wasn't even that expensive, but it meant the world to someone who believed in baseball like Sister Mary Bernadette did. She put the mitt in the bag. After a deep breath, she walked out the door of her little room and into the biggest dream she'd ever had.

Moss Thompson stood outside St. Francis with Father Michael trying to figure out what to say. Excuses had always been easy for Moss, a rare gift usually doled out to those who couldn't survive otherwise. He had standard, highly believable stories to explain why he was late to meetings, why he was late with the phone bill and why he had earned the bulge around his middle. This was something he could do well, but Moss was having trouble deciding how you explained to a seventy-something priest that nuns don't just walk out of the convent and onto a major league pitching mound.

"Father," Moss began, "you didn't tell me that you had a major league prospect for me to look at. If I'd have known, I would have brought a scout." Moss smiled at his idea. "You know, they're the ones who evaluate young talent for us."

The old man surveyed his church, planning the renovations soon to be paid for. "You are the manager, right? You decide who plays, right? Why on Earth would I go to anyone else?"

Moss kicked at the dust near his feet. "Look, Father Michael, I know I owe you an awful lot. When I was a kid, I couldn't have asked for a better priest, but—," Moss choked a bit.

"But?" Father Michael raised his eyebrow.

"The truth of the matter is that I just can't show up to spring training with a pitcher nobody's heard about and just put her on the team." Moss spoke quickly now. "It's just not done that way. There are the drafts and the minors and all sorts of things, not to mention that the owner has to sign her to a contract." Moss looked down. He couldn't bear to look Father Michael in the eyes. "That's just how baseball works."

"It's because she's a woman, isn't it?" Father Michael's voice trembled again.

Moss took his cap off and rubbed the top of his head. "Well d—, sh—, dagnabit that's part of it. Do you know how it's gonna look if I show up to spring training with a woman and explain that I discovered her in the boiler room of St. Francis Church in Wanuga, Nebraska?"

"You missed the point, Peter. You tell them it's a miracle," Father Michael corrected.

"I don't mean to be disrespectful, but most people out there don't exactly stand in line to see the next reported miracle."

"Well they should!" Father Michael put his hands behind his back and puffed out his chest against the world.

"I believe you, Father, but I just don't think I could sell management on a contract for a miracle."

"I see your point. We'll just keep that part of the story to ourselves for now. In the meantime, why don't you tell them that she's the answer to your prayers?"

"My what?" Moss tried to imagine telling the owner, C.W. McDermott, that he wanted to give a contract to a nun that was the answer to his prayers.

"Don't you see? Everybody knows the Memorials need another starter to make a run at the pennant." This was true. "Sister Mary Bernadette is that starter, and a cheaper starting pitcher you won't find. All we ask is for the Major League minimum. That should cover repairs for the church and take care of Sister's expenses." Father Michael clapped his hands and rubbed them together.

"The Major League minimum?" Moss stammered.

"Why, of course. That's the figure we need. We aren't greedy, but we think that's fair. Just imagine how it will be when you explain how the addition of Sister Mary Bernadette is going to bring your club the pennant."

Moss grabbed for the railing next to the steps of the church. Father Michael might want to see that meeting, but Moss had his career to consider. Owners, he believed, would frown on managers who find baseball salvation in the form of pitchers who wear habits instead of getting treated for them.

Moss rubbed his face with both hands. He knew that Father Michael was the kind of man you couldn't sort of say no to. But you had to say no, or he never stopped. Moss repeated over and over to himself that he could do it. It was a technique Ned Burnside, the team psychologist, had suggested to a few of his younger players to boost their confidence when facing big league pitching. Moss repeated his mantra louder and louder inside his head. His confidence grew. He snapped his head back and looked Father Michael right in the eye.

The moment was broken as Sister Mary Bernadette bounded down the front steps of St. Francis wearing a light cotton sweatsuit. Her blue eyes sparkled in the afternoon sunlight. She smelled faintly of grease remover but more than anything else, she beamed.

"I'm ready," she called out.

Moss had seen that glow before, but never in a woman. It was the look of wonder he'd seen in the eyes young men the first time they'd entered the Florida clubhouse for the Washington Memorials at the start of spring training. The eagerness to put on the uniform, and the desire to dive into mud puddles, if need be, for the opportunity to open under the big lights in a major league stadium. Moss knew the feeling intimately. He knew how much this next part would hurt.

"Father Michael, I—. I just don't think I can help you out here. It's nothing personal, Sister, but all I have is Father Michael's word that you're a great pitcher. That's good enough for me, but my bosses don't like to get scouting reports from the pulpit of a church. I should know. I scouted for awhile." Moss hoped this was the end of the most bizarre day of his life.

Father Michael's bushy eyebrows knotted in deep thought and agitation. The clergyman couldn't understand Moss's lack of belief in this miracle, this answer to his earnest prayer. The priest looked at his church. The building was likely to fall over if a stiff enough wind came along. He wanted to drag Peter into that building, sit him down in the front row and give him a sermon the baseball manager would not soon forget. But then the old man reminded himself of the complexities of faith. It had been an early member of his own faith that had inspired the phrase "doubting Thomas." That's when it came to him. Father Michael clapped his hands again and noticed that Moss winced in pain and grabbed his stomach.

"You wait right there." Father Michael tottered off around the back corner and left Sister Mary and Moss alone on the steps.

Moss went from the anticipation of victory to extreme discomfort in about two seconds. He wasn't the most social individual in baseball to begin with, and he certainly didn't think he had much to say to a nun, especially one to whom he had just denied spring training.

Silent, Sister Mary didn't move. The brightness in her eyes had dimmed. She scolded herself for being too willing to believe such a thing was possible. It was happening all over again, only this time there wouldn't even be a game. That's when Father Michael returned.

"Here we are." Father Michael emerged with a catcher's mitt, a baseball and a bat. He dropped everything but the dinged and scratched piece of oil-stained lumber, which he presented to Moss.

Moss looked with disbelief into the large round eyes of the parish priest. "You can't be serious?"

"You said it yourself. You've been a scout."

Moss refused to take the bat. "Father Michael, hasn't this gone just about far enough?"

Father Michael took a dramatic step toward Moss, and then his voice started to tremble. "I'll make a bet with you. Take one at bat. If she gets you out, you take her to Florida."

Moss didn't want to do it, but he knew Father Michael needed a firm "no" before he would quit. Moss took the bat and led the way to the dusty, old baseball diamond across the street. It was the field where Moss had first learned to play the game. It was the site of all of Moss's early triumphs. This was his field. If he had to embarrass the nun to end this, well that was just the way it had to be.

Chapter 3

"This isn't exactly the miracle you outlined to me," Sister Mary said as she rolled the baseball in her fingers. She stood with Father Michael on top of the dusty pitcher's mound on the ragged field.

"Well, sometimes miracles take different forms," Father Michael stated.

"This is the living legend of Wanuga," Sister Mary countered. "This is his field. What were you thinking?"

Father Michael took the baseball from Sister Mary and examined it. "Peter doesn't believe in this miracle. This is our only way of proving it to him."

"I don't know if I can do this."

"You have to. The future of this church is at stake." Father Michael turned and yelled to Peter. "Are you ready yet?"

"I'm ready," Moss answered, as Father Michael walked to home plate without another word to the young nun. Sister Mary tried not to look at Moss. She had heard so many stories about this man, and each one ended the same way. If only that manager hadn't pulled him in the ninth inning of that World Series game, Moss would've been as famous in New York as he was in Wanuga. A few feet off home plate, Moss took a final practice swing. He tried to recall any sage hitting advice he could remember.

Moss was a pitcher who had spent the better part of his career in the American League where the designated hitter bats for the pitcher. This rule allowed him not to embarrass himself against the best pitching in the world, but it also destroyed most of his once good batting skills. In the few seasons he'd played in the National League, Moss learned to bunt. Bunting was important, and Moss always tried to learn the most important things.

"Come on and get in here," Father Michael chided Moss from behind the plate. "I'm not getting any younger."

Moss kicked the dirt from the tennis shoes he wore and tried to take comfort in the fact that he was a former major leaguer. Most of all, he reminded himself that this was his park. He stepped up to the plate.

Moss set himself in the uneven dirt of the box. He heard Father Michael's knees crack, as the old man crouched in the catcher's position. Moss then eyed the young woman on the pitcher's mound.

"All right now, Sister Mary. Right down the old pipe." Father Michael flashed signs to the young woman, who nodded.

Sister Mary crossed herself once then dug her right hand into the mitt. The weight of her dreams almost pushed her to her knees, but she breathed deeply and started the sequence.

As the breath left her body, her mind cleared. She placed the ball on her fingertips, digging the nails of the pointer and middle fingers into the red stitching of the cover. She forced herself to view the plate as a large zone and refused the urge to pick a target. She came set, and with a small step toward home began the motion. Her right arm came from the side in a three-quarter throwing motion. At the release point, her hand simply stopped. The only added motion was the flicking of the two fingers she had dug into the ball. The nun watched as the ball floated toward the only baseball legend she'd ever met.

At first, Moss thought he was in a movie because the ball flew at him in slow motion. He squinted to pick up the rotation — there was very little. Moss swallowed hard. He recognized the pitch. A breeze wafted across the infield and the ball began to dance. His grip tightened and he lunged early at the ball. He missed.

"Strike one!" The priest called.

Moss swore silently and shook his head. The priest threw the ball back, and Sister Mary Bernadette caught it deftly and regrouped. Moss stepped back into the box.

She again went through her routine, but with new confidence.

"Wait, wait." Moss whispered the word over and over in his head.

The second pitch seemed even slower than the first. He waited and waited. The ball hung two feet from the plate as if it sat on a tee for him to swat. The coach threw all two hundred pounds behind his swing, but as the bat reached the plate, the ball died — dropped four feet almost straight down — and dipped outside. Moss missed badly.

"Strike two," Father Michael smirked.

Moss was mad now. He didn't like being down 0 and 2 in the count to a nun from a small Catholic church in a town with two stoplights. He was a former major leaguer. He set his chin and dug in with all the ferocity of young man trying to win a job in spring training.

Sister Mary's resolve grew as well. She was one pitch away from a dream. One pitch from getting back to baseball. She cleared her mind and threw with the true belief that the pitch would do its job.

In his worst nightmares, Moss never imagined he would be standing in the middle of Nebraska on a dusty old ball field, on the wrong side of a bet to a pitcher who threw the most misunderstood pitch in the history of the game — the knuckleball.

The knuckleball is an enigma pitch. With practically no spin to keep it straight, control was a secondary concern. This one seemed faster than the first two and danced in the light cross wind blowing through the diamond. Moss grimaced. He had seen what a pitcher with a good one could do in the majors. He knew what to call a pitcher with a bad one too — lunch meat. This, unfortunately, looked like a good knuckleball. Moss dug in and timed his swing perfectly.

His mouth dropped open wide as the lumber connected with the ball. There was no sharp crack of the bat, instead more of a thud or a chip. The ball trickled out in front of him and rolled to the feet of Sister Mary Bernadette, who bent down and scooped it up. Moss stared deep into the resolute eyes of the nun.

Every manager prides himself on knowing the rulebook inside and out. The ability to produce a trick or a spin on a rule that suits his own needs is part of the game. Moss knew his grounder wasn't going to get him out of this. In the midst of disbelief, the bet echoed in his head. "If she can get one out, you take her to Florida."

Moss knew a ground ball wasn't an out until somebody with the ball stepped on first base before he did. Moss ran.

Sister Mary Bernadette wanted to yell out in celebration, but she couldn't. She was, however, struck by the odd sight of Moss

Thompson running down the first base line. Why was he doing that? Then the bet replayed in her head, and she knew that this man was trying to welch via a technicality. That's when she dug her shoes into the dirt and sprinted toward the bag.

Halfway up the line, Moss turned to see Sister Mary charging the bag. He strained his fifty-year-old legs as they sprinted for a loophole. She was faster than Moss had speculated. She made up his advantage, and the two were about even in their quest for the bag.

A few strides from first base, Moss realized he wouldn't win. He could only hope to tie. Ties went to the runner, so that would be fine for him. Moss's face kept changing to darker shades of red, and veins popped farther and farther out from his neck, as the belief grew that he was going to salvage his baseball pride in two short strides.

Sister Mary's anger grew. She respected people and expected the same from everyone else. This race to first was unethical, underhanded and, worst of all, underway. She clutched the baseball harder and looked for speed from a divine source. In the end, she got it.

The field had not been raked in several days. A large clod of hard dirt sat in the baseline, unnoticed by Moss. The coach planted a foot firmly on the loose piece of field and began to stumble.

Sister Mary stretched out with her last stride and pounded the top of the bag. Dirt flew up and trailed her as she carried on into foul territory. Moss stumbled over the bag a second later, too late to save himself from an ill-advised bet.

"That about does it." Father Michael moved as fast as he could out to where Moss stood, hunched over trying to breathe.

"Pl— Please reconsider, F— Father," Moss stammered and coughed.

"A bet is a bet. Now you don't want to be considered a welsher, do you Peter?" Father Michael looked sternly at the man who gasped for breath.

Moss shook his head. He remembered his mother's words when she heard that Moss had gone to Aksarben to bet on the horses.

"Gambling's a sin. No good comes of it."

It was bad enough to lose a baseball bet to a nun. Then to have your mother's voice in your head saying, "I told you so." It was almost too much for the manager. As he finally got his breath back and could stand, he had to admit that his mother had been right about this one.

Sister Mary Bernadette had grabbed her bag and was waiting impatiently by the car. She knew this afternoon was proof positive that prayers were answered, even if that answer was ten years in the making.

Moss saw the nun at the car and began to hobble in that general direction. Dread filled him. He usually enjoyed spring training, but this year would be different. This year he had a major problem. He knew exactly whom he had to go to, the one man who might understand and, more importantly, be able to help.

Chapter 4

The first time Moss saw any fear in the eyes of Sister Mary Bernadette was when the engines on their jet whined to a higher speed as their plane readied for takeoff from the Lincoln Municipal Airport. She retrieved her rosary and closed her eyes, while she whispered an inaudible prayer.

Moss himself only hated one thing about flying, coming down. Landings annoyed his ears, and he was not adept at popping them to relieve the pressure. That was one of the biggest drawbacks to his visits home to Nebraska. It was extremely difficult to get flights into the state without having to make connections. This flight would go as far as Chicago, where they'd have to transfer to the plane bound for Florida and his rendezvous with his own reckless bet. A stab of tension welled inside his stomach. He rummaged through a pocket and found the packet of antacids. He chugged half the tablets, chewed twice and swallowed. Even the maximum strength pills had stopped working five years ago, but there was some comfort in the ritual.

Sister Mary didn't open her eyes until the plane crested the clouds. This was her first flight ever. She hadn't thought it would take this long for her to ride in a plane, but then, as her father used to say, "Life usually doesn't work out exactly as planned."

Her father was a bulky man built to survive the harsh winters of the northern Sandhills. He was quiet to a fault, but no one ever questioned his work ethic. He was a good Catholic who married a good Catholic and had nine good Catholic daughters. Sister Mary Bernadette's given name at birth was Anne Stanicek, daughter of Hank and Irma. Sister Mary had always favored her mother's angular figure, her deep brown hair and her sparkling blue eyes. She was born in the middle, so most of her childhood memories were of clothes coming down from above or moving on below. Five of her sisters had left home to find their way. Three ended up in Lincoln after attending the university. One married an orthodontist in Denver and constantly wrote home about skiing. The fifth became an English professor at Dana College. This caused a bit of a fuss in the family because Dana College was founded by Norwegian Lutherans.

The youngest girl never went to college and married the son of the lumberyard owner, who built her a big house in Valentine. She had a baby now. The oldest married a young rancher with a penchant for showing horses, so they traveled a lot. Then there was Nina.

Nina and Anne — now Sister Mary —had spent the most time with their father, taking care of the ranch. Both women were expert horsemen and ropers and had long ago learned to tolerate the smell of singed cattle hair at branding time. Hank Stanicek was not a young man anymore, and Nina had stayed at home to take over the spread.

Although proud, Hank and Nina had felt a sense of loss the day Anne had come home from college and announced she intended to take up the habit. Hank had always hoped Anne would one day work the ranch with all the love that he had put into it. He'd also figured she would be there to take care of him when it was time to put him out to pasture.

So true to form, Hank had spent most of that day alone. Ranchers aren't people who can take too much socializing as a rule. They need time to ponder things. It's more than being careful — it's a way of life. Anne had found Hank behind the barn looking at the large green yard that stretched out for an acre or two. She had presented him with the worn out piece of leather that he liked to call a baseball glove. Hank had used that mitt to teach nine children how to play catch. She had held it out to her father.

Hank had smiled at the glove and taken it in his weather-beaten hands. A father's memory gets flooded sometimes with all the images of a child growing up. Hank had known he was about to cry, but that wasn't something a rancher did. He'd grabbed the ball, pounded it into the mitt and motioned for Anne to move off in the distance. Then he'd crouched down in a catcher's stance and smiled.

His daughter had pumped twice and kicked. She'd thrown him a knuckleball, the pitch the old rancher had taught her in high school so that she could stay on the boy's team. It had fluttered in the ever-present Nebraska wind, traveling in a slow arch toward her father. Like so many throws before, this one had been a strike.

"When did you learn the knuckleball?" Moss asked as the plane reached cruising altitude.

The question startled Sister Mary out of her memories. She sat up abruptly and put her rosary away. She shook her head and tried to pop her ears. It was the first real thing he'd said since the ball field that afternoon.

"My father taught it to me so I could stay on the high school team."

"You played high school baseball?"

"Yeah, and college"

"College?" Moss asked in disbelief. "Where did you play college baseball?"

"Kearney State."

Kearney State was a small Nebraska college, NAIA, but it was a legitimate program.

"You really played at Kearney State?" Moss repeated.

"You don't believe me, do you?" Sister Mary accused.

"I—" Moss stumbled over his words, as it dawned on him that he had just called a nun a liar. "I never heard about a woman playing college ball."

"It happened. You can call them if you want."

"I'm sure it did," Moss said, but mentally made a note to call the college. "And then you just decided to become a nun?"

"It wasn't quite like that. There were other things involved."

"Family pressures?"

"You really want to know, don't you?"

"I am taking you to spring training. I figure I should at least get to know you a little bit. Besides, it has to be more interesting than this airplane magazine I've been reading." Moss's tone was softer and kinder now.

Sister Mary considered him for a moment, and then decided.

"Okay, I'll tell you," she said. "But I warn you, you may not believe it."

Chapter 5

"I was a senior in college when I received my call to the church," Sister Mary Bernadette began. "It was the last game of the season between my team, Kearney State, and our rivals, Hastings College. The winner took the top spot in the conference and got to go on to the national playoffs. That's a pretty big deal at a small school like that. Since I had the best year, the coach picked me to pitch the game."

"The week before the game, I dedicated myself to keeping sharp. I threw often. I also tinkered with new pitches, in particular the screwball. As a kid, I remember how Fernando Valenzuela dominated hitters with it. I believed that if I could throw it, maybe I might go someplace and pitch for somebody. It isn't an easy pitch to learn, as I found out, but I practiced hard."

"The day of the game came, and it was a close one. We were up by one run in the final inning, runners on the corners and two outs. Coach had visited the mound once in the inning already to see how I was, but I knew I could finish. I really knew it. Freddy Marks, our catcher, laid down the sign for the curve, but I wasn't going to throw the curve. I shook him off again and again until he finally slapped his glove, conceding to my decision."

"I have always believed that the only true test of a pitch is under game conditions, when you need a strike. So I threw the screwball."

"The ball immediately slid off to the left. I wanted to pluck it out of the air, to redo it. Freddy made a diving stab, but the ball rolled passed him and on toward the fence. The runner broke from third."

"I have always been good on fundamentals, Mr. Thompson. I go to first when the ball is hit to the right side. I back up the catcher when I can. And I cover home on wild pitches, every time."

"Harvey Brickenhammer, the man on third who now charged down the line, was a celebrity at Hastings College. He'd just been drafted to play offensive line in the NFL. He wasn't very fast, but he was huge."

"Freddy made a great play just to get to the ball. He tossed it to me as I covered home, exactly at the moment that Harvey covered me. I got the out, but I also got knocked back five feet and out cold. That's when I saw her."

Moss looked at her questioningly, but remained silent.

"She wasn't easy to make out at first. There was just too much light. I squinted, and the light lessened a bit. It was the Virgin Mary hovering just above me. She smiled with such warmth and compassion. Then she looked down at me and said, 'I have a job for you.' I knew what she meant; she didn't have to say anything else, but she did anyway." Sister Mary looked out her window at the clouds hovering just off the plane.

"What? What did she say?" Moss asked.

"She looked at me with these huge, kind eyes and said, 'Don't ever throw the screwball again.'"

"When I woke up, I was a bit miffed. She is the Holy Mother, but who is she to tell me which pitches I should throw? At first I was mad, but I got over it. She was right, and I never threw another screwball. I guess she was just preparing me to do without some things. I finished college, but from that moment on, I knew I would be a nun. I couldn't just turn my back when the Virgin Mary took the time to talk to me. I guess that's why I took the name Sister Mary Bernadette. You see, the same thing happened to her."

Moss interrupted, "I know, I saw the movie."

"Then you do understand."

Moss sat still for a moment. He didn't consider himself a deeply religious man, but he cared enough to still call himself a Catholic. He was uncomfortable with the thought of someone actually seeing the Virgin Mary. He liked to view the world as one big baseball league. The franchises had been handed out years ago, and there wasn't much expansion. Most people were assigned to a minor league club and tried to work their way to the majors, which in Moss's mind would happen when you expired. Life was just a matter of how high in the system you could get before you got the call to the show.

Moss turned to Sister Mary. "Do you share this story with a lot of people?"

"I used to, but everyone back home has heard it," she said.

"Just for now," Moss picked his way delicately, "why don't we just keep this between you and me?"

"Don't you believe me?" the sister asked earnestly.

"I — well, of course I believe you, but then we're both Catholics. I'm just saying that religion doesn't come up much in the clubhouse, and — it might be better for you if it didn't," Moss offered weakly.

"I'm sorry, Mr. Thompson, but it's who I am. I just can't change for baseball."

Moss rubbed his face. "I'm not saying you should change, just not be so vocal. Hey, if you ever need to talk about religion, I'm there for you. It's just that some of the guys have their own views on things, and it might go easier for you if you didn't mention having a vision."

"You mean they'll act just like you did when you heard?" Sister Mary asked.

Moss didn't answer. He took out his antacids again and chugged a few more tablets. His mind whirled as he pictured himself in front of C.W. McDermott presenting this new pitcher. He saw Sister Mary shake his hand and tell McDermott that she didn't throw screwballs because the Virgin Mary told her not to. Moss felt a headache start to form behind his left eye.

He cursed Father Michael for putting him in this position, and plotted his strategy for getting out of this with his career intact.

Chapter 6

"You want me to sign a what?" Buddy Wilson was a short, wiry man with bulging eyes who preferred standing to sitting. Consequently, there was an overstuffed chair in his living room back home that had never been used.

Moss sat on a couch as Wilson paced back and forth trying to decide whether or not to call the men in the white coats.

"When you said you were going home to fish, I had no idea what you were after," Wilson went on. "We are in a unique position here, Moss. We may be a contender after only six years in the league. Despite this fact, you want me to hire a side show!"

"Buddy," Moss began, wishing he had a bottle of antacids to swallow, "we need another starter."

"She's a nun, Moss. Do you understand the difference between spending the last two years of your life riding a bus in the minor leagues and lighting candles and crossing yourself? Do you?!?"

"I admit that it's a bit — odd," Moss offered.

"Odd? Odd! It's damn foolishness. Moss, you and I go way back to the days before free agency. You pitched in this league. How can you sit there and tell me this nun can play ball?" Buddy placed both hands on his hips and stared at Moss.

"I can't, Buddy. I know this seems crazy. Trust me, I had a whole plane flight to think about it, but I took some swings against her, and — she has potential." Moss smiled slightly.

"You took swings against her?" Buddy shook his head. "Did anyone under the age of fifty take swings against her?" He stared down at Moss.

"No, but —"

"But nothing, Moss. I hate to break the news to you, but you are not the major leaguer you once were."

"Now wait a minute there, Buddy Wilson. You may be many things, but even as a pitcher I was a better hitter than your sorry little shortstop butt ever was!" Moss yelled.

"What?" Wilson stared blankly at his friend.

"You heard me. I could still hit even today. These guys on the hill now aren't so tough." Moss rose as his knees cracked.

"Maybe, but how fast can you get down the line to first?" Wilson asked.

Moss hung his head, ashamed of what he had become. He patted the pudgy stomach he now lugged with him and stared into the turquoise carpeting of Buddy's hotel room.

Wilson watched his friend, the man who had picked him up from more than one barroom floor during his own horrendous streak of 30 games without a hit. Wilson remembered the taunts of "Mendozo Line" every time he took the field. He remembered Moss using that talented right arm of his to lay out some cuss who decided to offer an impromptu editorial on Buddy Wilson's play at shortstop in a bar in Philly.

There were relationships in life that don't operate on the favor system. They are formed on a deep understanding and respect, a complete belief that the other guy will always come through for you. That's the way Moss and Buddy were. Buddy realized that he couldn't just dismiss this man. No matter how cutthroat he had to be to earn the title of general manager, there were still a few ethics Buddy Wilson could not put away. That's when he sat down.

Buddy turned to his long time friend and looked him straight in the eye. "All right Moss, why are you bringing a nun to spring training?"

Moss was shocked to see Buddy sitting down. The general manager's question landed on him like a cold splash of water. Moss tried to find the words that would somehow make sense, but the sentences just wouldn't form. So Moss did the only thing he could do — he told it straight.

Moss cleared his throat. "It's like this, Buddy. My priest back home can't come up with the money to keep my old church going. So he asked me to give this nun a major league contract, which would keep the place afloat."

"Are you out of your mind?" Buddy asked.

"Look, I tried to tell him, but, well— you wouldn't understand. You're not Catholic."

"I still don't understand why you just can't say no."

"I sort of made this bet about whether or not she could get me out in one at bat."

"You didn't?" Buddy pleaded.

"I did. It's true what you said about me not being able to get down the line like I used to."

"She got you out?"

"Yeah, she did," Moss answered.

"So what we have here is a payoff of a bet." Buddy rubbed his eyes. In the code of conduct among men at this age level there were certain rules that were unbreakable. The list was small, but never welshing on a bet was one.

"This is serious. You lost a bet to a priest."

"I didn't mean to. Honest, I didn't. I just figured that it was impossible to lose to a nun."

"You were never a good gambler, Moss." Buddy strained to use every brain cell and find a solution. "So the bet was that if you lost you would take her to the bigs and give her a contract?"

"Not exactly," Moss said. "I believe it was that if I lost, I had to take her to Florida. The rest was implied."

"That's it," Wilson said leaping to his feet. "You brought her to Florida. You fulfilled your end of the bet."

"Buddy, I can't go out on a techie like that. Not to a priest," Moss stated matter-of-factly. He still felt guilty over his attempt to welch the first time. "Father Michael won't be happy until he hears she's pitching."

Buddy's eyes lit up at Moss's words. "Okay, okay, what about this? Say we put her on the roster. Say we even let her pitch in some early practices and maybe even a game. She gets shelled. There's no way it works. I, as General Manger, have to say no. She goes home early, and we can get down to business."

"I—" Moss thought for a moment. He didn't see a problem. He was just the coach. Father Michael had to understand that. "I think it might work."

For the first time since that tiny ballpark in Wanuga, Moss felt like his old self again. He was excited for spring training to begin. He wanted to get to work and try to win a pennant. Most of all, he wanted to end his debt to a wily priest over two thousand miles away.

"The only problem I see is McDermott," Buddy went on.

"I know." Moss sank again under the weight of the thought of the owner.

"I can probably sell him on the media angle. I mean, a woman invited to a major league camp doesn't happen every day. Good press, followed by the reality of the situation, and then a hopeful thought that the gender barrier might one day be broken. That sounds good."

Moss was astounded at how adept Buddy had become at working out the long-term media strategies.

"She'll work for the minimum. That's always good when dealing with the owners. Saving a church — that's decent. We'll try and downplay the nun thing, maybe. There's only one problem." Wilson turned to Moss. "Why is she here? What does she have that makes her a viable major league prospect besides a priest with a marker?"

Moss answered in a measured tone. "She can throw the knuckle-ball."

Buddy Wilson sat down again. A fleeting image of the pitch dancing across an infield toward a flabbergasted batter popped briefly into his mind. "Is that what she got you out on?" he asked.

"Yes." Moss nodded.

Buddy shook his head. Fantasy shouldn't interfere with business. Besides, his job wasn't to dream. But this one dream might be useful to convince McDermott to take the risk. After all, Buddy knew that McDermott was worse at gambling than Moss.

Chapter 7

"Sex! That's it, isn't it?" C.W. McDermott sat on the couch in his large hotel suite in baggy shorts and a hat to hide his bald spot. He was a tall, looming figure with fish-belly white skin and thin lips. "Which one of you idiots slept with who?"

"Sir, you didn't let me finish," Buddy said evenly.

"Somebody did, and somebody else took pictures. It was the Dodgers, wasn't it?" C.W. had read the old stories of espionage between football teams in the '70's and '80's. He took them as gospel and remained convinced that everyone else in the National League was out to submarine his team's chances.

"It wasn't the Dodgers," Buddy said.

"So you admit it was somebody!" C.W. McDermott had made his fortune in one of those pyramid product schemes where you convince someone else to bother their friends, relatives and complete strangers constantly to buy whatever you're selling. People jumped at this chance to be ostracized for a franchise fee and the hope of moving up. If they convinced enough people to take up the sales mantra, they moved onto the title of Grand Poobah to the chosen. That meant people paid you for the right to bother their friends, and you paid some of that money back to McDermott.

"Who was it, Buddy? I pay you good money not to screw up like this!" C.W. was about to stand. That was a bad sign.

"It wasn't him," Moss began. "I brought her here."

"I should've guessed somebody like you, no family, living alone would get trapped in something like this." The truth was that C.W. was also single and lived alone. "You realize the team comes first. You'll have to resign. Buddy, start the paperwork."

"She's a nun." Moss now realized that regardless of everything else this now meant his job.

"A what?" C.W. relaxed back on the couch. "You brought me a nun to play baseball?"

"She's not just a nun, sir. She's a nun with a knuckleball," Buddy stated.

"A knuckleball?" C.W. asked.

"A knuckleball, Mr. McDermott." Buddy could see thoughts jumping around inside the old man's head. "Let me ask you this, sir. Why hasn't the gender line really been broken in big time sports? I mean, why hasn't a woman ever made a big league team?"

"That's ridiculous. Everybody knows why." McDermott scoffed.

"Exactly. Athletics are based on strength, speed and size. In every one of these categories men have an edge over women. That's just biology, except when it comes to one thing, Mr. McDermott — one solitary thing in the world of sports that doesn't require the player to be of overwhelming power. That is the knuckleball." Buddy let the words sink in.

"Not exactly exciting material, though, the knuckleball," McDermott thought out loud.

"I disagree. I went to a small college in Texas, a real think tank. Apart from myself, there really wasn't anyone of talent on that baseball team. But we always got two or three games a year scheduled against the big boys to earn some money for the program. It normally became a turkey shoot, except when this one short, skinny kid with glasses pitched. Do you know what he threw? The knuckleball, sir, that's what. Those muscle-bound boys from the big schools swatted and cursed at that ball dancing around in front of them all afternoon. He scared more than one major program as he kept us in those ball games."

"So you stayed in games, but you never won," McDermott pointed out.

"We didn't have a team like the Washington Memorials."

McDermott scratched his left leg near the knee. "We're pointed toward the pennant, Buddy. And now you come here and ask that I approve a sideshow?"

"Not a sideshow, sir, but a fifth starter at the major league minimum." Buddy had waited to talk salary until now.

"The minimum?" C.W. asked. "Then something must be wrong.

No player worth any salt asks for the minimum."

"She's a nun. They don't keep a lot of material goods," Moss answered from his chair.

"That's what I call weird." McDermott scratched his other leg. He was a member of the All Lights Church, which considered itself on the leading edge of redefining religion. Their basic belief was that God had been broken up into tiny balls of light and distributed around the world in the form of enlightened humans. Their religious quest was for people to go out and try to identify who, indeed, possessed the inner light. The earliest days of the church had led most to believe this was a small number, and as soon as the pieces were gathered, the rapture would occur. That changed after the All Lights Church conference of 1981. The theologians proclaimed that the light was more widely spread than previously thought. They developed a test that consisted of a tuning fork and the trained ear of one of the "Keepers of the Light," a small group based out of Idaho who could pick up on the correct frequency. McDermott had paid all expenses for one of them to test him. After receiving a sizable donation from McDermott, it was determined that he had a little light inside.

C.W. had always been proud of that, for as the church had taught, those who carry God are rewarded for their burdens. "I suppose Catholics are still in the Middle Ages on this kind of thing," C.W. said to Buddy.

"She's cheap. She's a fifth starter, and she's a free promotional event guaranteed to increase merchandise sales," Buddy stated.

McDermott thought for a long while. The truth was that Buddy met with him every day. Every day, Buddy told him that they need a fifth starter. Nobody in the system was ready to come up yet and the two had been considering trading one of their top young prospects in hopes of acquiring a solid starter.

"Buddy, I have always trusted your judgment. I have been rewarded for that with the building of a contender." McDermott stood. "This request is highly unusual, but I will grant it. My only stipulation is that her tryout is fair. I will not have anyone mucking about and crying over how the Washington Memorials bend over backwards and have different standards for nuns that pitch for us. Is that understood?"

Buddy shook McDermott's hand. "Yes, sir. And thank you."
Buddy smiled as he led Moss from the room. He'd known exactly
how McDermott would react and that C.W. would place some kind
of restriction on the deal. That was C.W. McDermott's way. Buddy
recalled a clause in his own contract that stated he would be immediately terminated if he won more than two games of golf against the
owner during any consecutive thirty days while serving as the
general manager for the Washington Memorials.

"Buddy," Moss stopped his friend in the hall. "Thank you for all
this. And that last part was brilliant. Soon this whole deal will be
over and we can get down to winning a pennant."

"Remember, Moss, the idea is a fair tryout."

"Fine, fine, but we both know how it's going to go." Moss
slapped Buddy on the back.

Buddy Wilson didn't answer because he was deep in thought. It
was so tempting to believe. As a professional evaluator of talent,
Buddy knew choosing size, strength and speed would always fill the
rosters of sports with men. But this knuckleball, this was different. It
was almost a magical pitch in his mind. He could see how it might
work, and right there, at that exact moment, was when Buddy
Wilson became the first person outside of Father Michael who
believed the nun had half a chance. Buddy made a note that he
should meet her soon.

Chapter 8

Sister Mary did not sleep well the night before the first day of spring training. As a child, her dream had been to play major league baseball. She'd spent all of her free time practicing and improving. She'd taken the jeers of small town high school crowds and college fraternities who'd found new insults to hurl when she was busy beating their teams. At first, it had been hard to take. She couldn't understand the nastiness of the words and found herself questioning her ability. It had been her father who had sat her down at the kitchen one afternoon to talk about it.

He'd sat her at the dinner table and looked her squarely in the eye. "No matter what's said out there only one thing counts — whether or not you believe you're a ballplayer. I believe you are. Your coach believes you are. But that don't mean squat until you believe you are."

Sister Mary had spent two years mourning baseball. She could not walk away from the call she'd received. In another person, baseball might have been number one and religion number two. Sister Mary was not that person. She had finally accepted her path and reasoned that the Virgin Mother didn't appear on a daily basis to people on Earth. Whatever was in store for the young nun must be important. Sister Mary had found happiness in her lot, finally. Although there were still times when she remembered hot August afternoons in the middle of family vacations to Kansas City. She had watched the fountains dance at Royals Stadium while George Brett batted, silently praying that someday she would become part of the fabric of major league baseball.

The knock on the door startled Sister Mary out of the past and into a prayer newly answered. It was nine a.m., and she opened the door.

"Good morning, Sister Mary Bernadette. I'm Buddy Wilson, the GM of the Washington Memorials." Buddy Wilson stood outside her door at seven in the morning in crisp khakis, a polo shirt and a briefcase.

"Where's Coach?"

"He went on ahead to the stadium. I wanted to meet you and take care of this contract before we get out to the field." Buddy pulled a thick pile of papers from out of his briefcase. "Just sign here, and we can start spring training."

Sister Mary took the pen he offered and paused just a moment over the line for her signature. She breathed deeply. She remembered the jeering of the crowds. She remembered her prayer, but mostly she remembered her father. She signed her name on the paper. Today she was a ballplayer.

"Good," Buddy took the document and put in back in his briefcase. "Now when we get to the field, I made some special arrangements for you."

"Special arrangements?"

"You'll see when we get there."

Sister Mary grabbed her sport bag and her special mitt, the gift from her little league team. She followed Buddy out the door.

"I get to meet the other pitchers and catchers today, right?" Sister Mary asked.

"Oh yes," Buddy sighed. "Today you get to meet the guys." Buddy led on toward his car. The truth of the matter was that Buddy wasn't too worried about the nun meeting his pitching staff. No, he figured the problem would start when the pitching staff met the nun.

Chapter 9

As a group, they'd posted the third best earned run average in the majors last year. They had power, cunning and just enough confidence when averaged out among the whole unit. They were the main reason many preseason analysts in sports magazines all across the country had picked the Washington Memorials as *the* contender in the East. Most of the publicity posters had pictures of one or more of them, particularly since two of them had just successfully renegotiated their long-term deals. That's why the media wanted to talk with them. That, and the fact that the first week of spring training was just pitchers and catchers.

Amy Springer parked her rented Chevy Cavalier in the small parking lot outside of Deaver Stadium, the Florida residence of the Memorials. She grabbed her tape recorder and her notebook and trotted toward the field. Amy's press badge read *The Washington Herald* and the cap she wore displayed the two marble columns of the Memorials' team logo. Amy was the beat reporter assigned to the Memorials. She originally got the job during the expansion year and was shrewd enough to hang onto it through the expectations of the coming season.

She read her notes on the pitchers and catchers while she walked. This was a dangerous habit of hers, and she just missed hitting the corner of a Winnebago. As it was, she didn't even notice it. In fact, it didn't even enter her mind, because across the way she saw Jon John.

He was a massive young man with a ruggedness often found in men who disdain the razor for all but two days of the week. He stood six feet four inches tall and weighed two hundred and forty pounds. He was a quiet kid from a ranch in Montana whose father had taught him to approach everything straight on. In his first two years in the majors, he'd only thrown fastballs. He'd refused to throw the tricky pitches, as he called them. He didn't like them for the same reason he only hunted with a large knife. He was a mano-y-mano man to a large degree, who said nothing and threw hard — very hard.

"Jon John," Amy called out.

Jon John stopped and looked back at Amy. He nodded without saying a word as she caught up to him.

"Is your slider coming along?" She asked the tall rawboned pitcher.

Jon John nodded again and walked away. That was all anybody every really got out of that pitcher. Amy made a note that he was positive about the pitch. Adding the slider had made Jon John almost unhittable last year and put him squarely at the top of the Memorial's pitching rotation.

That rotation was here today, somewhere. There was the wily lefty, Marion Pierce; the party boy, Richard Day; and the skinny-kid Jose Martinez, whose forkball kept opposing batters up late at night. Amy craned her neck around trying to find one of these arms. She needed an interview for her daily update from spring training. Where were all the pitchers?

"Hey Amy! Want a quote?" Amy spun around as the tall, dark form emerged onto the field to bask in the sunlight as if it was his own personal spotlight from God.

"Sure Max, go ahead," Amy answered the man.

"This year, I kiss the butt of anybody who hits a dinger off me." He smiled.

"Are you sure you want me to print that?" Amy asked.

"Absolutely."

"And what if you surrender one?"

"Not going to happen."

Mad Max Standish was the team's closer and had more confidence than most teams. He kept most of the confidence in his glare. More than one major league hitter confided in Amy that looking into Max's eyes during the ninth with two out was like facing evil itself. Evil that caused you to make sure your helmet was on tight.

"You know, I could make some private time available for you,"

Max offered with a wide grin.

"Hey Amy!" The massive voice boomed across the ballpark. Dean Larson was a throwback player to the days before Astroturf, night games and television. He was a stocky 40-year-old catcher with a large smile and big hands. Today, he was also the best excuse for Amy to leave Max behind. She quickly crossed to Dean who stood near the first base foul line.

"Dean, how are you?" Amy asked.

"Been better, but not much," Dean answered as he ambled over to where Amy stood. Dean was a journeyman catcher, whose list of former teams numbered eighteen. A defensive specialist with occasional pop in the bat, he had signed on two years ago to develop young pitchers, and he had stayed after free-agent signings had taken away most of the cash for a big-name catcher. Dean had accepted everything for what it was and strapped the shin guards on each day with enthusiasm.

"Who's the number five pitcher?" Amy asked the catcher.

Dean pointed past Amy toward the outfield grass to a crop of rookies and has-beens who had answered invitations to vie for a roster spot. They were playing catch with each other, warming up for the tryout to be the last starting pitcher on a powerful team.

"I suppose whoever it is, he's out there." Dean almost laughed. Any other year he'd pick one of the kids, probably not old enough to drink legally yet, to be brought up on a trial basis, but this was a different season. Unless you played for a few of the dynasties in sports, you mostly got one or two shots at a championship. This year was the Memorials' opportunity. Many of their players were free agents next year, and ownership didn't have the money to retain everybody.

"I don't see too much talent out there," Amy said flatly.

"You know, I've been thinking of taking up pitching myself," Dean answered in his familiar Minnesota accent. "I think I might be the guy." Dean smiled at Amy, who chuckled. He slid his left hand into the catcher's mitt and walked slowly toward right field where the other catchers were.

As Dean walked away, Amy could tell that Dean Larson was the slowest man in camp. Amy knew that catchers rarely possessed much speed, but Dean was slow, even for a catcher. His teammates used to say the only way Dean could hit a triple was if all three of the outfielders fell over dead on the same play. Dean laughed at the joke along with everyone. His easy-going nature made him the unofficial team captain. That was a difficult task in a world of larger-than-life endorsement contracts for men that may or may not be as big.

Amy made a few more notes concerning the stability of the organization. She jotted down some thoughts on how Buddy Wilson had been able to keep the pitching staff intact one more year for a pennant drive, but the question of the fifth starter remained. She looked up to scan for Buddy, but what she saw stopped her pen completely. Sitting at the entrance to the ball field in a new uniform was a woman slipping on a pair of cleats.

Chapter 10

Sister Mary Bernadette sat on the bleacher and looked back at the Winnebago parked just outside the entrance to the stadium. Buddy Wilson had arranged for it late the previous night because he felt it was necessary for something he termed "team chemistry." When Sister Mary had pressed him further, Buddy had finally admitted his doubts about how a bunch of guys would react to a nun in their dressing room.

Sister Mary did not fight the decision. She surprised herself when she realized she hadn't thought about this particular problem in any of the dreams she'd had as a kid about playing baseball in the big time. For now, she decided the Winnebago was a good place for her to locker.

Sister Mary's hands shook as she struggled with the laces of the first shoe. Despite Father Michael's divine beliefs, she knew she had to prove she was a ballplayer. She told herself again and again that this was exactly what she'd always hoped for. She finally got the first shoe tied.

Instead of picking up the other shoe, Sister Mary grabbed the mitt. The gift from her little league team back home calmed her. They'd always told her they believed she could play baseball. In Sister Mary's experience, there was nothing stronger than the belief of children. She felt confidence again, at least enough to take the field. She quickly began to tie her other cleat, but stopped when someone interrupted her.

"Excuse me," Amy Springer said as she approached the sitting nun.

"Yes?"

"That's a lovely uniform," Amy started. "I didn't know you

could get Memorials uniforms at the sports stores."

"You must be able to, although I really couldn't say. They gave me this one," Sister Mary answered, a bit peeved by someone wanting to discuss shopping at this critical moment.

"They as in —," Amy prompted.

"Coach Moss and Mr. Wilson." Sister Mary finished tying her shoes and grabbed her special leather mitt. She wondered exactly who it was this woman *thought* handed out uniforms.

"So you're here at spring training as a player?" Amy asked.

"Why else would I be here?" Sister Mary shook her head and jogged toward the outfield. Amy skipped in her heels, trying to keep up.

"Do you mean the Washington Memorials have brought you in for a tryout?"

"Yes."

Amy's left heel broke and she had to stop. She yelled ahead. "What's your name?"

The young woman stopped and turned. "Sister Mary Bernadette." Without a beat, she turned and continued on to the outfield grass to stretch.

Amy's mind went numb. She told herself that this had to be a nickname but there was something in the way she had said it, so directly, so forthright, that told Amy that "Sister" wasn't a nickname. She hobbled back to the bleacher to retrieve her briefcase, which had her cell phone. She was about to dial when she saw something more important than calling in the scoop. On the other side of the infield, Moss Thompson and Buddy Wilson stepped out of the dugout.

"Hey Coach! Hey Buddy!" Amy yelled as she hobbled toward the two.

Both men scanned the infield and saw Sister Mary moving toward the outfield. They looked back at Amy Springer, cell phone in hand. It was finally a chance to use that algebra class from seventh grade. Both did the math and realized a shouting reporter plus a nun with a knuckleball equaled questions they didn't want to answer. Buddy and Moss wished this problem would go away, and it almost did.

Amy was not a patient person. She wanted answers and wanted them now, but walking on one heel was a task best left to circus acrobats, not reporters. She managed two long strides before the weight of her bag threw her off balance. She made one lurching effort with her right leg to stay upright, but the attempt proved unsuccessful. Amy landed in a partial split, her bag spilling out onto the infield. The phone never left her hand.

"You know, we could just start practice," Moss thought aloud, hoping Buddy would see the logic in leaving the press in a dust cloud a little longer.

Buddy looked at his coach and then at his team. Baseball was a team game. Players must work together, but to do that they must perform well as individuals. The pitchers and catchers who stretched in the outfield hadn't noticed the arrival of the nun yet. They were all too busy focusing on what they had to do. He realized the importance of getting to them first and making a proper introduction.

"Buddy, Moss, could you give me a hand?" Amy yelled as she rose to her feet kicking both shoes off toward the first base bag.

Buddy rubbed his tired eyes and shook his head at Moss. Moss had gotten him into this, and even if he didn't hold the same kind of hope that Buddy did for Sister Mary's prospects, shouldn't Moss be the one to face the music?

"Moss, go help the lady up," Buddy said.

"Are you out of your mind?"

"You're always telling me how they still treat women like ladies back where you come from," Buddy answered. "Well, prove it."

"Key word here is lady."

"And I suppose you want me to go over there and talk with her."

Moss kicked the dirt. "You are the general manager, and I expect she wants to talk about player moves."

"I bet she does." Buddy glanced back at Amy. "I think she should talk to you."

"Why's that?" Moss asked.

"Because if she asks me why we got a nun with next to no experience trying out for a major league team, I might just have to tell the truth. Now you've got to ask yourself, do you want the whole world to know that you lost a bet to a priest?" Buddy asked, looking directly into Moss's eyes.

Moss spat into the dirt and shook his head. He cursed himself for being a Catholic and an impatient hitter.

"What do I tell her?" Moss asked.

"You'll think of something," Buddy answered and walked off to the outfield grass.

Moss hiked his pants up around the spreading area of his waist and sauntered over to where Amy Springer scrambled to collect her things.

"It's nice to see that you made the trip." Moss smiled broadly and falsely.

"Oh, I'm here every year," Amy answered tautly as she brushed herself off.

"It's good to see you, and on behalf of the organization, we look forward to seeing you during the regular season as we try to bring home the series for our fans." Moss had worked on that line all winter. He thought those words, with the right tone, had just the right mix of humility and bravado necessary for him to be seen as the confident general about to lead his troops into battle.

"Cut the crap, Moss. I want to know about her." She pointed at Sister Mary, now gracefully stretching down to touch her toes.

"Her, yes — well, she's here to try out for the team." Moss smiled. He tried to hide the tension in his grin. He wanted Amy to believe that this woman in spring training was the most natural thing in the world.

"Moss, without going too far overboard, let me summarize this issue for you. Are you, or are you not considering a woman for a major league roster spot?" Amy waited.

"Those are pretty strong words."

"Well then, tell me, what are all those people stretching in the outfield doing here?" Amy answered back.

"This is spring training, and they are — spring training." Moss wanted to run away, but now that Amy had removed the impediment of the heeled shoes he didn't think he was fast enough.

"Moss, don't double talk me"

"It's not quite so simple as that."

"Look, I'm not dancing with you on this. Why is there a woman in the outfield, in a baseball uniform, during spring training?"

Moss scratched his shoulder, then his knee, and then he took off his cap and scratched the top of his head. It was a peculiar thing he'd noticed as a player. When the pressure of a big ball game came down, he got all itchy. Then he began to sweat. Amy glared at him.

Moss cleared his throat. "Look, it's —"

"Spring training is a chance for us to take a long, hard look at potential prospects for all levels of baseball," Buddy Wilson said as he strode up behind Amy.

Moss breathed a long sigh as he looked up into the steely blue eyes of Buddy, who stood planted firmly behind the reporter.

"So this woman is here as what, a pitcher or a catcher?" Amy didn't miss a beat.

"She's a pitcher," Buddy answered confidently.

"Where's she from?"

"Nebraska, a small town there."

"Who found her?" Amy continued.

"Our scouts are constantly looking for new prospects, and she was found in the normal way that young people across this country are discovered," Buddy answered.

"And just where, in your memory, do they have a lot of female baseball players, Buddy?" Amy said.

"We prefer to see her not as a woman, but as an athlete out here to compete for a job among other athletes." Buddy was smooth now. He could go on for hours like this.

"Let me get this straight. You guys bring a woman into spring training and try to pass it off as just another jock trying to make a team?" Amy's eyes opened wide with shock.

"Yeah, that's exactly how we see it," Moss blurted back at the reporter. Buddy winced a little. Moss wasn't the coach of the Memorials because of his speaking ability.

"You guys may be breaking the gender barrier in baseball here. This is possibly the biggest story of the decade." Amy's eyes glowed with the aura of awards, TV spots and the label of "scoop." Most reporters get few opportunities to completely outdistance the entire journalistic community. This was her big chance.

"Look," Buddy started in his best fatherly tone. "There's a lot of truth to what you're saying. I agree that this could be something — special."

"You're darn right it could," Amy stated.

"But on the other hand, look at it from her perspective. There is an awful lot of pressure on her right now. She's got a very difficult task ahead, a task that requires the utmost concentration. Now imagine what will happen if you print an article about how the Washington Memorials are trying out a female pitcher. Any chance she had at being out of the limelight as she strives for this goal will be lost. It could ruin her concentration. It could cost her a spot. Now, do you want to do that?" Buddy nodded in the reporter's direction.

"As soon as the games start, everybody's going to know," Amy said. "She can't expect to be treated like just another high school big shot trying to make a team."

"Could you give her at least a couple of days? Just to get settled in?" Buddy cajoled.

"I'll think about it," Amy answered. "I might be more inclined if I could get an interview."

"An interview? I don't think that's a possibility," Buddy stated. "It's her first day."

"Then I'll just print what I have." Amy turned to leave. She counted two steps before Buddy cleared his throat.

"She gives you an interview and you'll hold off?" Buddy said to Amy's back.

"I said I'd consider it."

"That isn't much of a deal."

"This is a big story, Buddy. If I get the sense that anybody, and I mean anybody, knows and is ready to print, I'll have to go with it." Amy now turned for emphasis. "You have to understand my position."

Buddy understood her position, but more importantly he understood his. He had no choice, and Amy knew it.

"Fine, you get the interview. You hold the story."

"As I said, I'll do my best."

Buddy made deals for a living. Amy's body language told him that there was an eighty percent chance that she wouldn't print anything. Considering the circumstances, Buddy thought that was the best he could do.

"Thank you." Buddy motioned to Moss to come with him. The coach stepped quickly.

"Just one last question." Amy caught the two men with her words. "Her name, Sister Mary Bernadette. Does that mean she's a nun?"

Buddy turned and sighed. "As a matter of fact, it does." He grabbed Moss's arm, and they walked briskly away.

Amy gathered her belongings and trudged off toward the stands. She stopped only to collect her shoes.

"You were brilliant," Moss started. "We keep this out of the media until the tryout, and it'll all just go away." The coach looked for a response from his friend, but Buddy had stopped. The general manager stared off into the outfield.

Sister Mary lay on her back with her right leg tucked under her body in the hurdler's stretch. She evidently took stretching very seriously, as her concentration shielded everything from her mind. That had to be the reason she didn't notice the half circle that had formed around her. One by one, each pitcher had looked over at the new prospect to size up the player, only to be forced into a second look. The other pitchers and catchers now stared at the female form occupying the Memorial uniform, stretching with the intent of doing something athletic today.

Buddy went from a standstill to a trot. Moss scampered at his side. Both wore worried looks on their faces. The unfortunate delay to deal with the press had kept them from being with the other players when Sister Mary joined them.

From out of the middle of the throng of players, an older man stepped forward. He was in uniform, with a permanent scowl etched on his thin face. The man was Boney Freeman. He took one look at the female stretching on his outfield and the scowl grew sterner.

Chapter 11

Sister Mary Bernadette tried her best to stretch without shaking. Something powerful in the grass of this outfield kept reaching up and twisting her stomach. She forced herself not to look at the men who prepared themselves around her. They all seemed to be more than seven feet tall, weighing two seventy-five — all of it muscle. She had seen lots of big guys in her time, but nothing like this. The sister felt alone again, but only on the inside. She had this strange feeling that someone was extremely close to her, watching her. She didn't look up, only concentrated on stretching. If she had looked up, she'd have seen the man standing over her. His name was Boney Freeman, and he didn't stand tall.

Boney Freeman spent every waking moment of his life stretching himself skyward, trying to push his frame to the height of five feet eight inches. He was unsuccessful. Bony was the Memorials' pitching coach, a hard and driven man who expected more out of a person than even he thought he could get. He figured it was always better to push for the unattainable than settle for the present status of the player. It was the way he played.

He'd pitched for ten major league seasons with three different teams and had almost won a pennant in the year before he was cut for the final time. Most pitchers, even in Boney's day, were large, raw-boned slabs of beef with powerfully built physiques. Boney had lifted weights since he was a freshman in high school, but he never bulked up close to the large men who occupied the staffs he pitched on. Instead, Boney resembled a ferret out on the mound. His neck seemed to be permanently stretched out, as he glared at the catcher while he waited for the sign.

During his first minor league campaign, one large clean-up hitter had noticed Boney's size, the skinny body with the large cranium that pushed the skin tight around it. The man, a first round draft choice, told a friend that the wispy kid looked like a skeleton. It didn't take long for the leap from skeleton to Boney to occur.

Boney was small, but he had generated great arm speed through some loophole in physics that even avid fans who were scientists never quite figured out. He had learned five different pitches during his tour through the minors, and could throw all for strikes. He was always regarded, even in his playing days, as one of the best baseball minds ever. Unfortunately, Boney wasn't remembered by the public for his mind, but rather for one of the most infamous bench clearing brawls of all time.

The game had been at the Astrodome against the Giants, with Ty Jones on the hill for San Francisco. Ty had surrendered back-to-back homeruns to the two and three hitters in the bottom of the fifth inning. Next had come Lawyer Milton, the cleanup hitter for Houston — Boney's team. Lawyer had been in the hunt for the triple crown and his success pointed his team toward a possible pennant. Ty Jones had been rocked by the last two hitters, and he figured it was time to take back the inside part of the plate.

The thwack of ball on skin had echoed throughout the ballpark. Lawyer had gone to one knee, holding his wrist. The team doctor had rushed to his side and had immediately known what every fan feared. It was broken.

Boney Freeman, a rookie at that time, had walked by Lawyer Milton as they took the power hitter back into the clubhouse. The young, gaunt pitcher with beady eyes had looked the All Star right in the eyes.

"This will not be forgotten," Boney had assured him.

The next inning, Ty Jones, plunker of Lawyer Milton, had walked up to the plate to face Boney Freeman. Boney's biggest asset throughout his career had been his control. He had pinpoint placement, so regardless of any report to the contrary, Boney had known exactly where his fastball would go.

Ty Jones had smiled before the pitch. That had just made Boney angrier. The fastball had started out high, and Jones relaxed. Boney still vividly recalled how the pitcher's eyes had popped open when the ball began to tail in, but at that point it was too late. Jones had tried to dive away, but the pitch caught him in the helmet with a mighty thwack. The impact had buried Jones in the dirt of the batter's box, where he lay writhing in pain. Both benches had erupted from their dugouts and charged the mound.

Boney Freeman had never been a man to wait for someone to come and get him. The moment he'd seen the first Giant hit the field, Boney had run screaming like a wild man toward the visitors' dugout. He'd met the Giants' catcher at the third base line and submarined him before being swallowed whole into the ocean of Giants' jerseys. He had gone punching and kicking. Before it ended, Boney had been accused of biting, scratching, clawing and hitting people from behind.

It had taken thirty minutes to break the ruckus up, and of course the last man pulled from the pile was a bloodied little pitcher named Boney. He had been thrown out of the game and suspended for two more. The team had been crippled by the loss of Lawyer Milton and finished out of the running. They had, however, invited Boney back for another season.

Boney Freeman's "us against them" mentality was tough to take at times, but the Memorials couldn't argue with the results. He was a man of severe opinions, and at that moment he was about to have one.

"Excuse me miss, but is there a reason you're taking up space on my outfield during my spring training?" Boney's top lip quivered in a show of anger.

"I'm stretching, so I don't pull something," Sister Mary said.

"As a coach, I can understand that. What I don't understand is what in the hell you're doing in a Washington Memorials baseball uniform."

Sister Mary halted her stretching and rose to her feet. She looked sternly at the short, gnarled man and took one step forward. "I'd appreciate it if you wouldn't curse when I'm around."

"Excuse me?" Boney asked.

"I don't think cursing makes you more of a man," Sister Mary said, putting her hands on her hips.

"You don't, do you? Well I don't give a damn!"

Sister Mary wasn't used to being cussed at, at least not since she'd taken her vows. "Sir, I've asked you nicely."

"Well, I got news for you. This ain't a nice place. And if you don't like it, you can get the hell out of here."

"Boney!" Buddy shouted out to the coach, now only two steps away from the pair.

"Do you ever listen to yourself? Does that sound appealing to you?" Sister Mary asked soberly.

"I ain't appealing. I'm a baseball coach," Boney screeched.

"Not much of an excuse."

"Look here you little —"

"Boney." Buddy grabbed his pitching coach.

"Do you see what we got here?" Boney sneered at the nun.

"I see her, and there's something you should know," Buddy started.

"What in the hell should I know?"

Buddy said calmly, "Boney Freeman, I'd like you to meet Sister Mary Bernadette."

"Je—, she's a nun?" Boney said incredulously.

"Convent and everything," Moss added.

"Then will somebody — anybody — tell me what she's doing in a Memorials' uniform on my field?" Boney looked at Moss and Buddy.

"Now that's a very long story," Moss began.

Buddy stopped Moss. He knew this required the direct approach. "Boney Freeman, this just happens to be one of the exciting, young pitching prospects we'd like to take a look-see at this spring." Buddy's expression didn't change. He fought to make the speech sound as natural and as ordinary as if he were introducing the next Warren Spahn.

Boney's mouth dropped open, and his lungs didn't function for what seemed like an entire minute. The scrappy coach tried to think of anything to do or to say that made any sense. Then he cracked a smile and started to laugh.

"Are you all right?" Moss asked.

"You guys. You guys are too much," Boney rambled. "Okay, okay. Which one of you thought this one up?" He laughed again. "Which one? Come on, this is the best spring training prank I've ever seen. I mean a nun pitching in the majors." Boney tried to laugh longer, but it was painfully apparent that no one else was. This included the athletic-looking nun next to him.

"Boney, can we see you a minute?" Buddy said. Moss, Boney and Buddy walked off a little ways. The other pitchers just gawked at Sister Mary, who went back to stretching.

"Look, Boney, we need another arm and we don't have any money left. This gal has talent. I know it. I realize this is highly unusual," Buddy began.

"Highly unusual? Highly unusual! Do you understand what you're trying to do here? Do you? Women got no place out here with the guys. It's the last safe place a man can spit, belch and scratch without having to apologize."

"Our job is to win a pennant. That's why she's here." Buddy assumed his stern negotiator's face.

"All right, fine. I agree. But let's give one of our guys in the minors a chance," Boney argued.

"She hasn't been handed the job," Moss said. "She's got to earn it like everyone else."

"I smell a promotional gimmick, that's what I smell. McDermott just wants a sideshow for the start of the season so he can get on TV."

"I'm telling you, she's legit," Buddy's voice grew.

"All right, then, how come I never heard of her?" Boney asked.

"She played in Nebraska," Buddy offered.

"They got newspapers there. Somebody should've written something. I mean a woman pitcher in baseball, that's better than most of the freaks they've got on front pages today."

"She had to take care of religious obligations first," Buddy said. "She's been away from the game for awhile."

"She's been away for awhile! You bring me a nun and the best you can tell me is that she's been away for awhile?" Boney shook his head.

"It's not like we didn't scout her," Buddy added.

"Who scouted her?" Boney asked.

Moss began to sweat. Boney was a pure baseball man. The idea of telling his pitching coach that this nun had a tryout coming to her because he lost a bet to a priest wouldn't sit well. Moss knew he needed Boney's expertise with the staff to help get the team to the pennant and beyond. That's why he chose his words carefully and painfully.

"I did," Moss said. "I saw her pitch at a ball field in Nebraska." Moss winced a little. "She pitched well."

"Against who?" Boney wasn't satisfied.

"Former major league talent," Moss said.

"So she looked good against wash-outs, big deal." Boney kicked some dirt.

"I wouldn't call them wash-outs, exactly." Moss's pride was hurt.

"They aren't playing now, so they don't count," Boney countered.

Before Moss could answer, Buddy pinched Moss discreetly. The pain brought him back down to Earth. Moss took a moment to collect his thoughts.

"Boney, I'm telling you as a former major league pitcher that this kid's got talent. We owe it to ourselves to take a look at her. If we don't like what we see, we've lost nothing but the plane ticket," Moss finally said.

"She's got a contract, Boney," Buddy added. "She is going through spring training."

Boney bit his bottom lip in resignation. He hated having things rammed down his throat, but he knew in the end, Buddy and Moss would win. That was their job.

"Okay," Boney started, "but don't expect any special treatment from me. She's gotta make the commitment that every other man out here does."

"I wouldn't have it any other way." Moss smiled.

Boney started back to his pitchers, but stopped after a few steps. "What does she throw?"

Moss answered, "The knuckleball."

Boney's eyes rolled up into his head. "Je—." Boney caught himself and looked at his new pitching project. The little coach shook his head and scratched his scalp. "She's already got me screwed up in the head," he muttered as he walked slowly toward the group to get ready for the season. Buddy and Moss gave Boney room to start his practice.

"All right, you guys," Boney addressed the group of pitchers. "I'd like you to meet our newest pitching prospect, Sister Mary

Bernadette." Boney paused so that everyone could take a good look at the nun in uniform.

Sister Mary didn't like the spotlight much, but she realized that these were her teammates. As she looked over the group of large, unshaven men, a sinking feeling began to gnaw at her stomach. Maybe this wasn't such a great idea after all.

"The Sister here comes from the diamonds of Nebraska after having faced the toughest competition that old, broken down ballplayers can provide," Boney yelled.

"Excuse me?" Sister Mary asked.

A cold chill went through the staff again. No player had ever stood up to Boney on a his first day, especially not twice.

"Is there a problem?" Boney asked.

"I don't think that's a fair description of my past."

"You don't think it's fair. Did you hear that fellas? She don't think it's fair. Well let me tell you something about fairness and baseball. This ain't a fair game. Some fat guy with a chest protector is going to stand sixty feet, six inches away from you, surrounded by 40,000 people trying to decide whether to boo or cheer, and you're going paint the corner with the sweetest pitch you've ever had the good fortune to throw in your short life. And he's gonna call it outside. Then tell me, Sister, are you going to storm up to home plate and scream at the top of your lungs, 'that's not fair?'" Boney's face was red.

Sister Mary didn't budge and didn't blink. She kept herself just barely under control in the face of the barking Boney. She bent down and picked up her mitt, slipped it on her hand and pounded it once with her fist. She found comfort in that baseball glove, a little love in the harsh world she had stepped into.

"Now, do you have anything else to add?" Boney asked Sister Mary. The nun was silent. "Good." Boney turned toward the infield. "You know the drill boys — and female. It's the same thing every year. Line up on the pitcher's mound, and let's start ingraining going to first on grounders hit to the right side. I want to see some hustle!"

The pitchers all ran off toward the infield to get ready for the best-known and most boring spring training drill ever devised. Sister Mary ran alone, to the side of the great mob of players. The other prospects measured her with the contempt rivals have for each other.

The regular staff wasn't entirely sure it was a good idea for their future with Boney as a pitching coach to talk to her, so they kept their distance. But everyone, to the man, was intrigued. Whatever she could do, it must be special — or at least interesting to watch.

Chapter 12

Sister Mary Bernadette allowed herself to limp only after all the other ballplayers left the field for the locker room. The muscles used for being a nun turned out to be very different than the ones used to play baseball. In her hand, she carried a large tube of sports rub. The trainer had offered her two, but she took only one to prove her mettle to the team. She regretted her pride as she opened the door and slipped into the Winnebago.

"Hello." The woman's voice would have shocked Sister Mary under normal circumstances, but today, the nun was too tired to scare. She was not too tired to be annoyed.

"Hi," Sister Mary said shortly, wondering what this woman was doing there.

"My name is Amy Springer, *Washington Herald*. I cover the Memorials for the paper." Amy stood and offered Sister Mary a hand, which the nun shook.

"Can I help you?"

Amy smiled. "As a matter of fact you can. I want to interview you for the paper."

Sister Mary knew that baseball had reporters who interviewed people. She hadn't really thought that would apply to her when she'd agreed to this scheme. After all, she was only supposed to be the fifth pitcher.

"Does this have to happen now?" Sister Mary asked.

"Sister Mary," Buddy spoke up. The nun turned to see the general manager standing in the back of the Winnebago. "This is a normal part of being a ballplayer. We want to have good relations with the press. Amy Springer is our beat reporter, and she has agreed not to print anything if you do an interview with her now." Buddy studied Sister Mary's reaction.

"Why does she want an interview if she isn't going to print something?" Sister Mary asked warily.

Buddy responded. "I meant to say, she won't print anything right away. Give you a chance to settle in. Get used to baseball again. This is the best thing for the team." Buddy gave her his best fatherly look.

"If it's best for the team," Sister Mary answered softly.

"It is," Amy Springer stated warmly as she took out a tape recorder. "Now if you'll excuse us, Buddy."

"I thought I'd stay," Buddy said to Amy.

"I don't think so," Amy answered slowly to emphasize that Buddy would be leaving.

Buddy balked for a moment. He knew she still held all the cards, and at best this was a long shot. But what was the worst that could happen? He decided not to press the issue and moved to the door.

"Be gentle," he said to Amy. "It's her first time." Buddy left.

Sister Mary collapsed into a chair and tried not to think about the pain in her body.

"Now then," Amy began. "My first question is the most obvious, I suppose. How does it feel trying to break the gender barrier?"

"The what?"

"The gender barrier. You understand you are trying to be the first woman to play in the major leagues?"

"I hadn't really thought about it much."

"You'd better start, because it is a big deal," Amy offered flatly. She gauged the nun's reaction and knew that Sister Mary really hadn't given it all that much thought. This would lead to a lot of silence, so Amy changed the subject. "You had a pretty rough day out there with Coach Freeman. Is everything okay between you and him?"

"Honestly, I couldn't say. We've only known each other one day," Sister Mary offered, although she did think the coach was a bit rude.

Amy put her pad down and looked right at Sister Mary and asked, "How did it feel out there today? To be a part of major league baseball's spring training?"

Sister Mary thought a long time about the question before she smiled. She said, "I don't know how to describe it."

"Was it good, bad? What was the emotion?" Amy continued.

"I —" Sister Mary stopped again. "This is difficult to explain."

"I have time."

Sister Mary began again, but halted. Finally, her eyes lit up. "I can answer your question, but not here and not now."

"Excuse me?" Amy Springer asked.

"Meet me here tomorrow morning at five."

"You're kidding, right?"

"No, trust me. If you want me to answer the question, come tomorrow morning at five."

"I'm not a morning person."

"If you show up at five tomorrow morning, I can give you an answer."

"Why not now?"

"I just can't; you'll have to trust me on that."

"Why should I trust you? I just met you."

Sister Mary shot her a knowing smile. "You can trust me. I'm a nun."

Amy Springer considered the young woman for all of five seconds. "I'll meet you tomorrow morning, but you have to promise to be candid with me. Not just about this question, but about anything I ask."

"I promise."

"I'll hold you to that, as a nun." Amy stood.

Sister Mary showed the reporter to the door and opened it. There, on the top step, stood the catcher Dean Larson, wet hair recently combed.

"Hello," Sister Mary said, somewhat surprised at the visit.

"I didn't know you had company." Dean looked at Amy who smiled at him.

"I was just leaving," Amy replied and stepped past the catcher to the ground below. "Tell me, Dean, did you ever think you'd see a woman in baseball?"

"There's one thing I've learned," Dean answered. "Each time you play a baseball season, you're bound to see something new."

"Can I quote you on that?" Amy teased.

"As always," Dean responded. Amy turned and walked slowly away. Dean returned to Sister Mary. "Your first interview?"

"Yeah," Sister Mary said.

"Get used to it. The better you get, the more you do."

"She seems a little pushy."

"That's most reporters," Dean smiled. "Look, I just stopped to see if you had any dinner plans tonight. If you don't, I know a diner. It is a generally-held tradition that this diner is the first place most rooks eat on the first day of spring training."

"That would be great. Just let me change and shower."

Dean nodded and Sister Mary went back inside. She sat down gingerly on a bench and felt the aches again.

She peeled the white and blue uniform with red piping from her body and tossed it near the laundry bag in a corner. Buddy had assured her that every major league team had someone who did the laundry. She, as a player, was to worry about other things.

It was the first time in her life anyone had offered to do her laundry without a catch. As a child, she had traded many chores around the house and ranch to get out of laundry, but this was something great. Somebody was actually paid to do her laundry. She settled back into the softness of the long, cushioned bench seat and smiled. This was heaven, a place where you never did laundry.

Sister Mary stepped into the tiny shower for a long, hot soak. She tried to lose herself in the water as it carried the sweat and the dirt of an afternoon of baseball down the drain. As small amounts of steam rose, the day began to fade. She fought hard to keep it. She had just participated in a real practice on a real field for a real major league baseball team. Baseball had returned to her.

She turned off the water and stepped from the shower into a soft, warm towel. She dressed quickly and rolled her dirty clothes up into a bag. As she tied the strings to the bag, she saw her baseball mitt lying near the door. She picked it up and remembered a life a thousand miles away.

The memory made her a little homesick and a lot uncomfortable. Nuns weren't usually given special Winnebagos and laundry services. She also knew that nuns weren't usually asked to become major league pitchers to save their churches. Maybe the rules relaxed a bit under abnormal conditions. There really wasn't anyone to ask for guidance right then. There was no Father Michael, no other nuns around. For the first time since she had arrived, Sister Mary began to feel alone.

"Are you ready?" Dean asked as Sister Mary dropped the bag on the bottom step outside the Winnebago a few minutes later.

"Yes," she replied and followed Dean toward the parking lot, and an unexpected meeting with Moss who was just exiting the locker room.

"Where are you two going?" Moss asked the nun and the catcher.

"She's having dinner with me tonight, Skip," Dean announced.

Moss almost couldn't respond. He hadn't planned on the nun socializing with the team. "Have fun," he finally managed to reply, although deep down, he really didn't mean it.

Moss did not want his team getting to know Sister Mary. She was supposed to be here for a short time and then leave. Hanging out with the ballplayers would only make it more difficult when he cut her and sent her back to Father Michael. He hoped that time would come soon.

Chapter 13

Amy Springer sat at her desk in front of her laptop and stared at the broken shoe prominently displayed in the middle of two notebooks. She had been like this for two hours. The paper had called twice asking about her story for tomorrow's sports section. She had told them she hadn't finished it yet. The better answer was she hadn't decided yet.

Amy knew the pitfalls of being a woman in a world dominated by men. She had been in many a press box listening to fat men who had failed to make high school baseball teams go on and on about the "bums" and the "spoiled children" who played the game in front of tens of thousands. And when large-breasted women crashed games to get a kiss, Amy was left out of that discussion as well.

She had played college softball for a mediocre team in the Big Ten as a second baseman whom her coach described as more cerebral than athletic. She had survived against the competition by shrewdly positioning herself in the field and drumming the concept of going with the pitch into her head. She had batted eighth, always, and made one fielding error in four years.

Unlike many of her colleagues, she had faced eighty mile-per-hour pitches. They were rising fastballs, which are harder to hit. She had more appreciation for the skill it took to play the game than most of her peers, but in the end she had learned that didn't make you a good reporter.

No one wanted to hear how difficult it was to hit a baseball, or how small the strike zone was becoming. No one cared about the mechanics of the double play. What the public wanted was heroes and goats A melodrama played out a hundred and sixty two times a year. A different script each day that unfolded with sound bytes, highlight clips, and shrewd analysis of the mental condition of key players. In this way, sports reporters were much like theater critics.

She fought to resolve the issue before her. She was a clear thinker most of the time, and she boiled down her salient items list to two things: Sister Mary needed all the time out of the spotlight she could get, and this was the biggest baseball story Amy Springer was ever likely to break. She understood she could not have it both ways. She had to make a choice.

Amy got up from her desk and poured herself another cup of coffee. She had vowed never to take up smoking and had decided caffeine was a safer and saner addiction. This was her sixth cup. Amy paced around her desk twice. The first time she imagined the rush of press tomorrow afternoon once her story hit the sidewalks. The second time she imagined one of those network dweebs scooping her in front of millions. The phone rang.

She once again told a lie to her editor. She said she was just finishing the polish before sending it down. She collapsed into her chair, wishing the answer would just strike her. It didn't. Instead, she wondered what it must be like to actually wear the uniform on the field, to be one of the players.

People always told her that sports were overrated, that there were other things in life that should get more attention. Amy never bought it. After all, there weren't five national cable channels devoted to opera. Millions of people didn't tune in to watch somebody read Mark Twain. Sports defined the United States as well as anything. It gave the nation drama, heroes, and most importantly, something to talk about when one couldn't think of anything else to say. She couldn't count how many times she'd said or heard, "See the game last night?"

She wanted to step onto a field on a steamy summer night in August and hear the anthem play. She wanted to stand in the box facing the pitcher and play the mind game of guessing what the next pitch would be. She wanted to see the hot shot to the right side and dive to glove it. She wanted the athlete's life, but she knew she could never have it.

She, for better or worse, was a sports reporter complete with all the baggage of the lifestyle. She was single because she traveled too much and men tended to shy away from a woman with strong shoulders who played second base better than they did. She traveled with the team, so her home was rarely well kept or lived in. It was fast becoming apparent to her that her life was her work. That's how she made a difference. That's how she made a living. That's how she'd be remembered.

Amy rose quickly. She walked to the desk and sat down at the keyboard of her computer. She quickly typed two sentences and smiled. It was the same grin she'd had after she'd guessed right on a pitch and drove it through the gap in right center. She typed two more sentences, then picked up the phone.

"Chief, save me more space. You're not going believe this."

Chapter 14

Sister Mary and Dean Larson sat in a booth in what was possibly the defining example of diner architecture of the late twentieth century. Dean ate his hot beef sandwich like he did everything else — slowly. He savored the gravy. Sister Mary worked her way around a cheeseburger platter.

"So, is your first day of spring training everything you thought it would be?" Dean asked.

"Yes and no," Sister Mary answered without looking up.

"Don't let Boney get to you. He's been yelling his head off since the day he was born. You can't change him. You just have to work with him."

"It doesn't seem that he wants me here."

"You're probably right." Dean swallowed a large spoonful of mashed potatoes.

"He hates me then?" She asked.

Dean chuckled and put down his fork. "No. It's not that he hates you. He's just very careful about caring until he knows you're going to be around a while. You see, Boney is the ultimate team player. The last guy whose loyalty to his team supersedes all. If you're on his staff, then Boney will go to the wall for you. That's just the way he is, but it means he gets pretty attached to his pitchers. Every time one of them is traded or sent down, Boney takes it hard."

"That doesn't help me much now, does it?" Sister Mary asked.

"No, but then that's not what spring training is all about. The number of people who want to be here is far greater than the few who ever get chosen. If you do make it, the scrutiny and the pressure are worse than anything you feel now."

"You make it sound awful," Sister Mary replied.

"Sometimes it is," Dean answered as he downed another forkful of mashed potatoes.

"If it's so bad, why are you here?"

Dean thought a minute and rubbed his chin. "I guess because I couldn't ever bring myself to do anything else besides squat behind home plate and try and make a batter guess wrong, then snap the ball to third after another strikeout."

"I'll be a disappointment to you then, because I don't strike out too many."

"What do you throw?" Dean asked too quickly, as if the entire evening had led up to this question.

"The knuckleball," Sister Mary stated.

The gears clicked in Dean's brain. The logic of her presence in spring training made sense now. She wasn't a mutant woman with a ninety mile-an-hour fastball. She had the enigma pitch, the most difficult thing in the world for a catcher to handle.

"Sister Mary throws the knuckler. Could be a headline."

"Sister Mary Bernadette," the nun corrected him.

"What?"

"My full name is Sister Mary Bernadette."

"It is, is it?" Dean said as his lips parted into a broad smile.

She asked, "Why are you're smiling?"

"Every ballplayer needs a nickname, and I think I've just figured out yours."

"That would be?"

"All in good time," Dean answered. He paid the bill and the pair walked back to his car. They drove back toward the hotel under a cloudless, starry Florida sky. As they got closer to the hotel, Sister Mary sensed the catcher growing more serious.

"Thank you for showing me around," she said.

"Well it's nice to get to spend time with a person not all caught up in the show," Dean responded. "I'm from Minnesota, small town. I hear you're from Nebraska?"

"Born and raised."

"That's nice," Dean said. "I miss Minnesota sometimes. Too da— darn hot down here all the time. Washington's a little better, I suppose."

"Is it a nice place to live?" Sister Mary asked.

"If you like a lots of asphalt, lots of traffic kind of life. My real house is just outside of Minneapolis. Always thought one day I'd be traded to the Twins. I've just got an apartment in D.C. It's all right, I guess."

"And your wife?" Sister Mary asked.

Dean Larson's eyebrows popped up. "Who told you I was married?"

"You've got the groove of a wedding ring dug into your left ring finger. I figured you don't like to wear it when you play."

The catcher sat quietly for a few moments as two bugs, transfixed on the headlights of his car, splattered into the windshield.

"I'm sorry. I don't always guess right," Sister Mary offered.

"No," the big man said. He looked over at the young nun and found something different about her. Her eyes were so large, so blue, so comforting. He imagined she could stare someone calm. "That's okay. She and my daughter live in our house near Minneapolis. I guess you could say things are not in proper order right now."

"That's too bad," Sister Mary said and waited for him to talk.

"It's nothing to be sad about. It's just two people trying to figure out how they're going to live side by side."

There were moments in her life when Sister Mary felt things so strongly that she had to say them out loud — things most people missed. She had one of those feelings now. She felt she probably shouldn't say anything, but in the end she couldn't stop herself.

"She wants you to give up baseball, doesn't she?"

Dean drove a few miles before he answered. "She thinks it might help if I were around a little more. Says she feels a little like a single parent. It was easier when it was just the two of us. We could travel. That's all changed now."

"Is that why you asked me to dinner tonight?" Sister Mary prodded. "Because you wanted to talk?"

Dean chuckled and shook his head. "No, that just happened. This isn't my normal nighttime routine during spring ball, but then you're not exactly the normal ballplayer either."

"I don't know how different I am."

Dean chuckled, "You are, trust me on that. That's why we always take the rooks to dinner. We need to know what kind of person he, or in this case she, is.

"Did I pass the test?" Sister Mary asked.

"Well, I like you, and I hope you make the team. We could use someone like you around. I hope you're as good a ballplayer as you are a listener."

"I am," Sister Mary said with more bravado than Dean Larson imagined a nun would have.

"That's good to hear, because I've caught every guy here, except you. Buddy has no trade bait for pitching, so the way I see it, I'm pretty interested in your right arm."

The car stopped next to the hotel, and Dean waited for Sister Mary to get out.

"You can park. I don't mind the walk," Sister Mary said.

"I'm not going in directly. I usually take some time to myself every day. It keeps my sanity." Dean smiled.

Sister Mary Bernadette opened the door of the car and then looked back. She had one of those feelings again. "This is your last season, isn't it?"

The large man took his time before he answered, "It just might be."

"You're not very comfortable with your fate in the hands of a nun on the mound are you?"

"Honestly," the catcher sighed, "no."

She waited for a moment and stepped to the pavement. "Thank you for this evening. It's the closest thing to comfortable I've felt since I got here."

Dean smiled broadly. "I'm glad you enjoyed it."

Sister Mary stepped away, but Dean caught himself like he'd forgotten to mention something. "Hey!" He yelled. "Can you stay later tomorrow?"

"I — sure. Why?" Her eyes squinted with confusion.

"I thought we might work on a few things. Get you a little more prepared for when everyone else shows up. I've been hearing scouts talk, and — well, the more prepared you are the better for all of us."

Sister Mary grinned broadly. She grabbed the door to the car but stopped before she closed it.

"By the way, what's this nickname you thought of?"

Dean gave her a grin that displayed every tooth. "You'll find out tomorrow."

She closed the door and walked slowly to her room thinking of nicknames and home.

Chapter 15

Sister Mary woke up in her hotel room the next morning at four. She dressed quickly and took the only city bus running at that early hour to a stop near the ballpark. Since her days at the convent, Sister Mary had kept the schedule demanded by her father back on the ranch. Early mornings were her time to prepare for the day.

She walked the two blocks from the bus stop to the stadium leisurely, taking in the dew and the freshness of the day. While she walked, she balanced a baseball on the back of her spread fingers, rolling it from side to side, up and down. She spun the little white sphere in a circle, then up her arm and down again. She had learned this game as a child and still enjoyed it.

She turned the final corner into the stadium and her pace quickened. Something about being near baseball gave her a burst of energy, a burst that stopped short at the door to her Winnebago. She stood there in a moment of awe, wonder and utter confusion. There, stuck above her door, was a piece of athletic tape. In handwritten black letters was scrawled the name "Bernie". It was the fulfillment of Dean Larson's inspiration the night before.

It wasn't a glamorous name or one that particularly inspired fear in the opponent. Sister Mary knew this as she sat down in the cool confines of the mobile home. In her private thoughts, she had wished for something more literary like Sister Strikeout or the No-Hit Nun. Bernie was a name that brought images of mop-haired guys in tie-dyed shirts with red colored lenses in their sunglasses.

She knelt down and crossed herself, clasping her hands the same way she had since her early days of Sunday School, and prayed.

"Dear God the Father, thank you for this beautiful morning and the chance to once again make good on Father Michael's belief in my abilities to help save St. Francis. I realize this may be a little petty, but I was wondering if you could see your way clear to do something about this nickname business." Sister Mary winced a little, knowing that God had much on His mind that was more important than her nickname. "I realize it's a small thing, but I mean, Bernie? I know there have been some less than stellar nicknames in the past, but this is me. I mean sure, everybody that's on this team seems to have one —." The words rang in Sister Mary's ears, and she knew. She knew that a previous prayer had been answered. Bernie, regardless of anything else, meant that in at least one person's eyes, Sister Mary Bernadette belonged on the Washington Memorials. She said a quick "Amen," then dressed and went to the ball field.

Amy Springer stumbled out of her car at precisely one minute after five. She carried an extra-large bucket of coffee, laced with sugar to keep her awake. She had not seen this particular hour of the day since early in her college education. Under any other circumstances, the reporter would grumble and curse the morning. Today was different. Today she knew she was about to scoop the world, and that was a feeling strong enough to buoy the natural tendencies of someone who hated the phrase "crack of dawn."

She wore a sweatsuit for comfort and because it was on top of the pile of clothing in her hotel room. These were two extremely important factors for the sleep-deprived reporter. The morning was just cool enough to make the outfit comfortable. She walked stiffly to the door of the Winnebago and knocked. There was no answer. Amy knocked again and looked up at the top of the door. She squinted and read the word "Bernie." The nickname made her laugh. She was sure that somewhere there was a nun unhappy about being rebaptized with a baseball name.

Amy turned from the mobile home and moved slowly to the field. Her first thought was that her interview was late, which made her mad. She decided to look around a bit, knowing that if she stopped moving she'd fall asleep. She walked to the field gate. That's when Amy saw the nun.

"Good morning!" Sister Mary yelled and motioned for Amy to join her on the infield.

"How cute," the reporter mumbled to herself. "She wants to talk on the field. Great." Amy entered the field and absent-mindedly pulled the gate shut behind her. She walked up to the nun, who bounced with the energy of sunrise. Amy hated that.

"How are you?" Sister Mary asked.

"To tell the truth, I'm not much of a morning person," Amy said evenly.

"But I have your answer," Sister Mary said. "Just put this on." Sister Mary held out a baseball glove to Amy, who looked at it in confusion. "I don't know whose it is. I found it in the regular locker room. Don't tell anybody, because I'm not sure I was supposed to go in there. I just figured they wouldn't mind if I borrowed it. I mean, they've got all kinds of gloves back there."

Amy didn't move. This was not happening. This couldn't be happening.

"Really, I don't think they'll be upset. I mean, they'll probably not even know." Sister Mary offered the glove again.

"What does this have to do with my question?"

"You asked me what spring training felt like. Well, I don't think I can really tell you. I'd rather show you." Sister Mary offered the mitt a third time, and this time Amy tentatively accepted it. The reporter slid the piece of leather over her left hand.

Sister Mary backed up a few yards and produced a baseball. Amy fought to keep her mouth from dropping open. This woman meant to play catch with her at five in the morning. Sister Mary lobbed the ball easily to Amy.

The tiny smack of the baseball on the leather of the glove snapped Amy wide awake. She opened the glove and touched the ball. As she did, she looked around her. She was standing on the infield of a major league spring training field playing catch. Despite all her attempts to control it, a surge of excitement rushed through her body. For years she'd watched and written about this surface. Today she participated in its function. She set the ball in her hand and snapped a throw back to the nun.

The pair exchanged several tosses in silence. A trust began to develop between them, the trust of playing catch. It was born of believing the other person wouldn't throw the ball too high, or wide right or wide left. The belief that the next throw from the other person would be catchable.

"Do you have the answer to your question yet?" Sister Mary finally called out.

"I think I do. Do you mind another question?"

"Go ahead."

"The name on your door out there, Bernie. Was that your idea?"

Sister Mary stopped mid-throw and laughed. She doubled over in amusement, as did Amy. "No, it wasn't my idea."

"Men have funny ways of showing affection," Amy said as she composed herself.

"I suppose they do. But to be honest, as terrible as the name is, I feel more like a part of the team now." Sister Mary was serious. She resumed throwing.

"Do you want to tell me why you're attempting to make the roster of a major league baseball team?"

"Besides the fact it was my childhood dream?"

"Besides that."

Sister Mary considered the woman. Moss had told her not to tell the truth, but she had a tough time lying. She decided that Amy could handle it. "It started with Father Michael, a prayer and a broken window."

Sister Mary spilled the whole story, including the part about the Virgin Mary telling her not to throw the screwball. Amy listened almost in disbelief for over an hour.

Amy was a cynic who didn't practice organized or unorganized religion. The concept of miracles and visions was not easy for her to accept. It bothered her that Sister Mary's earnest recount of the story made it believable in some odd way. That, and how she now felt closer to the nun. Sister Mary probably would have said a lot more if the traffic hadn't showed up.

Car tires screeched in the parking lot. Men's voices rose as TV crews fought for position outside the clubhouse. The front gate, which had locked when Amy pulled it shut, rattled as reporters tried to force it open to get to the young pitcher. Amy suddenly felt out of place, and she was sorry that the magic of playing catch was fading. She felt even worse when she turned to face Sister Mary.

The nun stood in shock, as a few men cursed as they tried to climb over the barrier.

"What are they doing here?" Sister Mary's eyes were wide with the terror of so much attention.

Amy thought of lying to the nun. She even began to try, but found she couldn't. "I wrote an article last night for the paper."

Sister Mary's eyes dropped. "You said you'd wait."

"I said I'd think about it, but I never promised." Amy felt bad for some reason. This wasn't how journalism was supposed to work.

"I see." The coldness in Sister Mary's voice cut deeply.

"I —" Amy began, but didn't finish. She watched the nun stare at the crowd like a deer caught in headlights. "Go to the locker room," Amy instructed.

"What?"

"You're not ready for a press conference."

"Protecting your exclusive?" Biting words seemed out of place on the nun's lips.

"I really don't think you're ready for a press conference. Do you?" Amy shot back harshly.

Sister Mary knew the reporter was right. It was one thing to answer questions one on one, another to face a throng of reporters shouting questions and demanding answers. She suddenly felt like she had something to hide, which troubled her.

"No, I'm not," Sister Mary said evenly.

"Go to the locker room now and stay there until Buddy gets here." Amy saw that a few brave souls were on top of the fence now. She looked at the door to the dugout. There stood a dark figure Amy instantly recognized. "Get going, or they'll trap you out here," Amy urged.

Sister Mary began to move.

"There's a guy standing at the door to the locker room. He's a reporter. No matter what he asks, just say 'no comment.'" Amy was deadly serious.

Sister Mary stood next to Amy now. "I need the glove. It isn't mine, and I need to return it."

Amy reluctantly slipped the mitt from her hand and gave it to the nun, which was more painful than Amy thought it would be. Sister Mary grabbed the mitt and turned without a smile. Amy felt Sister Mary's disappointment as she jogged back to the locker.

"Good morning," the tall, dark man said, in a confident voice that almost stopped Sister Mary at the door to the locker room.

"May I have a word?"

Sister Mary never stopped. She said, "no comment" and disappeared inside. She had seen the man's eyes, and felt only coldness in them. That's what made her slam the door shut.

The man lit a cigarette and waited at the door. He figured she had to come out sooner or later. He could wait, and he knew she would talk to him. After all, he was Johnny LePlant.

Amy Springer gathered herself together and walked toward Johnny. Her face hardened and her eyes glared. Her feelings of guilt over Sister Mary's reaction to the press stampede lingered, but they were set aside for the moment. This wasn't a time for an apology. It was a time for revenge.

Chapter 16

"Hello, Johnny," Amy said, as she slowly walked up to where the dark figure leaned against a brick wall.

"Was that the scoop everyone's talking about?" Johnny motioned to the locker room door.

"Maybe," Amy answered. "I guess you'll just have to wait and find out."

"I doubt it. I plan to have an exclusive by noon." Confidence oozed from him. It came from the three books he'd written and the two editor-at-large positions he'd held at prominent sports magazines. He was considered famous, which only made him worse to deal with. Amy never begrudged Johnny his success. It just constantly reminded her of the biggest mistake of her life.

Johnny and Amy had started together at the *Herald*. Johnny had the Wizards beat, while Amy trod behind the Memorials. Few fellow writers wanted to discuss the inner workings of either franchise often, so Johnny and Amy became a kind of club unto themselves. Then the Redskin's job had come up for reassignment when long-time area favorite Peter Naughton retired to write fly fishing books.

Amy still remembered with horror the day she'd arrived in her editor's office, just after Naughton's departure, to find Johnny offering Russell Harris, editor-and-chief, an expensive cigar. In those days, a person could still smoke in the office. She believed that Russell secretly liked the fact that the stench of smoldering rolled tobacco announced his arrival a full two minutes before he actually got there. It gave his employees time to think. Time to wonder why on earth Russell Harris was on his way to see them.

Russell had taken the cigar from Johnny and lit it. He'd turned and noticed the other reporter and barked, "Amy, good to see you, good to see you. Come on in here."

Russell was a tough-minded former military sergeant who minded the details and believed in very little massaging of egos. Amy had entered as the cloud of used tobacco poured out of Russell's nose and mouth and hung in the air.

"Now, Naughton has left real sports to go stand in a river somewhere and write about his heavy-weight bouts with a creature ten times smaller than he is." Russell did not like fishing. The only times he's ever gone, he'd cast his line out into the pond, then started drinking cold beer after cold beer. "So that leaves me with a spot to fill with the Redskins."

Russell had pushed his chair back from his desk a few inches. The chair winced out loud, as the editor bent forward and pulled open the bottom drawer. A hand had gone inside, fished for a moment and produced a red coffee can.

"I got this brainstorm last night," Russell had said. He loved the word brainstorm, which translated for Russell as taking credit for someone else's idea. "Now, I've put the first three games of the season on slips of paper inside here. You each select one and that's the game you cover. I decide after seeing the coverage of each game who gets the job." He'd smiled, satisfied with himself.

"Didn't you say there were three?" Johnny had asked.

"Whatever is left will be Naughton's farewell to the Redskins. Big circulation on that one I think." Russell had picked up the can in his large right paw and shook it. He'd offered it to Amy. "Ladies first."

Amy had bristled under the notion that after all her service, the reason this butterball of a man wanted her to select first was because she didn't have a Y chromosome. "No, Johnny can go first." She'd crossed her arms defiantly.

Johnny LePlant had needed no prompting. He'd stepped right up to the can and plunged his hand inside. He'd come back with a small slip of paper. As he'd unfolded the wad, Amy's defiance had begun to break a bit. She'd realized she had just given away the first opportunity at the most important draw of her life. She'd calmed herself slightly by repeating over and over again, "It's not that bad. It's not that bad."

Johnny had read the slip silently before he'd announced the

game, and the words had him grinning before he ever spoke. Amy
still felt the burn of those two words in her nightmares.

"Dallas Cowboys." Johnny had consciously restrained himself
from jumping up and down. Amy had restrained herself from
running her head into the wall.

The Cowboys-Redskins games made up one of the greatest and
most-watched rivalries in the National Football League. Some of the
contests were the stuff of legends. They were games that even
famous people had trouble getting tickets for. On the Redskins'
schedule, there was no bigger contest.

Johnny had stepped away from the can of fate and offered his
spot to the almost frozen Amy. She'd stepped forward hesitantly and
poked her smaller hand into the can. She had felt both strips of paper
immediately and tousled them around. She didn't believe in the
supernatural, but in times of desperation even a cynic can hope for a
miracle. As she'd paused over the one lying up against the wall of
the can, a strange surge of excitement had run through her body. She
had clutched at the slip of paper and brought her destiny back to the
outside world.

She had opened it quickly and read it out loud, "Cincinnati
Bengals." The words had rung hollow in Russell's office. She was
set to cover a once promising expansion team, now the doormat of
professional football.

The last slip had been the Minnesota Vikings, and that game had
turned out to be even more thrilling than the Redskins game Johnny
got. Paling in comparison, the game against the Bengals had been a
dog that scratched itself to conclusion in high humidity at RFK on
an afternoon better spent rereading the operations manual of a riding
lawnmower. She had tried every trick she knew to catch the attention
of Russell Harris, but that was hard in a fifty-two to three blowout,
where the backup quarterback played the entire fourth quarter.

The Redskins job had gone to Johnny. He had turned it into a
gold mine, as he rode the wave of excitement around their last Super
Bowl win into a litany of great articles. The executives who ran the
national magazines and television networks had noticed him quickly.
Soon, the Redskins beat became secondary for him. During the off-
season he wrote commentary on just about everything, especially the
issue du jour and how it impacted sports. That got him a book,

Season Remembered, an insider's account of the last Washington Super Bowl, which finally allowed him to leave the newspaper business. Like everyone else during those days, he'd sold an option on a screenplay that never materialized.

Amy had been offered the local pro basketball team, the Wizards, to cover if she didn't want to continue with the expansion baseball team. It was tempting at the time. C.W. McDermott was widely considered too much of a free spirit to truly run the franchise. The Wizards, however, didn't look to compete any time soon, so she had stayed with baseball. It was the national pastime after all, whatever that meant.

In her own private moments, Amy played the game of pick the slip over and over in her head. In her dreams she went first and selected the Vikings. Johnny got the Bengals. The readers would compare her coverage of the final moments of the Vikings game to the stirring finale offered by Naughton of the Cowboys contest. Johnny was left in the shadows of flashbulbs as Amy was ushered into the club of elite sportswriters.

She tried to limit the fantasy to once a week. The letdown after it finished was too much to take sometimes. Later, she had been offered the Redskins' job, but it was after the dismantling. After most of the men who gave the city the Super Bowl had left. The Memorials, on the other hand, had quietly built themselves up over the years and entered this year as serious contenders. This time she passed on football for a shot at the World Series.

"I bet it feels good to scoop everybody." Johnny sat down on the bleacher and lit another cigarette. His remark brought Amy back to the present.

"I can't complain," Amy replied dryly and refused to sit.

"The rush is pretty amazing. For one whole day, everybody wants to talk to you." Johnny dropped the cigarette to the pavement and crushed it with his heal. "Enjoy it, Amy. It doesn't last long."

"Thanks for the advice."

"By the way, anything you can tell an old friend about this woman?" Johnny asked.

"Read my column in the *Herald,* Johnny."

"You know you can help me out here, or you can stand in my way. I can help you, or I can hurt you. The choice is yours."

Amy considered the offer for a second. "You know what, Johnny. I'll take my chances."

"Suit yourself, but it's a shame to burn bridges over such a tiny story."

"If it's so tiny, what are you doing here?" Amy stood her ground.

Johnny turned and walked away, unhappy and unsatisfied. He kept his cool and his tongue. In his own mind, he wondered if this was just a sideshow. If it was, Amy would look stupid, and Johnny would make her dunce hat for her. If it wasn't, she held an advantage on the biggest story in a decade. Johnny would wait. If the nun was for real, the story would be his. He would make sure of it.

Chapter 17

Mad Max Standish got to the locker at nine that morning. The hotel where he stayed had problems with its hot water, so the famed relief pitcher decided to use the shower in the stadium. He arrived to a sea of reporters and became slightly irritated that none of them wanted to talk to him. He even tried to strike up a conversation with a few of his favorites, only to be rebuffed. The reporters claimed they had a story to send in. Mad Max finally gave up trying to be noticed and went to the locker room.

Max took a long, hot shower. Steam filled the whole locker room in puffs of haze. Max finished and dripped back to his locker with his towel wrapped around his waist. In front of the shrine of headlines, Max let the towel drop to the floor. That's when he heard the gasp.

Max spun around, naked, to find Sister Mary lying on a bench with her hands now pressed firmly over her eyes.

"What are you doing in here?" Max quickly piped up.

"I'm sorry. I'm so sorry."

"Sorry? Why are you sorry?"

"I didn't mean to see anything."

Mad Max looked down and realized he was standing in front of a nun, stark naked. He quickly grabbed a towel out of his locker and wrapped it around himself.

"It's okay now. I'm covered," Max offered.

Sister Mary gradually pulled her hands down from her eyes. A towel did not constitute much clothing, but it was better than nothing. "Thank you."

"By the way, what are you doing in here? You've got a whole Winnebago to yourself."

"Those reporters outside want to talk to me."

"And the problem is?" Max sniped back.

"I've never talked to reporters before. And there are so many."
Sister Mary looked at the cement floor in embarrassment.

Mad Max Standish looked over the nun with contempt. Not only
did he fail to understand not wanting to be interviewed, but he also
felt angry over a herd of reporters that would rather talk to this
unproven woman than to him. That's when he decided to have some
fun. "You know you have to talk to them, don't you?"

"I do?"

"It's a rule about being a ballplayer."

"I didn't know that."

"Yeah, so you better go out and answer some questions. You
don't want to get in trouble, do you?"

"No, but what do I say?" Sister Mary asked.

"Whatever comes to mind. But if you want to leave a mark, you
have to add something to the quote. You know. Guarantee the World
Series, something like that."

"I don't think I want to leave a mark," Sister Mary replied.

"Oh, yes you do. Everybody does. You play this right and
people will line up to talk to you."

"That's a good thing?" Sister Mary asked.

"Yes. Why play baseball if not to be remembered? And trust me,
the only thing that survives after a career are the headlines." Mad
Max reached into his bag and retrieved another article. As Sister
Mary watched, he taped it on his locker.

"I'm still not sure what I'm supposed to say."

"You watch SportsCenter, right?" Max sighed.

"Actually, no."

"You have cable?"

"Church couldn't afford it."

"You read the papers?"

"The local one."

"How local?"

"Population seven hundred."

"What kind of sports news have you seen?"

Sister Mary thought for a moment. "Local sports, high school,
little league. I tried to read the box scores."

Mad Max Standish's frustration finally broke, and he smiled. "Would you be more comfortable if I were there?"

Sister Mary wasn't totally at ease with Max, but she was less comfortable with the press. "Would you come?"

"Sure. Now let me dress out and we'll go out and meet the press."

Moss and Buddy arrived at the ballpark shortly after nine. They'd had a meeting over breakfast, and were now ready to face day two of the nun in camp. The mob of reporters clustered around the locker room caught both men off guard. Frenzy like this meant only one thing: Amy Springer had written her story. This was the bad news. The odd news was that the group huddled outside the locker room door, which seemed to be locked. Buddy realized that the reporters hadn't figured out Sister Mary was in the Winnebago. He quickly steered Moss to the mobile home and knocked on the door. There was no answer.

"Sister Mary!" Buddy whispered loudly. He pounded the door again. There was still no answer. Finally, he tried the door. It swung open.

Buddy and Moss cautiously entered the vehicle. Both were aware of some primordial force that made them worry about walking in on Sister Mary just exiting a shower. When they were finally brave enough to look, all they found was empty space.

"Where is she?" Moss asked.

"I don't know," Buddy answered. "Where would she go?"

"Maybe she isn't here yet."

"Maybe," Buddy answered, but he privately believed something was wrong. Wrong enough to make him sweat as he peered out the window at the mob of reporters poised at the locker room door.

Dean Larson entered the locker room from the field side. He found the front door locked and surrounded by reporters foaming at the mouth, ready to do battle to maintain their interview turf. Dean knew that news of a woman in camp had leaked out. There was no other reason for the herd of reporters this early in spring training.

Dean moved down the row of lockers easily. He enjoyed the silence. Most of the team wouldn't be here for another hour. Halfway to his locker, he stopped abruptly. There on the bench was the cheapest, smallest and scratchiest piece of leather that had ever been called a glove. He'd seen it yesterday at practice. It belonged to Sister Mary. This was bad. Spring training was a fertile crescent of pranks, particularly the sophomoric kind. Dean began to scan the locker room. While pranks on guys who were just out of college or the minors were humorous, pranks on nuns might not go over as well.

The front door to the Winnebago swung open and a woman walked in. Unfortunately for Moss and Buddy, it wasn't the woman they were looking for. Amy Springer stood before them.

"You printed it, didn't you?" Buddy asked without emotion.

"I couldn't wait. I couldn't risk it."

"I understand, and I'm sure you understand we're disappointed," Buddy stated.

"What's past is past. I think the important thing is the future." Amy sat down. "Having a woman on the team is going to change things. You haven't thought about it yet, but trust me. I have."

"And let me guess," Moss grumbled. "You have the answer?"

"As a matter of fact, I do." Amy leaned forward.

In the locker room, Mad Max Standish rolled his eyes as he watched Sister Mary pace back and forth in front of the door.

"Are you ready yet?" Max seethed.

"What kind of questions are they going to ask?" Sister Mary fretted.

"The same ones they ask everybody."

"Like what?"

"Why did you start playing ball? Were there any hurdles? How did you come to the Memorials? You got answers for those?"

"Well yeah," Sister Mary said. "But Coach Thompson told me not to tell anybody."

Max smelled embarrassment in that answer. He put a gentle hand on Sister Mary's shoulder and said, "They'll just find out anyway. Now are you ready?"

Sister Mary took a deep breath and nodded her head. Mad Max Standish unlocked the door and led the nun into a gauntlet of faces and questions.

"So, what do you think?" Amy Springer asked the pair of men sitting in the Winnebago.

"I don't know," Buddy answered thoughtfully. "What do you think, Moss?"

Moss wasn't listening. Instead, he stood and looked out the window. "Buddy, we have a problem."

Buddy jumped to his feet and saw Sister Mary standing next to Mad Max Standish and about to answer questions.

The clang of a large metal door swinging open and shut pricked the ears of Dean Larson. He had gone through the storage room and was ready to check out the laundry. The door changed his mind.

"Sister Mary!!"

"Sister Mary!!"

"Sister Mary!!" The voices rang out in a chorus of her name. It was odd and strange and almost amazing for the young nun. She waited for a moment before a single voice carried over the crowd.

"Sister Mary, I'm sure the world wants to know what brings a nun to spring training?" The voice belonged to the dark man she'd passed earlier that morning. He was even more imposing now. Her nerves grew raw as she started to formulate her answer.

Several yards separated the Winnebago from the crowd. Buddy and Moss ran ahead of Amy. Buddy cursed under his breath and vowed to have a serious discussion with Mad Max Standish.

"Well," Sister Mary began. She paused and tried to think of something to say. Nothing came into her mind, so she relied on the truth. "I guess I'm here because of the miracle that happened to Father Michael."

The entire press corps went silent as Sister Mary began the story. In the distance, Buddy stopped running. He was transfixed by her words, and knew this would be a nightmare. Moss now stood, as well. He blamed himself and a wily priest who was not there.

Sister Mary stumbled through the part about the church repairs and the broken window. The reporters hung on every word. Tomorrow would be a day for each one to show off their wit and wisdom in newspaper columns and TV shows, but the full glory of the miracle was not revealed to the reporters at this time. Sister Mary was interrupted. A large, veteran catcher emerged from the locker room and brought the proceedings to a halt.

"Hi, Dean," Sister Mary said weakly.

"Good morning. It's looks like you've been busy," Dean said to Sister Mary as he looked over the press corps.

"They came and this is what I'm supposed to do," Sister Mary said quietly.

Dean looked at Sister Mary and then glowered at Mad Max Standish. The relief pitcher had fought to control the laughter trapped inside him from the moment the whole "miracle" story had begun. Dean grumbled under his breath. "Max, we'll talk later."

"Sister Mary, don't you want to continue your story?" The voice was Johnny LePlant's.

"I," she began, but never finished.

"I think that's enough for one day," Dean Larson advised both the reporters and the nun.

"You heard the man," Sister Mary piped up, happy to have someone she felt comfortable with now in control of the situation.

"Practice doesn't start for awhile," Johnny countered. "I'm sure she has a little time." A chorus of voices seconded Johnny, surrounding the trio and refusing passage.

"Practice starts now!" The voice jumped around the parking lot with the force of a whirlwind. Everyone turned to see Boney with his signature scowl. He held a baseball bat in his hands, much like someone would hold a weapon.

"Give it up, Boney. We don't buy it," Johnny smirked.

Boney walked slowly toward the group. He let the bat tap the pavement, just hard enough to get everyone's attention. "I said practice starts now. Anybody got problems with that?"

"I'm not finished yet," Johnny glared back.

"Unless you plan to put on a pair of cleats and work off that tire around your middle, I suggest you leave baseball practice to the players," Boney shot back.

"And what if I did put on those cleats?" Johnny jeered.

"Then you'd be mine," Boney answered without missing a beat, "and we'd finally find out just how much of a man you are." Johnny didn't answer. Boney glared at Max, Dean and Sister Mary. "Did you not hear me? I said practice begins now!"

The three players ran for the field. Max cursed the hotel for not having hot water. Dean cursed Max for being an idiot. Sister Mary did not curse. She sighed in relief at having escaped the crowd of questions.

Behind them, Moss and Buddy shook their heads. How long before the next press conference? What would she say then? How would C.W. McDermott take this? They turned and walked to the clubhouse, leaving Amy Springer behind. Amy Springer would never apologize for running the story, but she knew bridges needed to be mended.

Chapter 18

A crowd of reporters sat in the bleachers, ready to chronicle the second day of practice for pitchers and catchers. Boney didn't like that, so he took his team to center field. It was the farthest away he could get from the stands. Max, Dean and Sister Mary started stretching. Soon the rest of the pitchers and catchers arrived, save one.

Richard Day straggled out of the dugout a half an hour after the second-to-last man showed up. His uniform was mostly on, but his eyes were bloodshot. Richard had indulged himself again last night.

"Day! Do you own a watch?" Boney scowled at his pitcher.

"Yeah."

"Do you know how to tell time?"

"Yeah."

"Then explain to me, if you have such knowledge, why you are always so late?" Boney's eyes got bigger.

"Relax, Boney," Richard began. "It's just spring training. Geez, don't you ever take a break?"

"You think I'm too tough, don't you Day?" Boney said quietly. "You'd rather I just let you have it easy. Listen to you complain about how much work baseball is. Be here for you emotionally. Is that what you want?"

"It's a start," Richard answered.

"There's just one problem." Boney's face contorted. "I wasn't hired to be a nursemaid willing to breast-feed your ego while you run in place. You want to win a pennant, you do things my way!" Boney stormed.

"If your way's so successful," Richard countered. "Why is it you've never won one?"

The team fell silent. Richard Day, man of leisure, had hit the sorest point in Boney's tense, gnarled body of anger.

Boney stopped and breathed once. Since his early days, he had tried to harness his anger — control it. He used to think he had been successful at it. That was before his second wife filed for divorce and took his kid to another city, which proved Boney still had a problem. Now when he got angry, he remembered them.

"You're right, Day. I haven't won a pennant, but I've been close. Just like you guys were last year. Do you know how many times you get a shot at the pennant? Do you?" No one said a word as Boney continued. "It's a small number, Day. Very small. I'm here to tell you that this year just may be your last chance." Boney's voice began to rise. "That means it's also my last chance. Now you can imagine my shock and horror when I realized that my last chance at that pennant rests on you. So believe me when I tell you that I'll be shot before I let you screw this up because you don't want to work!" Richard stretched and said nothing more.

Sister Mary watched Boney for an extra moment. Her mission had always been to save St. Francis back home, but now she realized there was more. She was supposed to be a part of this team and a part of their shot at winning it all. She saw how much it meant to Boney, and that made her worry. Worry that she might fail when the team really needed her.

Practice went about the same as the first day. More drills designed to make things second nature. They threw a little under the penetrating eyes of Boney. He walked down the line and stopped at Sister Mary. Cameras snapped in the distance as reporters tried to capture photos of the new pitcher's motion. This annoyed Boney, who had a vendetta against the press from his playing days. A misquoted story concerning his relationship with a nurse in San Francisco had pushed his first marriage over the edge.

In reality, it had been the job more than the story that drove his first wife away. She hadn't been able to take the great stretches of time alone when her husband was on the road. She hated for her son to see his father in one bench-clearing brawl after another. In the end, the split was probably for the best. Boney had only one passion, the game.

"Is that all the movement you've got on that sucker, Bernie?"

Boney stood behind her as she threw to one of the backup catchers. The name "Bernie" resounded across the corps of pitchers the way a pebble ripples water. It even caught the nun off-guard.

"I haven't thrown it under these circumstances in some time," Sister Mary said.

"Excuse me?" Boney's eyes lit up. "You come to a major league spring training and give me excuses about work? Is that what you are giving me, Bernie?"

"Not exactly —"

Boney interrupted. "I don't have time in the seventh inning of the NLCS to come out to that blessed heap of dirt they stupidly glorify as the pitcher's mound, to get in your face and ask you if you are prepared for the inning. Does that sound like baseball to you?"

"Well, no —"

"Finally. Finally, the new kid gets something right."

Sister Mary Bernadette drew her lips tightly together in anger. She stood silently with the ball in her glove and stared back at the coach.

"I want you to remember that, Bernie," Boney continued. "If it doesn't sound like baseball to you, then it doesn't matter between the foul lines. And just where exactly are we?"

She didn't respond.

"Bernie, where are we?" he persisted.

The weight of her teammates' eyes felt like several tons on her shoulders. For a short time she fought answering him.

"Between the foul lines," she whispered.

"Exactly. Now back to work." Boney walked on, with an air of disinterest like he had never spoken to her.

Sister Mary turned and threw her next pitch out of reflex. Her concentration was on anger and revenge and things nuns shouldn't think about. She thought the day had begun so well. This wasn't a good sign.

"Hey, don't worry about today." Dean Larson walked up next to her as practice ended.

"Don't worry? Don't worry? Are you serious?" she asked.

"Look, the media was here. They only wanted to talk to you, shoot your picture. This is baseball. Egos are as big here as anywhere."

"I didn't ask for this."

"You didn't have to. If Boney goes on and doesn't get tough with you, everybody else thinks you're a prima donna. They get jealous of your screen time. You're too raw to hold your own in the game of who's got the biggest headline," Dean said matter-of-factly.

"I'm not so sure." Sister Mary stopped and refused to walk further.

"Look," Dean began and moved closer to her so no one could hear. "Would you like to take some extra work? You know, try a few things out before the rest of the team gets here?"

Sister Mary considered this offer. "Do you think I need extra work?"

Dean nodded his head. "You've got some raw talent, but up here, everyone's got raw talent. The difference between making it and not making it is the amount of work you're willing to put in."

Sister Mary folded her arms across her chest. "Okay, when do we start?"

"First, I want you to go to the Winnebago and act like you're done for the day. Wait for the reporters to leave. I'll come get you. And don't tell anybody about this."

"Why?"

"I don't want anyone else to know you're taking extra work." Dean saw the crowd of reporters at the fence.

"Why?"

"Trust me." Dean smiled. "And just so you know, Boney respects you," he added

"How can you tell?"

"He called you Bernie. Nobody in baseball uses a nickname unless there is respect."

The news brightened her for a moment before she had to face the press standing between her and her Winnebago. She was saved, as Dean Larson stepped through and parted the media like the Red Sea. He quickly deposited Sister Mary inside her Winnebago and then waded back into the locker room.

Buddy and Moss stood next to the Winnebago's door to field the reporters' questions. They had prepared stock answers to what they figured would be the most anxious questions from the group. However, the first request caught both off-guard.

"Hey, open the door." Johnny LePlant called.

"Excuse me?" Buddy asked.

"You know the drill. The press gets access to the locker room. It's part of the deal." Johnny smiled knowingly.

"Are you out of you're mind?" Moss yelled. "What kind of sick pervert wants to go into a nun's dressing room?"

"Have you been inside?" Johnny posed his question to Moss.

To be sure, the coach was a man of outdated principles about men and women, but there was no way he was going to let insinuation draw a smug smile on a parasite who made money on other people's foibles.

"You want to come through this door, you gotta go through me." Moss glared at the reporter. "You don't have the guts, Johnny?"

Johnny started to sweat, but managed a stern visage. This was always an awkward moment. Reporters couldn't begin to take on professional athletes, even faded ones. But there was a vague notion of manhood at stake that Johnny and his counterparts all understood. The raw rage that always made sure bench-clearing fights made the highlight reels.

"The league rules are clear," Johnny went on.

Moss snarled and didn't move. Finally, Buddy put a hand on Moss's shoulder. He pulled his friend to one side.

Buddy addressed the group. "I realize that we must allow press access, but that doesn't mean we have no restrictive ability on that access." Buddy scanned the crowd. "Amy!"

Amy made her way through the sweaty men. She smiled the smile of someone who had figured checkmate out ten moves ahead of her opponent. She stood in front of the Winnebago.

Buddy knocked on the door. It opened a crack and the general manager whispered something inside. He looked back at Amy, and motioned her to go in.

"You were right," Buddy told the reporter under his breath.

"Of course I was," Amy answered and slipped inside, as Buddy and Moss stood outside and fielded more questions from every reporter imaginable, except one.

Johnny LePlant dialed his publisher and the magazine editor he freelanced for. He apprised each of the current status of the story and then asked each one for a favor. He had a plan to fix the situation, and that plan would begin tomorrow.

Chapter 19

Amy Springer stood just inside of the door of the Winnebago. Getting in was the easy part. Now was the tough assignment. Sister Mary sat in a chair in the back, frowning.

"How did practice go today?" Amy asked.

"Fine," Sister Mary stated flatly.

"The boys treating you okay?"

"Fine," Sister Mary said shortly.

"You're upset with me, aren't you?"

"Absolutely!"

"You know, they'd have come sooner or later," Amy said evenly. "At best, I could've held the story for one more day."

Sister Mary shook her head. "That's one more day then."

"Would it help if I said I'm sorry?"

The nun didn't answer.

"You know you have your job. I have mine," Amy was done giving ground. "This is part of being a big leaguer. If you can't handle this, how do you expect to survive?"

Sister Mary sat and looked at Amy. This whole media thing was too much. Why did it have to be this way? Why couldn't it just be about baseball? Sister Mary picked up her mitt and rubbed the old leather. There were always costs to getting dreams, weren't there? She looked up and took stock of Amy again.

"That wasn't much of an apology," Sister Mary said softly.

"I'm sorry," Amy stated. Then flipping a notepad she said, "It's time to get back to work. Boney gave you a pretty tough time today."

"No worse than he gives anybody else," Sister Mary answered.

Amy sat down opposite the nun. "I see Mad Max Standish is

your new press agent."

Sister Mary rubbed her temples under the memory of the morning fiasco. "Well, at least you got the whole story. The rest only got half."

"I'm not printing that story, at least, not most of it. I will include the stuff about the church needing repairs."

Sister Mary eyed the reporter carefully. That was unexpected. "All those other reporters seemed pretty interested in the miracle stuff."

"I imagine they'll write about it tomorrow." Amy chose her words carefully. This was as close to a true favor that she could offer.

"And you won't?" Sister Mary asked.

"Sister Mary, I've been alone in this business a long time. I don't say this often, but thank you. Thank you for the game of catch this morning. You have no idea how much that meant to me. So, I'm going to do something I haven't done in a long time. I'm not going to print the story everybody is going to print. You deserve better — at least from me." Amy stood and moved to the door.

"No more questions?" Sister Mary asked.

"No more questions," Amy replied and slipped out the door.

Sister Mary found herself alone and confused. She felt the desire to hold Amy Springer accountable for this morning's problems, but there was something about her.

Many of the reporters had left by the time Amy emerged from the Winnebago. Most had early deadlines, and evidently Moss and Buddy were firm about when and where access to the female pitcher would be granted next. Amy walked slowly toward her car. She felt Johnny's presence before she saw him.

"You think you've got another Jackie Mitchell, don't you?" Johnny LePlant inhaled the last of a cigarette. He threw the butt down and quickly lit another.

"I don't know yet," Amy replied.

"We'll see. Just remember that Jackie Mitchell wasn't all that good," Johnny sneered.

"That's open for debate."

"For you maybe, but not for the rest us. The truth is, I wish you the best." Johnny almost sounded sincere. "If the little sister pans out, you just might join the A list. If she doesn't, well that could be damaging."

"I'm a reporter, Johnny."

"Face it Amy, you've chosen sides already. If that nun goes down, every reporter that wasn't allowed in that mobile home is going to crucify you. I hope you've got disaster insurance."

"Johnny, leave me alone. You'd trade places in a second and you know it."

"I don't think so." Johnny finished the second cigarette and stomped it out. "Just remember, Jackie Mitchell never made the majors, and she at least came from somewhere." Johnny strolled toward his car.

Amy knew he was right. Jackie Mitchell had never played in the major leagues, but that wasn't entirely her fault. Everyone knew that, but most chose not to remember.

Jackie Mitchell was a female pitcher who'd signed a minor league contract with the class AA Chattanooga Lookouts in March of 1931. It wasn't facing minor leaguers where Jackie Mitchell had made her fame, but rather in pitching against the vaunted New York Yankees.

Jackie Mitchell had grown up in a very desirable place to become a baseball player. She'd lived next door to former major league pitcher Dazzy Vance, a star for the Brooklyn Dodgers. He'd taught her to pitch, and she'd pitched well. She'd thrown a side-armed sinker with great movement. Movement she would need when the Yankees came barnstorming up the coast from spring training and landed in a game with the Lookouts.

When Mitchell had been inserted in the first inning of the exhibition game, her team had trailed one to nothing, and the next batter stood ready to face the young woman. His name was Babe Ruth. The accounts of the game related that Babe Ruth struck out against Mitchell. That strikeout is debated to this day, along with the strikeout of the second man she'd faced, Lou Gehrig. Some said Ruth and Gehrig weren't trying. Others believed that the event was just a promotional stunt. Still others said it was real, that she did strike out two of the greatest legends of the game. The streak of strikeouts had ended at two as Mitchell walked the next man and was lifted. That had ended her stint for the game, but set off a furor that carried all the way to the office of the Commissioner of Baseball.

Kenesaw Mountain Landis, better known for his decision regarding the Black Sox scandal, had ruled baseball. He'd heard about this event involving a woman pitcher. He'd mandated that baseball was too strenuous for women and had promptly voided Jackie Mitchell's minor league contract. That had ended any hope of Jackie Mitchell making it to the majors.

Reporters knew the story. Amy knew it better than most. The allure was the idea that it could have happened. Most people never believed such a thing would ever occur again, but as long as the idea lived, there was hope that one day it just might.

Amy opened her car door. Was she too interested in this nun's success? Had she lost her reporter's edge? She couldn't answer immediately, and she knew that could be trouble. Johnny was right about one thing. The press would kill Amy if any signs of favoritism toward the nun were shown and her player failed.

Chapter 20

Two batting cages ran the length of the old shed next to the Memorials' baseball complex. Inside, Dean Larson moved in the dark, quickly and surely. He spent many hours in this place. He was as familiar with it as he was with any building he'd ever been in. This was his workshop. The place he honed his swing enough to keep him in the majors and playing baseball. He knew this was also the place to prepare Sister Mary for the task ahead.

"So what do I do?" Sister Mary, now in sweats and running shoes, stood outside one of the batting cages as Dean switched on the lights.

"Go into the first one."

Sister Mary complied. She picked up the bucket of baseballs that sat in one of the corners and carried it to the far end of the cage. She stretched.

"So what do we do here?" she asked matter-of-factly. That impressed Dean.

"You add another pitch," Dean said as he laced up his sneakers.

"I what?" The nun stopped and put both hands on her hips.

"You need another pitch." The catcher put on the rounded mitt and pounded his fist into the worn leather.

"Really," the nun began, "and just what do you suggest I throw at fifty or sixty miles per hour to major league hitters? Or should I just set the ball on a tee?"

She had fire. Dean liked that, sort of. Fire in baseball was like fire in real life. It was only useful when controlled.

"What have you thrown in the past?" the catcher asked without any hint of emotion.

"You're the big leaguer. I know that. But are you listening to me? College guys could crush my other stuff."

"What have you thrown before?"

His repetition, much like the way a teacher handled a second grader, rankled her. "I throw the knuckleball."

Dean slid his mitt off of his right hand and slowly walked to her end of the batting cage. His steps were measured and thoughtful. His face was stone.

"How many knuckleball pitchers are in the majors right now?"

Sister Mary scrunched her eyebrows in deep thought. "I don't know."

"Two, maybe three. Do you know why?"

"No." Her hands dropped to her sides in fists.

"When the pitch goes bad it becomes a game of slow-pitch softball against sluggers who can take a ball for a four hundred and forty foot ride with the regularity of Ex-lax. Don't you think it would be nice to change up on them occasionally? Give them something to think about, especially when that ball doesn't dance like it should?"

Sister Mary turned toward the small window in the back of the shed. It looked out over the manicured field of spring training. She slowly turned back to the catcher.

"I have a curve."

Dean smiled. "Do you have a fastball?"

"It's too slow."

"Maybe not. Remember, you're changing speeds. But we start with the curve."

Dean walked back down to the other end of the cage. He swept the plate with his foot and placed himself behind it.

"I want to see the curve," he commanded.

"Can't I throw a few knuckleballs?" Sister Mary asked.

"You're a nun, so I figure you don't lie. You can throw the knuckle or you wouldn't be here. From now on, when we're in here all you throw are curves and fastballs."

"But —" The nun began, but Dean stopped her with a wave of his hand.

"Remember, you have to imagine that you've gone four and two thirds. Two men on. The knuckleball is tired of dancing for the day and is quickly becoming a set up act for a three-run shot that puts a large "L" in the Memorial loss column. The pen is weary, and you've got to make it out of the fifth. What are you going to do?" He squatted and pounded his mitt again.

Bernie looked long and hard into her mitt at the ball nestled in the webbing. She stuck out two fingers and gripped the ball on the seams with her middle finger. She looked up at the Dean, who was a little over sixty feet away. She kicked and threw.

The ball started out just over her shoulder, spinning fast. At a little over halfway to the plate, it began to break. For a second, she smiled at her handiwork, but it faded quickly. The ball landed five feet in front of the plate, took two bounces and landed in Dean's mitt.

"That's why we're in here," Dean called out as he threw the ball back to her. She caught it, reset herself and prepared to throw again.

Chapter 21

The brain trust, as television play-by-play men liked to label the group, sat around a table with an open bottle of whiskey, cheap cigars and a worn deck of cards. Boney dealt.

"Seven card stud, one-eyed jacks and split-bearded kings are wild." The cards snapped out of the small hands like rounds through a well-oiled machine gun.

"Why, Boney? Why are there always two wild cards when you deal?" Buddy asked from his chair.

"It makes it more interesting," Moss piped up.

"It helps out bad hands." Buddy shook his head.

"It's my deal, the rules are clear, so live with it, Buddy," Boney snapped.

The general manager let out a breath. He sized up Boney's pile of chips and decided now was the time for questions, before Boney lost a lot and got cranky.

"Speaking of wildcards, Boney, how's the nun?"

Boney took his cigar out of the ashtray and took a long pull of smoke. He released it slowly. "Boys, I've been in this business a long time. I haven't seen many, but I saw one today. She's got it. She's got the knuckleball."

Moss's mouth dropped opened, and he almost lost his cigar. Sure she could throw it, but Boney sounded more excited about it than Moss was comfortable with. The last thing he needed was his old friend to start believing in the Sister.

Boney and Moss went back many years. They had been relievers together with the Kansas City Royals during the expansion seasons of the late sixties. They'd spent every game amusing each other in the bullpen of what is now Kaufman Stadium and watching the victories pile up for the other teams. Both had been gone before George Brett, the run at four hundred, the pennants and the series were even viable predictions.

"She's got it," Moss offered. "But is it any good?"

Boney rubbed his head as he tapped his cards, still face down on the table. "That's the tricky thing with knuckleballers. You never seem to know until they take the mound and face live bats."

"The rest of the guys report in a couple of days," Moss said. "Maybe we could figure out some kind of test?"

Buddy's eyebrows rose at Moss's suggestion. In the past few days, Buddy Wilson had become more and more convinced that this nun might actually have potential. He now forced himself to remember that Moss Thompson was his friend. When Buddy had been out of work, it was Moss who'd marched into McDermott's office and demanded that Buddy be given a shot at the job. It was Moss who had piled up the wins the past two seasons that put Buddy on the cover of one of the many sports magazines that crowded the shelves of newsstands. Buddy owed Moss a lot.

"I like tests. Tests are good," Boney said in his best impersonation of Patton.

"What do you think, Buddy?" Moss asked.

Buddy considered his cards for a short time. Then he looked up to face the two other men. "I think it's a great idea. The day after everyone reports, we have a mock game. She goes three to five innings and we take a look."

"Who bats?" Boney inquired.

"The regular lineup," Moss piped in giving Buddy a knowing nod. "Might as well throw her in and see if she can swim."

Moss smiled as he picked up the seven cards before him and started arranging them in his hand. Boney followed suit, but Buddy hesitated. He stole a glance at Moss, knowing that he had just pulled a fast one on his good friend. Buddy shook his head and raked his cards in as well. He had nothing, so he quickly folded and let Boney and Moss duke it out. Neither was any good at gambling. That's one of the reasons they hung out together.

Buddy's mind drifted to the new plan, the game between Sister Mary and one of the best hitting lineups in the majors. Most on the outside would consider the move dangerous for Buddy. It was too early, by conventional wisdom, for him to believe she could be successful, but Buddy saw the subject differently.

Those first few days of practice, his team would be at their worst. None of them were fighting for a roster spot, so he guessed they'd arrive a little dull. Buddy knew his players, and the sooner they faced this nun the better. Even if it was a disaster, if she just got a few outs it would be a wakeup call that hopefully inspired them to a pennant and beyond. If she were successful, it would be a time for a mass conversion on the subject of her shot at the majors.

Chapter 22

Amy Springer donned her uniform, a black dress, for her regularly scheduled game of strikeout at the hotel bar. She gave herself two nights every spring training to hope against hope. She was pushing forty with a job that kept her on the road or busy at night three hundred days out of the year. Game after game she sat alone. Afterwards, she ate alone. She went home alone. Spring training was different. Most games were played during the day, and stories had to be filed before six in the evening. In the silence of the nights, Amy remembered just how much her passion for her profession cost her.

Five years ago, Amy had started the black dress tradition. She randomly selected two nights when she knew most of the ball players and other sports professionals would be somewhere else. She put on the dress and the hope that just maybe, tonight she would not be alone. It seemed to her a little like playing the lotto, but then didn't someone always win the lotto no matter what the odds?

She climbed onto a stool near the bar. She pulled out a compact and checked her makeup. Dissatisfied, she pulled out a lipstick and made a few attempts at applying a fresh coat. Her actions more closely resembled a dentist filling his own cavity. She gave up and quickly snapped the compact shut to avoid lingering over the lines now creeping out from the corners of her lips.

"I'll have a whiskey, no ice," she softly called to the doughboy of a bartender.

The man poured the drink with all the verve of a mortician and solemnly served it to the reporter.

"Slow night," Amy offered as she scanned the room and laid three dollars on the bar.

The bartender considered Amy for a long moment, and then decided to finally speak. "The ballplayers aren't here tonight."

Amy almost spit her whiskey right across the bar. Since the beginning of spring training, the guy had said nothing to her. This was his maiden verbal voyage.

"What makes you think I'm looking for ballplayers?" Amy said defensively.

"Only women hunting big game come into a place like this dressed like that," the man offered with absolutely no change in his expression.

"And I suppose ballplayers equal big game?" she countered.

"Anybody in that tax bracket sees a lot of offers." He pulled out a rag and began to wipe the dark wood top of the bar. "But I wouldn't suggest you try that."

"Why not?"

"They don't usually go for the more mature type." He stepped back to avoid any thrown objects.

Amy sunk her fingernails into the bar. Well-known media types are supposed to be above shouting matches with bartenders. That was the reason she held back, she told herself. Deep inside though, she knew the man was right.

"Give me another." Amy threw the whiskey back. She glared at the man. He had no idea how tough it was for her to date. How many guys wanted a relationship with a woman who knew more about sports that they did? Unfortunately for Amy, she knew exactly how many men that totaled.

"Now, take me," the bartender said as he poured this drink and got closer to Amy's stool. "I'm the kind of man who appreciates maturity." He managed a half-smile.

"I'll bet you do." Amy briefly considered the doughy figure before her. Maybe if she had three or four more whiskeys. Or maybe not.

"Amy?" a voice tentatively called out behind her.

Amy spun around slowly, hoping for deliverance from the doughboy.

"Wow, I've never seen you wear a dress before." Dean Larson stood in front of her like an angel sent to brighten up a rapidly deteriorating evening.

"It's not like I don't ever dress up, is it?" Amy teased.

"No," Dean chuckled warmly. He caught himself looking at her legs for an instant too long. He flushed a little. "Just not so — elegantly."

"My, how you do chat up the ladies."

"Just one of my many talents." Dean cleared his throat. "Look, I'm just hanging out back there. Would you like to join me? That is, if you're not with anybody else?"

"No, I'm not with anybody. I'd love to join you," Amy answered.

Dean moved off toward a corner table. Amy paused and leaned over the bar.

"Do you know who that is?" Amy asked the bartender, now back to his somber self.

"Catcher for the Memorials."

"Just wanted to make sure." Amy turned and walked to the table. She slid into the corner and found it much smaller and cozier than she had first imagined.

"So," Dean began, "you coming back from somewhere?"

"Ah — yeah. A newspaper thing." It was a lie, but only a small one. "I've never seen you in here before."

"I was just was looking for a quiet place."

Amy looked around at all the empty tables. "It doesn't get any quieter."

"And you, what are you doing here?" Dean asked.

"Nightcap." She said and half-smiled. "You know, unwind."

He glanced sideways at her and smelled the perfume she wore. "It's nice to meet up with people you know."

"Always nice." She smiled more broadly now, even though she felt a rush of heat. "Usually this place is full of strangers."

"I know what you mean."

Dean and Amy had known each other a long time, but always across the distance of a sports column. They had shared more than one long conversation about baseball and movies. They talked about baseball, because both were passionate about it, and movies because it was the best way to kill an early afternoon before a night game.

"So," Dean started again. "You got any questions about the team?"

"No, I'm off duty tonight."

"Have you seen any good movies?"

"Not really," Amy began and floundered for something more intelligent. "I see so many during the season, I guess I just took a break. You?"

"Same with me."

Amy looked Dean Larson over very carefully. He was a man looking for something. That was obvious. She also knew enough about him to understand that there were strings attached. She glanced past Dean and into a mirror on the wall. She saw a woman overdressed, out of place and ready for something or someone new.

"Maybe we could catch a movie sometime?" Amy asked.

The question settled on Dean slowly, but not without impact. He almost beamed. It had been a long time since anyone had flirted with him. It felt good.

"Sure," he stammered.

"How about tomorrow night?" she pressed gently.

Before he thought twice about the offer, he answered, "Okay."

"Good. Say, the lobby? About eight?"

"Fine."

Dean and Amy finished a drink then and argued playfully about the worst sports movies of all time. After a few hours, Amy knew it was time to go. It was almost midnight when she stood.

"Tomorrow then," she said.

"I'll be there."

She walked briskly out of the room and paused only slightly to give a knowing look to the somber-faced man behind the bar.

Dean stared at his next drink for a long while in that corner. He'd come to the bar instead of phoning home. He knew the conversation would just be questions about his retirement. He couldn't face that this evening. He was too tired of the topic, and lately it was all his wife wanted to discuss. She never understood how important the game was to him — how much baseball meant to who he was. Maybe if she followed the game and lived for it like he did, she'd understand. But there were few women who held baseball in such high regard, women like Amy Springer. Now there was a woman who understood the game.

Chapter 23

Moss Thompson stood over a sink in the late morning in the Memorials' locker room. The water was running as Moss took stock of his chin whiskers in the mirror. Few of the players had arrived. Sister Mary was there, but she always seemed to be there. He lathered up the beard and cursed his bad break.

Moss liked to shave in the locker room. It was a habit he'd picked up in his younger days, and it suited him. He grabbed his razor and began, whistling because he felt better now than at any time since spring training had started. He had a plan to end the nun fiasco — a plan he believed would work. He'd bet anything on that. That's when Moss cut himself, but instead of cursing he smiled.

Moss considered the cut a sign from God. It was a reminder that this whole mess was the result of gambling. Moss applied a tissue to the cut. He stood there in the steam of the hot water and took a solemn oath. Because God had seen fit to get him out of a tough situation, he would forever give up gambling.

"Moss."

The voice shook him for a moment. The manager turned to see Buddy Wilson standing in the locker room with his arms crossed.

"What's up Buddy?"

"Have you been watching the news?"

"No."

"Johnny LePlant filed a discrimination claim with the courts," Buddy said. "A judge heard a motion this morning to lift our ban on the Winnebago."

"You're kidding, right?"

"I only wish I was. The good news is that we're safe for now.

The judge ruled that the proviso for media access to locker rooms was limited to major league players. Sister Mary is not one yet."

"Then there's nothing to worry about," Moss answered. "Day after tomorrow, the nun gets lit up and there is no problem, right?"

"You and I believe there isn't a problem, but this is the knuckle-ball, Moss. What happens if she wins?" Buddy asked carefully.

"Our guys work out during the winter. Most of them take batting practice religiously. Anyway, it doesn't take a week for them to get back into the swing. Don't worry, it's still a perfect plan, Buddy." Moss wiped the foam from his face and moved to his office.

Chapter 24

Richard Day was the first pitcher to see the notice. He had gone to the training supply closet for a new can of spray for his athlete's foot. The sheet flapped in the cross wind of fans and air conditioners that made the clubhouse bearable on hot days. He read it quickly and forgot about his spray.

"Max, look at this," Richard shouted as he showed Max the bulletin that he had taken the liberty to remove from its posted place.

Max quickly scanned the announcement that the second day of full squad workouts would involve an abbreviated practice game, no specific mention of the innings involved. The most enlightening part of the entire statement was the starting pitcher of record, one Sister Mary Bernadette.

"I don't believe this," Max said. "Hey guys!"

The entire locker room turned around to see Max waving a piece of paper over his head. They walked slowly toward the man, wary of spring training practical jokes.

"What's up?" Dean asked.

"It seems," Max began, "that our benevolent coaching staff has decided that Sister Mary Bernadette is to pitch a short game of shag the homers against our lineup on the second day after position players arrive."

Dean's mouth dropped open an inch, and he quickly shut it. "Where did you find this?" Dean grabbed the notice from Max.

"On the bulletin board, down there." Max pointed.

"That is not good," Richard added.

"Something's not right," Dean began. "Nobody pitches simulated games on the second day after the whole team is back."

"Serves her right," Max snorted and returned to decorating his locker.

Richard responded, "You're just sore because she's got bigger headlines than you."

"No," Max brayed. "She's been nowhere, guys. Have any of you heard of her? Well? Isn't it a tiny bit strange that nobody can remember news of a nun with a knuckleball? That isn't something you'd hide."

"No one heard of you before you got here," Dean chided.

"You ask me, in two days we find out she's just a freak show, and this practice game will prove it. Promo stunt is over and we can get back to being baseball players," Max snipped.

"We've all seen her throw, Max," Richard said. "She has the pitch."

"Having the pitch in practice is one thing. Having the pitch against live major league batters — that's entirely different." Max walked out of the locker room.

No one said anything for a long time. Gradually they all finished dressing and left. They had not been comfortable with the idea of sharing the field with the first modern day woman to wear stirrups and cleats. No one believed she would really make it. They were products of the system. Each one had been on a short list at one time or another only to see the chance snatched away for vague reasons, like bizarre early practice games. This wasn't fair in their minds, and to some, it made Sister Mary seem a little more like a ballplayer than before.

Dean Larson sat in deep thought. He knew Bernie needed more work. He also remembered he'd promised Amy Springer they'd see a movie, and it weighed heavier on his mind than he'd thought it would.

Sister Mary was their best shot at a fifth starter in camp. But Max was right. Pitching against live hitting was a very different thing, especially for someone who'd never faced major league bats. Dean rarely gambled, and now he knew why.

Jon John stopped in front of the catcher. The young pitcher removed his hat and ran a hand through his tousled hair. He looked intently at Dean. It took almost thirty seconds before Jon opened his mouth.

"Bernie," Jon said. A little smile played on his lips, as if it was some kind of punch line. He nodded his head and walked slowly toward the door.

It was the first time anyone except Boney had used the nickname. Someone else on the team was willing to give her a shot. Dean knew what he had to do after practice today.

Sister Mary emerged from her Winnebago ready to practice, but fully unprepared to answer the questions burning on the lips of the reporters who gathered around the door.

"What do you think of today's ruling about your locker room and visitation of the press?" one reporter yelled from the back.

Sister Mary had seen a bit of TV news that morning and knew of the legal actions involving her. "I'm happy."

"How happy?" Another voiced echoed.

Sister Mary shook her head in disappointment. How much detail was required for these people? "Just happy," she offered.

"Excuse me." The voice grated on her nerves. It was Johnny LePlant. "I understand you are scheduled to pitch a practice game day after tomorrow against the regular lineup. Are you confident?"

Sister Mary struggled to keep from asking questions. She was new to the whole press conference thing, but she was sure that asking them questions was a quick way to get in trouble.

"The practice game. Are you prepared?" Johnny continued.

"As prepared as I can be." Anger began to creep into her eyes.

"You did know about this, didn't you?"

"The information," Sister Mary started slowly, "came to me rather recently. Now if you'll excuse me." Sister Mary pushed through the crowd and onto the field. Her destination was a certain coach's office.

Johnny watched her walk away and took satisfaction in his surprise attack, relishing springing the tough question on an unsuspecting quarry. This had turned out to be a good morning for him, even if his legal action had failed. He had struck a blow for himself and against Amy Springer, who also was in the crowd. She'd asked no questions of the nun that morning, especially after the news about the practice game.

"Good morning, Amy," Johnny said with sick sweetness.

"Johnny."

"That's an awfully early practice game they're planning,"

Johnny said aloud. "Any idea why?"

"It isn't the first time a coach has made a weird decision."

"You knew about it, right?" Johnny asked in a tone that revealed he knew she hadn't.

"Truth is, I didn't," Amy admitted reluctantly.

"You need better sources inside the organization. Perhaps we can work together. Share some info? Maybe I can even help you with your sources."

Amy's lip curled in anger. Johnny didn't want to help. He wanted the only advantage Amy had ever held over him. She wasn't about to give that up, and she bristled under his patronizing offer, a mad so deep it twisted around inside of her and produced a lie.

"I suppose you got the jump on this one," Amy said, almost unconcerned. "So, tell me what you know about her secret weapon."

Johnny stopped short of a quick answer. His mind raced. What was she talking about? "You mean the knuckleball?"

"Don't play dumb with me, Johnny. You know, the secret weapon?"

"Sure, I do."

"What is it?"

Johnny felt uncomfortable. The kind of uncomfortable you get at a poker table when you hold three of a kind, but you have the worst feeling that somebody else has a better hand.

"You don't know, do you?" Amy shook her head. "Well, when you find out, you come talk to me." Amy turned and walked away. She knew Johnny would eventually figure out the bluff. Then he would know he had more information about the nun than she did. Her anger boiled under the afternoon sun. This was her story, her scoop. How dare anyone mess with that.

"Amy?" Dean called softly from near the bleachers.

Amy stopped too quickly and almost fell over. She turned to see Dean kicking the dirt with his shoe. The truth was, he was unable to stand still.

"How are you?" she asked.

"Fine. Look about tonight. I —"

"Say no more. It's fine," she crisply stated and held up a hand to stop him. She had been through this enough times before.

"No, really. I'm sorry. It's this practice game. Have you heard about it?"

"I have."

"Bernie's our best shot at the fifth spot. We've been working nights. She's just not ready for this yet, and I need all the time I can get to help her."

Amy considered Dean carefully. She knew there was something different about this nun, but few young pitchers inspired this kind of attention from major league catchers. She also knew that Dean was right. Sister Mary needed the work.

"I understand," Amy said quietly.

"I —," Dean stammered again. "I hope we can see that movie soon."

Amy's insides flipped again. He had just proposed a make up date. This was a new concept for the sports reporter.

"Sure. Just let me know when," Amy answered and lightly touched Dean's arm. He stayed a moment too long, and then went back to the locker room.

Amy walked slowly up into the bleachers. She thought of Dean. She also thought of Sister Mary and their morning playing catch. She wondered how the nun was taking the news.

Moss Thompson's head was down, reading notes, as he walked up the ramp from the locker room to the field. The voice stopped him before he got there.

"Coach." Sister Mary Bernadette stood in front of him.

"Hello, Sister Mary."

"Could I have a word with you?"

"Uh — sure," Moss stammered.

"Why are you making me throw a practice game on the second day of full spring training?" Her eyes narrowed.

"What happens during practice is a coach's decision. That's why they give me a supply of antacids in my contract," he answered gruffly.

"You promised Father Michael," she accused.

"As I tried to tell Father Michael, I don't make the rules when it comes to hiring new ballplayers. Did you think nobody was going to put you to a test before the season began?"

"This isn't about me," she said.

"Unfortunately, it is." Moss lightened his tone. "There is a lot of money in baseball. And I would love to be able to just hand over that minimum salary to you, but I can't. People have to earn a place on this team. There are no exceptions." That should do it, he thought.

"When does the next pitcher, after me, throw a practice game?" she asked.

The question caught him a bit off guard. There were no other practice games scheduled yet. "Probably not until sometime next week," he admitted.

"Why am I being treated differently?"

"Because —," Moss stopped for a moment. "Because nobody just shows up to spring training from out of nowhere and pitches at the major league level. Nobody. You've never thrown any minor league or even division one college ball. You come to me and want to know why you're being treated differently? Did you ever stop to consider what happens to most guys when they first turn professional? Did you?"

The nun stood quietly.

"They go to rookie ball, then single A, double A, triple A and then maybe if they are really playing well they get to come to spring training. This is a very special place, and it's very difficult to get here. Most never even get to step onto that field in uniform. Now, you didn't have to do any of that. You came right here and jumped over years of work and sacrifice. You're right. I am being unfair. Because you're here, I've got two or three other pitchers that aren't coming." This was a half-truth. Moss knew it deep down inside, but he wasn't in the mood for penance.

The realization that someone might be hurt by her time on the team hadn't really occurred to Sister Mary before. It worked at her conscience. She knew nuns were supposed to have compassion for others, but she had been sent here to do a job. Stubbornness grew in her quickly, a trait left over from her father and ranch life in Western Nebraska.

"You want me to throw a practice game tomorrow? Fine, I'll do it. When it's over, I want your assurance that from then on out I'm treated just like any other ballplayer."

Moss smiled. "You have my word on that."

Chapter 25

Moss stood outside the locker room that afternoon. He was ready to get the rest of his team into camp and pointed toward the new campaign. The last time the entire Memorials roster was together, they were cleaning out their lockers after a devastating loss to the Philadelphia Phillies. In truth, it wasn't just that one loss that had killed the team's chances of making it into the playoffs. That loss was merely the conclusion of a terrible losing streak, a streak that began on a single play, in a late season game in Los Angeles. The form of the disaster was a pinch hitter for the Dodgers named Dave Hansen.

The Memorials had led two to one, two outs in the bottom of the eighth and a man on second against the vaunted Dodgers. Jon John had gone the distance with a consistent ninety-five mile-an-hour plus fastball. The count was two and two to Hansen, as Jon John fired another heater. Hansen had whacked the pitch hard, right back up the middle. It had been headed to center field and a tie game when the smack stopped it. Jon John had reached out and caught the ball with his bare pitching hand. The fans had cheered as the pain began. Jon John's hand was broken.

It should've been a sign right there that the team was in trouble, but Moss had refused to believe it. He had simply watched from his seat on the bench as his team had fallen apart. It had started with the pitchers.

Jose Martinez and Marion Pierce had become the number one and two pitchers. Each dove headfirst into a slump. Richard Day, the new number three man, was never supposed to be more than a number four starter, especially with the amount he drank.

Young arms from the triple A farm club in Wilmington, North

Carolina had arrived daily. Relievers had started games, which left the pitching staff exhausted and thin as the Memorials traveled to Veterans Stadium for a three-game set with the Philadelphia Phillies, the two teams now tied atop the National League East.

Marion had lost the first game, but Jose Martinez had shaken off his funk for a complete game two-hitter. The final game had been winner-take-all, and Moss had no choice but to throw Richard Day. A choice he had regretted when Richard showed up to play in less than game condition.

Moss had spent the hour before the game in a shower trying to pull Richard together after another legendary pub-crawl. The pitcher had thrown up three times before grabbing his mitt and slowly walking out for warm-ups.

Richard's head had throbbed with a severe headache, so much so that for the first time in his career he hadn't even thought about pitching. He had simply thrown. The results had amazed and shocked Boney, who saw a whole new pitcher with an unbelievable slider.

Moss had sat quietly in the dugout as the innings had dragged by. Richard had blanked the Phillies through seven innings of play. Tommy Brown, the Phillies starter, had pitched better. He one-hit the Memorials.

In the top of the eighth, Richard had gotten a fly ball out then a sharp grounder. Moss had known Richard was fading, but he'd also known the arms of his bullpen were tired. There had also been Moss's own past to consider as he walked slowly to the mound.

"How're you doing?" Moss had asked Richard softly when he'd finally reached the mound.

"Great," Richard had offered.

"That last guy hit the ball pretty hard."

"An out's an out." Richard had looked at the cheering stands and felt the final out that would launch the team and him into the biggest party in baseball. "I can finish."

Moss had considered the pitcher and the hitter. He'd then remembered his own two weeks of torture after being yanked out of game seven of a World Series. "Go get 'em," Moss had said and walked quickly back to the dugout. He'd perched himself on the top step to view the coronation of his team.

Moss clearly remembered Richard's first pitch fastball to that next batter, especially when it glanced off the pinch hitter's bat and screamed out into the night and over the wall. Richard had gotten the next man out. Andejar Morales, the team's back-up catcher, had pinch hit for Richard in the top of the ninth. He'd promptly deposited the second fastball he saw into right field for a base hit.

Moss had jumped up in anticipation. There was one last shot for this team. Lenny de Haven, the starting left fielder and the team's best clutch hitter, had knocked the dirt from his cleats and planted himself in the box. Moss had felt the confidence grow along the bench.

The Phillies' reliever had missed high and outside with his first pitch. He then brought a fastball inside. Lenny had turned in a flash. The crack of the bat had brought an entire stadium to silence. All eyes went to center. Driver, the centerfielder, had sprinted back, back, back to the wall. Moss had climbed up to the top step of the dugout.

Moss had known the result instantly. A deafening roar had foretold the news that Lew Driver had measured the big fly to the wall in Veterans stadium and caught it. The play was had been shown over and over at least a thousand times before Moss could get his team off the field. He hadn't needed the replay.

The picture was etched forever in his memory, and the only way Moss knew how to get over it was to get started on next year. That began today.

"Hey skip," Freddy "Vitamin" Vitarello called out as he humped his gear up to the door of the locker room. Vitamin was thirty-eight and he and Dean Larson were the veteran leaders that kept the Memorial clubhouse focused. Vitamin's locker was a licensed health food clinic. He had more supplements than most college science textbooks. His regimen of yoga, strict diet and exercise served him well. Moss just wished Vitamin didn't spend so much time annoying the other players with his suggestions of herbs and roots to help them when they were ill.

"Vitamin, how are you?" Moss asked the big man.

"Ready to go," Vitamin answered. "Am I the last guy here?"

"Not yet," Moss stated. "Go on down and get settled in. I'll be there in a minute."

Vitamin nodded his head and disappeared inside. Moss turned back toward the parking lot and watched as the used Honda Civic of Toby Haynes pulled into a spot. Moss knew that this was Toby's season to prove he had all the tools. The kid was young, twenty-four, and had risen to the big leagues because of his defensive prowess as a middle infielder. Moss always told reporters that catching the ball was an underrated part of the game. Toby's offensive skills had leveled off last year. It was becoming apparent that Toby was destined to be a career .230 to .240 hitter. That wasn't good enough to keep him here. Buddy had three or four young infielders incubating in the various minor league levels. It was only a matter of time before one of them was ready to hatch. Toby was unpacking his trunk when the blast of heavy metal shook the air.

Moss almost laughed at the dirty old army jeep that careened into parking lot. Link Molanksy was the product of the fading all Polish neighborhoods in Chicago. He played third base without regard for his body and often his fielding percentage. He had some pop and some range, but it was his grit that Moss liked. Link hopped out of his jeep and marched right up to Moss as if ready to go to war.

"Now just what is all this crap about a woman on the roster?" Link demanded.

"Go on into the locker and we'll talk about it in a few minutes," Moss answered reassuringly.

"Well, for the record, it's crap!" Link snorted and pulled his cap lower on his head. He pushed on into the locker room.

Moss waited until Toby was ready, and they walked together into the teeth of the storm.

"A nun?" Da Bull Ramirez asked incredulously among the first-day chaos of the locker room. He was a giant raised in East Los Angeles. He played right field and was feared by every pitcher in the league because of his power. "We have a nun on the team?"

"Don't you read the papers?" Tommy Chang, the small but quick second baseman asked Da Bull from across the room.

"Da Bull don't read," Flip Toussant, the team's Dominican shortstop, chimed in. Da Bull snapped a clean towel at the much smaller man. Flip sidestepped right into Moss as the coach entered.

"Skip, you want to tell us what's going on?" Vitamin Vitarello stood in front of his locker with his equipment unpacked.

Moss stood in the middle of the floor. He knew this question was coming.

"We've brought her in for a look. It's just a tryout. Let me stress that point, gentlemen," Moss answered.

"Geez, Skip," Lenny de Haven started, "don't we do enough promotional stunts without something like this?"

"This is serious business," Moss stated, but didn't believe it himself.

"She's a girl for Pete's sake." Link Molansky bellowed. "Hell, what's next? We gonna let little kids play? Skip, this is a guys' game. Women just ain't equipped for it."

"We'll find out tomorrow," Moss said.

"Tomorrow?" Link asked.

"Didn't you read the bulletin board?" Moss asked loudly. "You boys have a practice game against the nun tomorrow."

"Excuse me?" Link's voice rose.

"You not up to it?" Moss called back.

Link growled, "I can play the nun anytime, anywhere."

"Good." Moss scanned the rest of the team. "I'd hate to be the team that got beat by a nun." Moss left them with that. Tomorrow the nun would lose, and he could get back to the job of redemption.

Chapter 26

"I don't want to talk about it," Sister Mary said as she laced up her shoes in the Winnebago.

Amy sat in a chair. "This practice game is not fair."

"I'm starting to believe Boney is right, baseball isn't fair."

Without saying another word, Amy stood and got the door for the nun. She watched Sister Mary wade through the reporters to the practice field and then sprint out to where the pitchers stretched. Amy remembered her first days as a woman in the press box. Those had been the toughest days of her life, as acceptance had come slowly. Amy shook herself back to the present, and the Memorials' ballpark where the whole team started to straggle onto the field.

The first day of practice for the everyday players turned out to be little more than a media day. Each reporter sought out that one player willing to speak candidly about a nun in baseball. Most of the players were veterans of at least one or two bulletin board comments that inspired another team to come out of a locker room and kick their butts. Subsequently, most followed the lead of Lenny de Haven.

Lenny answered every question about the nun with, "We have a lot of fine players in camp this year, and I'm looking forward to competing with them all." This statement became the credo recited endlessly to reporter after reporter by all the players except two.

Jorge "Da Bull" Rameriz refused to comment on the nun. His eyes widened each time she was mentioned. Da Bull was a devout Catholic, who'd lost his mother as a child and was taken in by the nuns who ran his private grade school. Jorge's father drove a truck and was gone a lot. The sisters made sure that the young Jorge stayed on the straight and narrow, which was not an easy task for the large young man with a quick temper. One nun had encouraged him to play baseball and had arranged for his first mitt. She'd made him practice every day, even in the winter. The nuns were the reason he'd ultimately left East LA and succeeded. Now he was a single man. He had long ago moved out of the protective shadow of the nuns and into a wide world that included a lot of things that the nuns hadn't ever told him about.

"Women are just not suited to baseball." Link Molansky had a crowd of reporters around him, because he refused to use Lenny's credo when talking about the newest pitching prospect. "It all goes back to the caveman. The caveman hunted because he was stronger and faster. Same is true today."

"So you're anti-women?" The question came from the back.

"Not at all. In fact, I love women. All kinds of women," Link added a wink for effect.

Boney watched with disgust from right field, then turned back to his pitchers. Boney decided his pitchers had already given enough time to the press. He also didn't want the nun to face another round of "meet the press." By barring all pitchers from the media circus, he couldn't be accused of giving special treatment to the nun. A few reporters attempted to get to the group in right field as they loosened up. Boney met them head on, and the message was clear. They settled for a few more pointed quotes from Link Molansky.

Sister Mary forced herself not to look at the men she'd spent countless afternoons watching on TV. These were more than just ballplayers. They were the reason newspapers had sports sections and television had sports channels. She especially tried to forget that this was the best hitting team in baseball last year.

Boney watched the young nun carefully. He saw that her eyes were different. The roaring fire he had once seen there had dwindled to an ember. He clenched his teeth.

"Bernie!" Boney commanded.

The nun stopped and took the couple of steps necessary to reach the pitching coach. "Yes, sir?"

"Bernie, what's wrong with you today? What kind of crap are you pulling out here? You're as sharp as a butter knife. Now get back over there and concentrate." He finished with a trademark scowl and stalked away. He fought the temptation to believe in her right arm. He knew it would only make saying good-bye worse.

Sister Mary Bernadette tightly gripped the ball in her mitt. Didn't anyone understand the pressure she felt? Didn't anyone care? Her eyes narrowed as her nails dug into the stitching of the baseball. Sister Mary Bernadette reared back and threw a fastball.

The snap of leather when the pitch hit the glove was less than threatening, and the catcher she threw to didn't seem to feel any sting, but it didn't matter. At that moment, it just felt good to throw something as hard as she could.

She sat alone in her hotel room that night. Dean Larson had left immediately after practice without saying anything to her. There would be no practice session in the shed. That was disappointing, but he refused to tell her why he couldn't work with her. Sister Mary reached over to the bedside table and picked up the telephone. It was late, but she had to talk to someone.

"Hello?" The tired voice of Father Michael crackled into her receiver.

"Father Michael, it's me."

"Sister Mary, how good to hear from you."

"Father, I— I'm in trouble." Sister Mary paused then. "I don't know if I have the strength to do this."

Father Michael's mind turned in high gear. Sister Mary Bernadette was many things, but uncertain was never one of them. "What seems to be the problem?"

"I have to pitch a practice game tomorrow against the Memorials. If I fail, I have a feeling they're going to cut me."

"But Peter is the coach."

"Coach Moss doesn't have the final say," she knew this wasn't quite right. She understood that Moss would be the first person to help her pack her bags for her flight home.

"I see." The old man had no surprise in his voice. "Well, we must have faith."

"You don't have to take the mound tomorrow." Why was he talking about faith and baseball?

"Did you forget the reason you are there?"

"We need repairs."

A warm chuckle filled up the phone. Father Michael continued, "No, you are there because of a miracle. And nothing, nothing can beat a miracle."

Sister Mary answered, "Miracles need a ninety mile-an-hour fastball tomorrow."

Father Michael paused. He turned his words around, "Sister Mary, do you remember the parable of the mustard seed? Tomorrow when you are standing alone on that mound, recall that if you have faith the size of a mustard seed you can move mountains."

Sister Mary found some comfort in those words, but not much. The conversation soon ended. She knew she needed sleep, but the batting averages of the Washington Memorials haunted her every moment. She tried to concentrate on Father Michael's words, but all she could do was pace. That was, until the knock on her door.

Amy Springer stood in the hallway wearing jeans and a white t-shirt. She held a bag of doughnuts and two cups of coffee.

"I thought you might need these," the reporter said and barged into the room.

"You know, it's pretty late," Sister Mary answered. She wasn't used to people just walking into her rooms.

"Don't worry. Its decaf," Amy assured the nun.

"I don't have anything to say for the paper," Sister Mary said in growing frustration. "To be honest, I've had enough reporters for one day."

"I'm not here as a reporter." Amy answered. She knew this visit violated several professional rules about journalism. She also knew that she was the only other person who could fathom what Sister Mary was feeling. "I'm here as someone who knows how hard it can be to be a woman trying to survive in a world of men, nothing more."

"With doughnuts and coffee?"

"Don't knock it until you try it."

The nun didn't move. She eyed the reporter warily. Amy pulled out a doughnut and took a bite.

"See, not even poisonous." Amy offered a doughnut to the nun.

"I'm not sure I should."

"Is there something in the Catholic faith against doughnuts? There's only a dozen here."

Sister Mary didn't answer.

"Look, I'm sorry about the other morning and I don't blame you if you never trust me again. Don't worry. I'll go. But before I do, I just wanted to thank you for that game of catch. I never dreamed I'd ever get to do that. I'm also sorry for just showing up tonight. I just figured somebody needed to show up and help you get through the night."

Sister Mary's father often said that sports had a transcendence that few things had. It brought people together across the widest gulfs. Sister Mary felt that now. She walked over to Amy and took a doughnut from the bag.

"So this is what you prescribe for pregame jitters?"

"Works for me." Amy grabbed a doughnut, and the two women ate and talked until one in the morning.

Chapter 27

The High Ground Bar was built on stilts, which allowed for three levels of drinking pleasure. The roof held the wine drinkers. The middle room was a smoky enclave serving hard alcohol to desperate people trying to make connections across small wooden tables. The patio on the ground floor was the center for heavy drinkers who wanted to be loud and rude to all comers. This is where Dean Larson brought the Washington Memorials.

Buddy Wilson had pulled Dean aside at the end of practice and delivered his plan to the catcher. Buddy had also pulled out a wad of money that was discreetly passed to Dean.

"No one comes in before five," Buddy had commanded.

Dean had announced in the locker room that everybody was invited out for a drink after practice, on him to celebrate the new campaign. Everyone had agreed to be there, except for Sister Mary. Dean didn't tell her about the party.

"Dean!" Vitamin Vitarello yelled from across the crowded barroom. "Help me find an outlet!"

The catcher lumbered across the patio, parting the sea of humanity that pushed up against one another to remain standing against the alcohol and the exhaustion from the speed of the music. Dean arrived at Vitamin's table. The first baseman sat there with an electric juicer and bags of fruit and vegetables.

"I can't find an outlet," Vitamin repeated and scanned the floor. He was the sort of health nut who'd take a juicer to a bar to make his own setups, which he'd spike with tequila or vodka shots from the bar. Vitamin believed the fresh produce took away the bad side effects of drinking. Dean tried to point out to him that the damage done by drinking had nothing to do with the mix.

"I don't see one, Vitamin," Dean said, now on his knees next to the wall.

"This is just great; just great! My body is my temple and now I have to desecrate it with substandard material."

At one time Vitamin had been a regular Italian kid from Brooklyn who ate like a horse at a trough filled with rich sauces and stuffed pastas. Four years ago, the transformation to health guru had occurred, along with the dissolution of his marriage. Now all Vitamin had was baseball. He had prepared for nothing else, and he was determined to play until he was fifty.

"One night won't kill you," Dean called out to Vitamin, who finally gave up and stood.

"I guess we'll find out, won't we?" Vitamin motioned for the waitress, and Dean circulated.

Lenny de Haven and Da Bull danced in the middle of the small wooden floor next to large speakers. Each one danced with a devastatingly gorgeous woman. Both women had long flowing hair and red dresses that ended about six inches above the knees and started six inches below the shoulders. Dean caught himself for a moment in the memory of an elegant black dress and the woman who wore it.

"Dean!" Link Molansky boomed out over the room. He stood up and motioned the Dean over to a back table. Flip Toussant, Andejar Morales, and Marion Pierce sat with the third baseman in a game of high stakes poker. Money lay on the table, not in neat stacks, but in slush piles.

"Play some cards." It was an order from Link. He was a direct guy who wasted few pleasantries on anyone. He led almost all the excursions to the horse tracks and held a private poker games for anyone who felt like dropping several hundred dollars.

"I'm on a strict budget this spring," Dean replied.

"Bull. You just bought a round, so there must be money somewhere," Link grumbled.

"Maybe. But that doesn't mean I want you to take it."

Link liked it when other people complimented him on his prowess. Link never bet on professional sports games. He knew where that line was, and if the third baseman was consistent about one thing, it was about honoring lines.

"Gooooooo!" The yell brought the entire packed room to attention. Mike Flowers and Tommy Chang hung from an exposed rafter near the roof. How they'd climbed up there wasn't entirely clear. On Tommy's cue, the two turned their backs to the crowd and let go. The stunned dancers below quickly raised their hands and caught the jumpers out of self-defense. Mike and Tommy were passed along overhead until a spot was found to dump them.

The two were known for their pranks and willingness to try anything once. This, however, was a special case. Both guys wanted another go at the stunt. The bartender, a mean man with a limp, stuck the barrel of a large bat into Tommy's chest and offered the suggestion that they find amusement elsewhere. Both smiled like the devil and slunk away.

Dean made his way to the door, and stood outside on the back stairs for a breath of fresh air. Richard Day stumbled up the stairs to the patio above. Richard grunted a hello to the catcher and was gone. Soon Toby Haynes appeared at the door and slid out onto the steps. He paused when he saw Dean.

"How are you doing, Toby?" Dean asked.

Toby stopped for a second. "Look Dean, don't take this the wrong way, but I'm not going to stay."

"What's wrong?"

Toby bit his bottom lip and then slowly released it. "I read the papers. I hear the talk: great glove, no bat. I'm on the edge. Everybody knows if I don't pick up the batting, I go down."

"That's a bit bleak, don't you think?"

"Tell me it isn't true," Toby challenged the older man.

"So what if it is?" Dean responded. "Lots of guys do a tour of duty then come right back for more action."

"How many times did you go down?"

Dean couldn't lie. "I never went back after I came up."

"I'm going to the batting cages." Toby slipped by him and down the steps.

Dean stood there a long time. He had seen that look of fear in the eyes of many guys who had worn the uniform through the years. Baseball was unforgiving. Nobody put much stock in seniority when it came down to numbers. Either you could do the job, or you couldn't. He always read the papers during the season, especially the sports pages where they listed the transactions. About once a month he saw a the name of a guy who'd been released because he wouldn't report to some minor league team. Dean had played with or against many of those guys. The fall was fast and hard, and it was Dean's greatest fear.

The crowd at the bar raged through the night and into early morning. Dean switched to coffee at three to stay awake. It was a quarter after five when the bartender finally kicked everyone out.

As they all waited in the parking lot for the taxis that Dean insisted on, Tommy and Mike hatched the idea of bagel batting practice. They would stop and pick up two hundred bagels and meet the rest of the team at the ballpark.

They took the first taxi and mumbled something about cream cheese and fish as they slid in after promises from everyone else that the whole team would show up.

Dean agreed readily. He didn't see the harm in hitting bagels with baseball bats. It was only much later that he'd understand just how significant that morning would become.

Chapter 28

At 5:45 a.m., the Washington Memorials, considered contenders for the championship, fell out of three taxicabs onto the parking lot of their spring training site. Dean paid off three meters with large tips, hoping to keep the drivers satisfied enough not to call the local paper with a tale of drunken ballplayers carousing around the city.

Soon after, Tommy and Mike arrived with four large bags of supplies for bagel ball. As the group turned to the field of play, the first pink reflections of morning broke over the far horizon, but it was still dark enough for mischief. Tommy and Mike led the way to the diamond. It was at the gate that the procession ground to a complete halt and mouths dropped open. There on the pitcher's mound, on her knees with eyes closed and hands clasped, was Sister Mary Bernadette.

"What is going on here?" Tommy asked.

"I think she's praying," Da Bull added from the back.

"At five in the morning?" Mike whispered.

"They get up early," Da Bull offered back.

"How would you know? Have you ever been in a convent?" Tommy snipped back to the slugger.

"Yes, have you?" Da Bull growled.

"As a matter of fact," Tommy began.

"Guys." Dean cut the second baseman off. "There is no point in figuring out who has or hasn't been in a convent, okay?" The two men shrugged their shoulders slowly under the burden of alcohol and silently agreed with Dean. "The fact is that she's using the field right now, so we'll just move on."

"She's just sitting there," Link mumbled.

"She's concentrating," Dean stated. "Everybody has their own ritual to get ready for a game."

"For what?" Flip asked.

"The practice game today," Dean said without emotion.

"Don't waste my time with freaks," Link seethed. "I want to play bagel ball, and I don't care if she wants to Hail Mary to every last saint in the world."

"She has the field." Dean measured himself up to Link.

"She's not using it." Link didn't back down.

Dean eyed the third baseman carefully. Dean had been careful to keep everyone happy and together. The last thing a team needed in spring training was a fight, which always led to a stupid injury that cost a club heavily in the race.

"I don't think this is something to get that upset about," Dean said coolly.

"I will get upset about it, Dean ol' buddy." Link's face started to turn red. "I'm not going to stand here while Sister Mother of Teresa takes time for a person-to-person with heaven."

"You are not going out there." Dean's face lost all expression, as the group closed in around the two.

"To hell with you. Do you think I'm scared of you? Do you?" Link's eyes narrowed and the crimson rose in his cheeks. "You think you're El Capitan, don't you? That's bull. We can't have a leader that's afraid of a nun, now can we?"

"You are not going out there." Dean's stance widened. His whole body tensed. Link turned to go. Dean dropped a large hand on Link's shoulder. The smaller man was ready for him. Link spun and kicked hard with his left foot.

Dean stumbled back with pain in his ribs. He had failed to bring the evening home without incident. His worst mistake was forgetting that Link grew up in a tough family and a tougher neighborhood where the normal rules of fighting were suspended. Dean's left shoe hit some gravel and slipped. Without his footing, he fell to the ground. Link took two steps toward the catcher.

"Stay down, Dean!" Link's eyes burned with fire.

"I'll stay down here, if you don't take the field." Dean said quickly, as he held his ribs.

"That's just too damn bad for you," Link sneered. "Let's go play some god—"

"Is there a problem?" Sister Mary stood next to Link now. She had appeared from out of nowhere, and Link's eyes were wide.

"Where in the hell —"

"I'd prefer it if you didn't swear," Sister Mary scolded.

"I guess that's just too damn bad," Link answered.

"There you go again. Do you not want to say something more interesting, or can't you?" Sister Mary stood her ground as Link moved closer.

"You know, you got a lot to learn about baseball."

"Sorry. I'm new at this," Sister Mary continued. "I overheard you guys want to use the field. I'm almost done and then it's all yours."

"We want it now," Link grumbled.

"I promise I'll be brief," Sister Mary answered.

"I said now!" Link staggered toward the nun.

"I said in a few moments," Sister Mary stated flatly. She knew it was important for them to respect her, but perhaps she had taken this a bit too far.

"Look, freak show. I don't care what idiot reporters say. You ain't a ballplayer. Now that's a field for ballplayers. As far as I'm concerned, you're trespassing." Link stumbled a little to the right. Alcohol fired his tongue now.

Sister Mary had a limit for weathering insults much higher than most people. Maybe it was because she was a nun, or maybe it was just the way she was, but regardless, there was a limit. Link Molansky had just crossed that line.

"I'm not finished yet." Her tone was slow and measured. She planted her feet in a wide stance and stood at the gate to the field. Link Molansky took one loping step toward the nun.

"You aren't going to touch her?" Da Bull moved to the front of the pack of players. "You can't hit a nun."

"I can hit this one," Link slurred.

"No, you can't." Da Bull stepped between Link and Sister Mary. "Nobody here wants to see that."

Link fumed. He'd just wanted to play bagel ball, but now that was all screwed up. He had warned Moss about a woman on the team. This was proof enough for him that it was a bad idea.

"Fine, you guys want to be pansies, go ahead. I don't care. But you!" He pointed to the nun. "You'll get yours this afternoon." Link stormed off, kicking a bag of bagels as he passed, spilling them out onto the grass.

"Are you on the way to breakfast?" Sister Mary asked when she saw the food.

"No," Tommy answered. "We weren't going to eat these."

"You were giving them to a shelter. That's so nice, but then why was Mr. Link so difficult?"

"He's just that way," Dean added with a groan as he got to his feet.

"Do you need help delivering them?" she asked Mike.

"We — uh, no," Mike said. "We can take care of that. Call a cab, Tommy." Tommy rushed off, glad to be out of the moment.

"If everyone doesn't mind, the excitement here interrupted my morning prayers. Excuse me." The men all nodded and walked away toward the locker room to crash except for Dean. He walked the nun part of the way back to the mound.

"You knew those bagels weren't for anyone to eat, didn't you?" Dean asked.

"Don't be silly. Bagels are always meant for people to eat."

Dean turned back to the locker room. He'd crash there with all the rest, save for Tommy and Mike who stood outside with three bags of food waiting to be picked up. Dean later learned that St. Mark's Methodist Church in nearby Orlando had received an anonymous donation of bagels for their morning soup kitchen. The pain in his ribs kept him from believing that the plan had been a complete success. He knew Link wanted revenge. He also knew that Bernie had more guts than he'd ever imagined.

Sister Mary waited until none of the players were looking her way before she knelt. Her knees wobbled from the rush of fear she'd fought to control throughout the exchange. She paused to regain herself. Sister Mary Bernadette then prayed for guidance, but mostly she prayed for the strength to meet the challenge of another wager against her.

Chapter 29

Amy sat in one of the captain's chairs in the rear of the
Winnebago soaking up the air conditioning. The day was hot and the
temperature continued to climb with each passing minute. She took
out her notebook. She wrote some cursory notes about this improba-
ble turning point in the history of professional sports but stopped as
the front doorknob turned. Sister Mary walked in. She took one look
at the notebook and sighed, "You're a reporter again, aren't you?"

"It's my job," Amy replied.

Sister Mary smiled. "Thanks for the lift this morning."

"It was nothing. I couldn't sleep anyway."

"I hope I give you a good show this afternoon."

Amy nodded. "Just remember, you've got the advantage."

"The advantage?" The nun asked.

"Imagine the pressure on that team today. Would you like to be
the one who fails to get a hit off a woman?" Amy stood up. "If I
know my team, they're sitting in front of their lockers praying they
don't look foolish."

"I don't think they pray much."

"Trust me," Amy said. "When it comes to baseball, a player will
pray to anything he thinks will help."

Amy left then to cover the game. Sister Mary asked for a
blessing for this woman. She didn't, however, believe that the
Washington Memorials were, at the moment, huddled in prayer next
to their lockers.

"Anybody got some aspirin?" It was the feeble cry of Flip
Toussant as he sat half-dressed in front of his locker and held his
head.

Malcom Kildrich, the trainer, took a bottle from his supply closet and tossed it to Flip. He didn't even try to catch it. He picked it off the floor, poured half the bottle into his mouth and chewed.

Dean Larson surveyed his work from a far corner. Lenny and Da Bull still slept on the bench. Tommy and Mike had picked up four cups of coffee each on their way back from the church, Tommy had two left, Mike had three.

Dean saw that Toby Haynes dressed quietly by himself. His tired eyes weren't the result of any party. He'd spent the night at the batting cages, but it hadn't erased his fear.

Dean winced from the pain in his ribs. The trainer had looked him over and told him that it was just a bruise, which meant it would still hurt. The pain reminded him of Link Molansky. Dean looked all over the room, but the third baseman was not among the team.

"All right, everybody, let's get out there," Moss commanded as he entered the locker room. He took one look at the remains of what used to be a ball club and shook his head. "Geez, who called for the suicide mission last night?"

"Just first day back celebration, Skip," Flip called out.

"Get yourselves together, guys. Unless being the first men to strikeout against a woman pitcher sounds appealing to you." Moss thought that little pep talk would be the last great nugget in a truly splendid plan.

Each member of the major league franchise gradually pulled himself together. Malcom Kildrich walked in a slow, somber cadence behind the team gathering the gloves, caps and sunglasses the walking wounded left behind, but would call for later. Each man stumbled out into the brightness of the dugout.

Moss studied the players with disappointment, as the group fell down on the bench. Moss saw none of the fire in their eyes that typified a major league baseball player except for one face. Link Molansky sat alone at the end of the bench. He'd been there since before Moss arrived at the ballpark. He sat like an attack dog waiting to be called into action.

Buddy arrived at the stadium minutes before Sister Mary took the field. His office had been working overtime fielding press requests. The skepticism that greeted him from reporters hung heavy over the field like high humidity. Nobody believed that a nun could stand on the pitcher's mound long against the Memorials' batting order.

Buddy slid into a chair next to C.W. McDermott in the owner's private box high above the field. It was actually a scouting tower that some of the coaches used to evaluate talent, but during a media circus like this, C.W. required a special place.

There was no announcer. It was just a practice game. Only one umpire was provided to call balls and strikes. The ground rules were simple. Sister Mary would throw as many innings as she could, up to nine. She got to rest between each inning, but in reality, her opposition never took the field.

In order to be as fair as possible, Moss allowed Dean Larson to catch the game, and Toby Haynes played shortstop. The rest of the club was mainly members of last year's AAA squad. They sheepishly took the field for warm-ups, while Sister Mary warmed up in a secluded bullpen.

Moss posted the batting order, with Andejar Morales hitting for Dean. The ump sauntered onto the field. He was Richie Keyes, a plump man with a big voice and a flare for the strike out call. Boney motioned for Sister Mary to come onto the field.

Cameras clicked and videotape rolled as the slender figure of the Nebraskan nun trotted up to the pitcher's mound. Dean met her there, and they waited for Boney to join them.

"Okay kid, this is it," the small, bald man began. "They're going to try and knock the living stuffing out of this ball I'm giving you." Boney rubbed the ball once for luck and slammed it into her mitt. "I have only one piece of advice. Get outs." He turned around and walked all the way to the dugout without once looking back.

Dean patted her on the shoulder. "I'm not going to get fancy back there, okay? We go with the money pitch, but I will call for variety. Expect it, and don't think you can shake it off. I know these guys. Trust me." He turned and trotted back to home plate.

"Play baaaallllll!" Richie Keyes call was dramatic and stylized because he realized this was more than just practice. This was the eleven o'clock news.

Sister Mary Bernadette stood alone on the mound fighting the urge to gawk at everyone around her. She looked down at the mitt she wore. It was the shabby leather gift from her little league team back home. She knew they believed in her. She rubbed the mitt for luck, then said a prayer. She breathed deeply as the first batter was called.

Mike Flowers walked slowly to home plate. His eyes drooped. His step lacked zest, but even in this condition he was faster than ninety percent of the men in the big leagues. He was a switch hitter up on the left side to face the right-hander.

Dean flashed five fingers for the knuckleball. Sister Mary came set and studied Mike' batting stance. He stood back in the batter's box, a few feet from the plate. Sister Mary knew his weak spot was low and outside. She kicked and threw, aiming at the far outside corner of the plate.

The ball danced little as it arced toward the plate. The pitch also began to fade back inside. Mike waited and waited, and then waited some more. Then he slapped at the pitch and smacked a hard ground ball.

The ball screamed out toward left. Toby Haynes flew into the hole. He stabbed the ball on a big hop. He spun without setting his feet and launched a throw to first.

The race between ball and player brought those in the stands to their feet. Mike Flowers regularly won this race.

"Yer out!!" Richie Keyes called from home.

Mike kicked the dirt in frustration. He would be forever known as the first major leaguer put out by a woman pitcher. Toby Haynes saw the play differently. He felt it proved his worth to a major league team. In the dugout everyone smirked. Mike had gotten good wood on the pitch. They were certain this would quickly become batting practice.

Sister Mary Bernadette kicked herself for her lack of faith. She knew there was no halfway believing in the knuckleball, you either trusted it completely or you didn't. This was supposed to be her strong suit, and yet on her first pitch she'd given in to doubting her pitch. Sister Mary stepped off the rubber and walked behind the mound. She had to find the belief again, and quickly.

"Batter up!!" Keyes called out.

Sister Mary took the mound again. She cleared her mind and focused on the faith. She took the sign from Dean and came set. She kicked and threw, but this time she closed her eyes. She didn't open them until the ball was well on its way.

Tommy Chang stood ready to clobber the offering from the pitcher, but his confidence faded as the pitch approached. The ball danced out over the plate. Tommy swore later that the pitch bounced up and down, side-to-side, and was the most amazing thing he'd ever seen. He claimed it even called to him to swing, which he did. The ball glanced off the top of his bat and became a high infield fly ball. Toby Haynes caught it for the second out and whipped the ball around the horn. Sister Mary's confidence grew. She had the faith again and retired Lenny de Haven on a ground ball to second. She left the field for a quick drink of water, then took the mound again.

Da Bull Ramirez used his at bat to pop up a foul ball to the catcher. Vitamin Vitarello grounded to second base on a weak half swing. Then a solemn Link Molansky stepped up to the plate. There wasn't a joke written that could've cracked a smile in the cement that was Link's face as he took his stance.

Behind the plate, the pain of the bruised ribs was beginning to bother Dean. He tried to focus on the game and called for the knuckler.

The pitch came in and ducked at the last minute into the dirt in front of home plate. Dean stabbed for it, but only feebly. Link spat and took a practice swing. He never left the box. Dean checked his gut one last time and put down two fingers for the curve.

Sister Mary's eyes grew large. Was he out of his mind? He wanted her to throw the curve in the second inning? She shook him off. He put down the sign again, this time with an added glare. She finally nodded, kicked and threw.

Link almost jumped out of his skin when he saw the looping curveball. He stepped too early and had to slow the bat to make contact. The ball looped into right field for a base hit. Link rounded first, but didn't challenge the arm of the right fielder.

Sister Mary glared at Dean, who called time and walked out to the mound.

"Did you see that?" she asked him.

"I said trust me, didn't I?"

"You were supposed to make sense when you called for a pitch."

"Next pitch, I want a fastball upstairs."

"Are you crazy? Are you out of your mind?"

"I have been a professional baseball player a long time, kid. I want it hard and high. Is that understood?"

Sister Mary gritted her teeth and nodded her head. Dean trotted back to home plate. Richie Keyes knelt behind him for the next pitch.

"Let's gooooo!" Richie barked, as Andejar stepped up to the plate.

There was no sign from Dean. Sister Mary came set. She looked back at Link, and then kicked. The crowd gasped as Link broke for second. Dean was already halfway up as the pitch flew home. He caught and released the ball in one smooth motion. It was only after the throw was gone that Dean felt the pain.

Sister Mary stood in shock on the mound. She'd never expected a steal in a practice game. A little voice inside of her screamed out, "Duck!!!" She flattened to the dirt. The throw sailed perfectly into the glove of Toby Haynes. He swept the dirt in front of the sliding Molanksy.

"You're out of therrrrreee!!!" Keyes punched Link out from home plate.

Link got up and brushed himself off as he marched to the dugout. Moss waited on the top step.

"What did you think you were doing?"

"I thought I could make it."

"Boney, you hear that?" Moss started. "Link thinks he's the manager now. Isn't that interesting?"

"She throws the knuckleball, Skip. Dean could steal second on the knuckleball," Link protested.

"This is a practice game, Link. What if you would've gotten hurt out there? No more crap. We play this one straight up." Moss ended the discussion.

Sister Mary sat down Andejar Morales and Flip Toussant to start the third. Batting ninth in the lineup was an actual pitcher. Moss had many failings, but he did try to be fair. That's why the manager gave the nun at least one pitcher to throw to.

The pitchers drew straws before the game for the distinction of being that person. Richard Day, the worst hitting pitcher in baseball, lost. He repeated over and over that he really did like women, but he just didn't want to be struck out by one. He wasn't. He grounded back to the pitcher for the third out.

Innings four, five and six went the way of the first three. There were four hits and a few walks, but the nun stranded every runner that got on. The game pushed into the seventh and then the eighth, and still the Memorials had failed to score even one run on the woman who now stood taller on the mound.

Moss grew more agitated on the bench throughout the later innings. The world wasn't supposed to work this way. These guys should kill her stuff. He took off his cap and rubbed his head as the ninth inning began.

"Now come on boys, you look like crap out there today!" Moss pleaded with his bench. He felt like a poker player staring at a huge pot and needing to draw the ace of spades to win it all. He reminded himself it was still possible. His best three hitters were due up.

Lenny de Haven, mister clutch last season, swung early and missed for strike three against the knuckleball. Da Bull followed by taking the first pitch he saw to deep shortstop, where Toby Haynes caught the high fly ball for out number two. Moss kicked and spat on the cement steps in the dugout. He didn't like this at all. He closed his eyes and hoped for deliverance in the form of Vitamin Vitarello.

Vitamin took the nun's second pitch to the gap in right center. He chugged around first and lumbered into second with a stand up double. Moss felt his redemption at hand. After all, Link Molanksy was due up. He'd looked the sharpest all day.

Dean called time and walked slowly to the mound. "Don't worry about Vitamin. He's got no wheels. Concentrate on Link."

"Do I throw him another curve?"

"Not this time. He'll be expecting it."

Later, Dean explained that the book on Link was that he couldn't hit the curve in pressure situations. It was only partially true, but Link knew it was on every scouting report in the major leagues. Link also knew that Dean knew it. Link had seen a steady diet of curveballs early in the count all day. The catcher hoped that Link had it in his mind that Dean would try and use his weakness to end the ball game.

Sister Mary pitched from a full windup. Her kick was small and the follow through smooth. Link's bat was too anxious. He knew the curve was coming, and this time he would laugh in the face of the scouting reports. The ball wasn't spinning, though. It floated.

Link planted his front foot and found himself staring at the fat side of a baseball hovering a few feet out in front of him and begging to be crushed. All strategies faded from his mind. It was like tee ball. He tensed his biceps and swung for the fences and retribution.

The ball dived to the left just as the bat reached it. There was no hard crack of wood. In its place, a dull thud that bounced twice to the waiting mitt of Sister Mary Bernadette, who picked it up and threw to first to complete the shutout. Link broke his bat as Dean trotted out to the mound to congratulate the new major league pitcher.

"Way to go, Bernie!"

Many of the players came up to her and shared their congratulations for a job well done. Each one referred to her as Bernie. It was the final step in acceptance.

Buddy Wilson watched the nun run quickly to her Winnebago, pursued by reporters who were stopped at the front door by the two security guards he'd hired that morning. C.W. smiled as TV reporters lined up along baselines to shoot their reaction to the incredible story that had just unfolded. The owner was ecstatic.

In the parking lot, Amy Springer made her way through the crowd. She walked past the security guards, who didn't bat an eye. She forced herself not to look back, not to gloat as she entered the door to the Winnebago. She wasn't sure if she felt better about her upcoming exclusive, or the reality that a new friend of hers had just done something nobody thought possible.

Moss stood on the top step of the dugout in disbelief. He had lost another bet. He knew he didn't have another arm anywhere close to what he'd seen on the field today. He was going to have to get used to the fact that a woman was in baseball and on his team. On the up side though, God had failed to come through for him, so his promise to give up gambling was now null and void. That was at least something.

Chapter 30

"You were terrific," Amy gushed as Bernie entered the Winnebago.

"It was just one game," Bernie shrugged, but the smile on her lips betrayed her true feelings. The rush still carried her four feet off the ground and filled her with confidence.

"So tell me, Bernie," Amy emphasized the nickname. "How does it feel to be the first woman in modern history to make a major league roster?"

"I haven't made it yet."

"You go out on the second day of spring training for the regular players and throw a shutout against that lineup, and somehow you believe that you don't own a roster spot? It doesn't work that way. People from here to California are going to line up for tickets to see you pitch."

Bernie wanted to shout, but there were just too many words of thanks and they overwhelmed her. As a kid, she'd fantasized about pitching in the majors. As a collegian, she'd never felt as alive as when she was pitching for Kearney State. There had been a time after she became a nun when she'd resented the call, because it had stopped her baseball career completely. She knew now, that as a player right out of college, she would've never had a shot like this. It was only as a nun that her dream was finally fulfilled. She offered a quick, silent prayer of thanks.

"All right, down to business." Amy brought out a tape recorder and sat it on the table. "We have an exclusive one-on-one interview to do."

Sister Mary would be introduced to the world as Bernie through the words of Amy Springer. The interview went fifteen minutes before Buddy Wilson opened the door and stepped inside.

"Great game today," Buddy offered in congratulations.

"Thanks," Bernie answered.

"I, unfortunately, am the bearer of the bad news part of being successful. We have to have a press conference."

"We're having one," Amy quickly added.

"The league rule, as well as team policy, encourages players to make available time to the press. There are a whole lot of reporters out there who want to talk with you."

"I haven't even showered yet," Bernie answered.

"You do that, and I'll wait outside and help you through it."

Bernie didn't exactly leap to take her shower. She'd spent most of her time at spring training avoiding the press. Now it appeared she would have to face them.

"Give me fifteen minutes," she said, and slowly walked to the shower in the back of the Winnebago.

"Amy, don't you think you should join your colleagues outside?" Buddy suggested strongly.

"Okay," Amy answered. "See you later," she called to the nun in the shower and walked out the door, followed by Buddy.

The press conference took place exactly fifteen minutes later. Amy was not there. She had her exclusive to work with. She only heard about the mess later that night.

"What statement do you hope to send by making the team?" a reporter yelled from the back.

"Statement? I'm not here to make a statement. I'm here to answer questions," Bernie said.

"Have you always played baseball?"

"Not for a few years."

"In an earlier press conference, you mentioned this was all due to a miracle." Johnny LePlant leaned casually against a wall in the back. "Anything else you think we should know about miracles?"

"I guess you could say you saw one out there on the field today," Bernie replied.

"Miracles tend to be one shot deals, Sister Bernie." Johnny drew out the name sarcastically. "Are you inferring that this was a single moment of divine intervention?"

"I'm afraid you don't understand miracles very well at all.

Miracles are rarely one-time things. Mostly they are meant for a whole lifetime."

"Do you foresee the miracle of a Memorial championship?" Johnny stood up and prepared to write.

"That wouldn't be a miracle," Bernie shot back. "I think this team has a good chance. It's a talented group."

"Well then, is there anything coming up that you're willing to call a miracle?" Johnny continued, undaunted.

"Yes," Bernie snipped at the reporter. "It'd be a miracle if you talked less than anybody you interviewed."

The other reporters laughed at Johnny's expense, and Buddy ended the press conference. He ushered her back into the Winnebago.

"Sister Mary," Buddy began when they were alone. "I don't think it's wise to talk about miracles like that."

"Don't you believe in miracles?" Bernie asked.

"This isn't about miracles. It's about the press."

"Do you believe in miracles?"

"I believe in you," Buddy answered her. "But I think it will be easier on everyone if you just don't talk about it so much." He then left her alone in her glory.

Bernie went to the door of the Winnebago. She wanted to thank Dean Larson for everything, but the mass of reporters stayed outside her door and didn't seem to want to budge. She would wait. It gave her time to think about what Buddy had said. She didn't know if she could comply with his suggestion. At that moment, she didn't care. She was a major league ballplayer.

The other players trickled out of the locker room. Dean lingered and sat alone in front of his locker rubbing deep heating rub into the left side of his rib cage.

The catcher strained to get the lotion into the right area of his back. The struggle caused him pain, and he grimaced. He stopped and pushed the wet hair from his shower out of his eyes. He wore a pair of ragged shorts and shower thongs. He poured more of the lotion on his hand and tried again.

"You look like you could use some help." Amy Springer stood at the end of the locker room.

Dean tensed immediately, sending a shock of pain down his

lower back. "It's just a tough spot to reach."

"I see that." She walked slowly toward him.

"Bernie was really something out there today, wasn't she?" Dean asked.

"She was, but I think she had some help. Sometimes we could all use some help," she added as she picked up the tube of deep heating rub. She squeezed a portion into her right hand. The hand slowly descended onto Dean's back with the utmost tenderness. He shivered, as the cool lotion and the warm hand made contact. Amy rubbed the lotion in a clockwise circle, around and around. The heat started almost immediately. He closed his eyes. She went on, perhaps a bit longer than necessary. Finally, reluctantly, she removed her hand.

"I should be going," she whispered and left the locker room without turning back.

An hour later, Bernie found her way through a deserted locker room to a small back room at the end of a long hall.

"You wanted to see me," she asked as she gingerly stepped into the office.

"Yeah, I did." Moss sat back in his chair with his feet up on the desk. "I wanted to tell you that you pitched a he—, a heck of a game out there today."

"That must be difficult for you to say."

"I'm not crowning you the next Sandy Koufax or Bob Gibson, all right? I'm just saying you had a good game."

"Thank you."

"Get some rest. You've got a lot of work to do."

Bernie stood and considered the manager a minute. If that was his best compliment, she understood why he wasn't married. "See you tomorrow."

The nun turned to leave, but stopped when Moss cleared his throat. "And the next time you talk to Father Michael," he began, "tell him that someday I might have to thank him for a miracle. Make sure you emphasize the word might."

"I will," Bernie answered and left for the hotel.

Hours later, when it was almost midnight, there was a knock on the door that woke up Dean Larson in his hotel room. He rose gingerly and opened the door. Bernie stood there, beaming.

"I just wanted to stop by and say thanks. I couldn't have done it without you."

Her sincerity almost overwhelmed him. "You did it yourself out there today. I didn't throw a single pitch," Dean answered.

"You know what I mean."

"I'm just glad it all worked out. Of course, now you're going to have six months locked up with us."

"I think I can manage that. It's got to be more fun than a convent." They both laughed.

"You should get some sleep. I have a feeling those media boys are going to want more interviews."

"I don't like that," Bernie sighed.

"Be careful what you say. Remember, no one takes more license with a quote than a sports reporter. Keep it simple, and you'll be fine. And always remember, it's not about who gives the best interview. It's who gets the most outs."

"I have just one question," she asked. "Why did you call for all those curveballs to Molanksy?"

"I'll explain it later, when we talk about preparation."

"Why didn't you tell me that when I asked you out there today?" she continued.

"I needed to see if you trusted me enough to throw something you didn't believe could work."

"So I passed?"

"Yeah, I'd say you passed," Dean said warmly.

Dean stood at his window for a time after she'd left hoping he'd done the right thing. She had faced his team at their worst possible moment. He had predicted to himself that the Memorials would score at least five runs, so the shutout had been a surprise, but her knuckleball was something to watch. The last pitch to Link had been a thing of beauty. Still, he reminded himself of all the great spring trainings he'd seen fizzle out after opening day. They'd taught him that spring wasn't summer, and it was only summer that counted.

Chapter 31

As the legal proceedings carried on in the courtroom, a different kind of trial hit the Washington Memorials. They opened the season with a four-game series in Los Angeles with the Dodgers. They lost by an average of four runs in each game. Moss bought out a small convenience store's entire stock of antacids.

After losing eleven to two in a night game to the Dodgers, the team boarded a late flight to San Francisco. Any hope that the media would remove its magnifying glass was dashed with the announcement of the starter for game one of a three-game series. It was to be the major league debut of Bernie, the nun with the knuckleball.

It was well on the way to one o'clock in the morning when the team's chartered bus dropped the Memorials off at the hotel. The team was mostly silent. They hadn't expected to start this badly, and the idea of a rookie stopping their losing streak gave no one confidence. Most of the players, however, were tired enough to sleep, except for Dean Larson.

The catcher finally gave up and got out of bed at 4:30 in the morning and padded his way to the restroom to splash cold water on his face.

The water felt good and clean as it washed over his cheeks and dribbled off his chin. The feeling was fleeting. Dean couldn't stop the Jumbotron in his brain from replaying the nightmare of the first four games.

"It's early." He'd chanted the mantra on the plane last night. He'd chanted it before he went to bed, and now he chanted it in his mind in the early morning hours. He knew it was only four games, but something felt wrong. Bad things kept happening. Throws skidded by cutoff men. Pitches just missed the outside corner.

Dean splashed himself again. He shook his head clear. He reminded himself to focus on what he could control instead of what he couldn't. Bernie took the hill today, and he knew the cameras had already started rolling. She was about to break the gender barrier in baseball. That was supposed to be some great thing, but it didn't really matter to the catcher. All he wanted was a win.

"Focus on what you can control," Dean repeated to himself again. It was a quarter to five, and he knew Bernie rose early. He never figured out if it was because she was a nun or because she was raised on a ranch. He'd ask her later, but if she was up, there was no reason to believe she wouldn't be open to discussing more game plans on how to pitch the Giants.

He threw on a pair of practice shorts, tennis shoes and a t-shirt. He picked his way across the room and opened the door silently. He slipped through the door without once disturbing his roommate Vitamin Vitarello's sleep.

Dean quietly walked down the hall. His sense of purpose grew rapidly. This was the right thing to do. It was positive. It was the only thing he could do. He reached her room and was about to knock when the door swung open.

"Ahhhh!!" Bernie screamed and then immediately stopped. She looked quickly up and down the halls to see if anybody woke. No one appeared.

"What are you doing here?" Bernie whispered.

"I came to see you."

"At 4:45 in the morning?"

"I couldn't sleep. I figured you'd be up. I thought we could discuss game plans."

"Not now," she answered matter-of-factly. She slid into the hallway dressed in sweats, sneakers with socks, and a baseball cap.

"Not now?" Dean asked. "You got other plans?"

"As a matter of fact, I do," she said and slid past him. She walked briskly down the hall.

"Wait a minute," Dean whispered loudly. "Where are you going?" He ran to catch up with her.

"I have things to do," she answered as she got on the elevator.

He jumped on behind her. "What things?"

"I don't think you'd understand."

"Try me."

The elevator arrived at the lobby. She got off and walked to the front desk. The clerk saw her coming and met her at one end of the counter.

"Good morning. You must be 12F," the clerk yawned.

"That's me. Is it ready?" Bernie asked.

"Is what's ready?" Dean asked.

"Right out front. Will your friend be joining you?" the clerk asked, as he eyed Dean Larson.

"I don't know," Bernie answered.

"Friend?" Dean asked. "Do you watch baseball?"

"No," the clerk said flatly and returned to his desk.

Dean slapped a hand to his forehead as he whirled around. Bernie watched the front doors slide open and stepped toward the hotel's courtesy van parked and running outside. Dean bolted the length of the entrance and slid between the closing doors. Bernie opened the van door, and the driver smiled at her. She started to close the door, but Dean caught it. He held it open.

"Where are you going?" Dean asked.

"Does it really matter to you?"

"You're about to start a game for my team. It really does matter to me," he stated.

She thought a minute. "I'm going to the stadium."

"What?"

"I'm going to the stadium. Either get in or stay here," she announced rather matter-of-factly.

Dean hopped into the back of the van. The driver turned. "Thank you for riding with us, Mr. Dean. This is an unexpected surprise." The driver stammered nervously in the presence of the catcher.

"He really is very nice, most of the time," Bernie assured the driver. Her voice calmed him. There was something different about her speech, her expressions, that calmed and soothed those around her. So far as he knew, the only people resistant to her powers were reporters.

They rode most of the way to Candlestick Park in silence. Visiting ballparks at five in the morning was not the normal behavior of a major league pitcher.

The van pulled up to the players' entrance of the ballpark and stopped at the security station. The guard looked in to see Bernie and Dean and immediately passed them through. The van stopped near the door to the visiting locker room.

"I'll be done at six," Bernie told the driver.

"And him?" The driver turned to Dean.

"I don't know. When will you be done?" Bernie asked the catcher.

"Six will be fine," he told the driver, and both of them got out of the van.

She walked into the locker room quickly, took a right then a left. She turned around twice and frowned. She put her hands on her hips and pondered the problem.

"You don't know how to get to the field, do you?" Dean asked.

"I don't," she said with amazing candor.

"This way." Dean shrugged and led her off down a dark tunnel and into the dressing room.

They quickly walked past the lockers and out another door. The runway to the field was long and dark, but Dean had been this way enough times not to need lights. They emerged into the dimly lit infield to the early morning sun and the sparkling dew on the grass. Dean stopped to take in the majesty of the park, empty and grand like an ancient Roman temple. Bernie walked straight to the pitcher's mound and sat down. Dean looked at the nun and remembered the morning before the practice game when the team found her on the field doing — something. He walked up to her.

"What are you doing?" Dean asked softly.

She looked up. "I'm taking some quiet time."

"Quiet time?" Dean asked. "You're praying, right?"

"At times," she answered. "Every morning I get up and spend some time in silence. I use the time to make sure I appreciate everything that God's given me. I pray to thank Him mostly, and to tell Him what I've seen. What I worry about."

"Like our losing streak?"

"No. I never talk about baseball with God."

"No baseball?" Dean had prayed only a few times in his life. Most of them were requests for a hit in a clutch situation.

"He gave me the opportunity to play baseball, something I never would've done under any other circumstance. Even when we lose, I can't really complain."

"So losing doesn't bother you?"

"Oh, yes. It does, but that's part of my human weakness. I'm afraid I lose that battle more than I win it. I do have rules. I don't ask for His help to win a baseball game. He's given me all the help I need to compete, so that's what I do."

Dean scratched his tangled mass of hair, the result of his tossing and turning in his sleep. "So what do you think and talk with God about on a pitcher's mound at five in the morning?"

"The important things."

"That's pretty vague."

"No, it isn't." She thought for a moment. "Do you remember that morning in spring training when the team found me on the field?"

Dean rubbed his ribs, which had almost healed now. "Yeah."

"The next morning, I was thankful for the gift that Mike and Tommy made to the soup kitchen."

"But you know they hadn't intended to do that?"

"Intentions don't always equal outcomes," she said and then closed her eyes to resume her quiet time.

Dean Larson looked up into the sky and was suddenly very nervous. He realized that his hopes to break the losing streak rested on the shoulders of this nun from Nebraska who sounded strangely like Kane from Kung Fu. He rubbed his hair furiously, and looked around for a clock. There wasn't one. He knew he had at least forty-five minutes left with the nun in silence. He sighed heavily and sat down on the mound with his back to her. How was he going to kill the time? Oh yeah, he reminded himself, the important things. That's what Bernie had said. She thinks about the important things.

He looked up into the starlit sky and smelled the dew hanging onto the blades of grass out beyond the dirt of the infield. The city noises were now just low hums. He reached down and touched the dirt of the pitcher's mound. He rubbed it in his fingers. It was lukewarm. He brushed it on his leg and as he did, he remembered.

The day had been bright and the uniform small. He'd had the Memorials make it up special to fit the body of a five year old. Becky, his daughter, had stood in full major league regalia, the home colors, and smiled in that all consuming way that he could look at for hours. He had even taken the trouble of getting his number on the back of the uniform. She was a spunky little girl with unlimited energy. She'd asked for the uniform one Christmas and it had taken months before Dean had been able to deliver. He'd even gotten her a tiny mitt.

He remembered her birth, how small she'd been. The feeling of responsibility and complete dedication to this little perfect creature cradled in his two monstrous hands. He'd sworn on that day that he would always take care of her. Fathers were like that about their daughters.

The small lawn tractor jolted Dean back to the pitcher's mound in Candlestick park. He shook his head clear of the— the— he didn't really know what to call it. He turned to see Bernie already standing and patiently waiting for him to join her.

"I think they're ready to work on the field," she said.

"I 'spect they are," he answered, and lumbered to his feet.

She walked slowly to the exit, and Dean trailed her. He wanted to ask her a few questions, but the thought of disturbing the last moments of peace in the morning prevented him. He finally managed to say something in the van on the way back to the hotel.

"What did you think about?" Dean asked.

"It's a private time, Dean," she answered. "I've always thought about it like a birthday wish. You're not really supposed to talk about it until it comes true."

"So you made a wish?"

"No, but it's the same principle." She leaned back into the seat. She looked refreshed, as if she had slept all night.

Dean turned to look out the window and realized that she was right. The moments he'd remembered were his and only he could fully appreciate them. But there was still a part of him that wanted to boast and wax about his child, his Becky. In the end he said nothing, because baseball started to creep back into his mind. By the time they got to the hotel, he was fully focused on the game again. As he turned his key in the hotel room door, the image of Becky in her uniform flashed in his thoughts again and then was gone.

Chapter 32

No one could remember this kind of media exposure for a game so early in the season. Cameramen fought for space in the media cage just to one side of the Giants' dugout. The contest was carried by ESPN as the featured game of the doubleheader. Even Lifetime had bid on the event.

Moss paced in the locker room, going through every nook and cranny of the four previous games hoping to find some change in the batting order to produce more runs. He stopped himself right after he penciled in Link Molansky to lead off. He walked over to a sink and poured cold water over his head. He figured it was enough to break the gender barrier in one game. Too much to debut an entirely new batting order as well.

Moss went over to his private locker and sat down with his clipboard. He had taken the liberty of memorizing several stock answers to the questions reporters kept asking him about the nun. His favorites were, "We treat her the same as any other player," and "She's part of a team, and in a team concept they're all just players to me." He'd written the last one himself. He looked at the clock. It was time.

"Welcome to baseball from the Stick! Tonight, the modern game breaks new ground. Pitching for the Washington Memorials is Sister Mary Bernadette." The announcer on the TV spoke in controlled excitement as the Giants took the field. The Giants were throwing a young arm named Darren Carr. Carr promptly sat down the first three Memorials' hitters on five pitches.

"Hey, Bernie." Moss called his rookie pitcher over before she took the field.

"Yeah," the nun answered.

"Stay calm out there. Remember, nobody ever put out a fire by panicking, and for Pete's sakes, don't embarrass me."

Bernie nodded to Moss, then trotted out to the mound amid the lights and sounds of her dreams. She wore brand new cleats and had a top-of-the-line glove. Buddy made sure she had the best, something she wasn't used to as a nun. She took a quick look around the stadium. Fans everywhere were waiting for her to throw. The nerves began as she set for her warm-ups. She threw six knuckle-balls and one curve that bounced three quarters of the way to the plate. None were even close to the strike zone. Sweat beaded on her forehead, and she wiped her sleeve across it several times.

Evan Fish, a recent acquisition to play outfield for the Giants, led off the first and became the first man to face a woman in the big leagues. He watched the first pitch float out over the plate, then bail outside.

"Ball!!" The umpire called.

Dean snapped the ball back to Bernie. He held out his hands and motioned for her to calm down. She kicked the rubber once and reset. She closed her eyes for a moment and remembered her secret, her faith in the pitch. She wound up and let her mind focus on the pitch itself and not the plate. The pitch came off her hand slowly. The entire crowd was mesmerized as it began to dance across the infield toward home.

This second pitch hung out over the infield longer. It begged to be crushed, and Fish couldn't help himself. The swing was early and high. The clunk of lumber on ball sent the pitch down the third base line where Link easily fielded it and threw out the runner.

That was the first recorded out made by a woman pitcher in the modern game. To Bernie, it meant she belonged, and that another batter would follow until her team made twenty-six more outs. That was baseball.

She escaped the rest of the inning without incident. The game continued that way into the fourth. Bernie pitched out of a runners-on-the-corners jam by inducing a ground ball double play. In the bottom of the fourth with one runner on, she brought another knuck-leball to Fish.

The ball hung too long, and to the horror of Bernie, the movement was minimal. Fish caught the pitch up in the strike zone and pounded the ball to deep left field. It became a double and the runner scored.

In the top of the fifth, Carr struck out Da Bull then walked Vitamin Vitarello on a high three-two fastball. Molanksy grounded into a fielder's choice. With two out, Dean Larson kicked the dirt from his cleats and walked to the plate.

He dug in and clenched his teeth. This Carr had a live fastball, and normally he would be expecting it, but not this time. Dean was a great first ball fastball hitter. The world knew it. He figured the kid would throw something else, probably the slider that Carr had worked so hard on in spring training. That was the pitch to look for, the slider.

The ball spun from Carr's hand, and immediately Dean picked the white spot on the side of the ball. It was the slider. He stepped forcefully toward the pitch and launched his bat through the strike zone. The crack of the bat echoed throughout the stadium. The ball arched high out over the field as it streaked into the sky and over the center field fence.

Moss led the cheers as the Memorials posted their first lead of the season. Bernie pitched the sixth, and the knuckleball stayed sharp. She came up to bat in the top of the seventh, and Moss pinch-hit for Bernie in an effort to extend the lead.

Bernie was thankful not to have to bat again. It was one thing to throw knuckleballs to these guys. It was an entirely different matter to stand in there and watch ninety-mile-per-hour fastballs rocket toward you. She had been up twice and struck out looking both times. In fact, she'd managed only one weak, late swing.

Andejar Morales flied out to third and started a one, two, three seventh inning for Carr. The bullpen held the lead through the seventh and eighth. They kept the Giants to their one run, but in the top of the eighth the Memorials padded their lead.

Dean Larson cracked his second homer of the day, a solo shot. Mad Max Standish struck out the side in the bottom of the ninth to record his first save. The Memorials won three to one, and Bernie went into the record books with her first victory.

The clubhouse rocked after the victory. Dean was hailed as an unlikely hero. It was only the second time in his long career that he'd had a multiple homer game. Bernie pitched well. All questions about whether or not she could compete were gone. Only two people were not completely consumed by the joy of victory.

Link Molansky still scowled at the thought of a woman on his team and believed she would bring eventually them down. This win was an aberration he told himself, a one-time freak fluke. She'd show her true self soon.

Buddy Wilson was called a genius, but he took all the praise from his peers with skepticism. He was a general manager. He couldn't help it. The majors were littered with pitchers with one-game careers. The test wasn't the first time you pitched. It was the second and third time that big league hitters saw your stuff.

Moss Thompson showered quickly, and even shaved. He had forgotten his intentions to get rid of Bernie. She was his discovery now. He dressed and picked up his clipboard. He studied his answers one more time.

The locker room was full of reporters, with the exception of one corner. Buddy had made arrangements so that one corner was curtained off. There, Bernie found privacy from every reporter but Amy Springer. Amy picked her way through the reporters and slid behind the curtain.

Amy could not contain her excitement. She hugged Bernie tightly, which threw the nun a little off balance.

"You did it!" Amy whispered.

"I know. We won."

"No, you did it. You broke the gender barrier. You took on the whole of male society in their arena and triumphed."

"It's my job," Bernie said plainly, but then a broad grin broke out across her lips. "It was something, wasn't it? I mean, I'd dreamt about what it would be like to pitch in the majors."

"How do your dreams compare to the real thing?"

"Nothing can compare to the real thing."

"Is that a quote?"

"I suppose it is."

Bernie dressed quickly and talked a bit more about her first start with Amy. The reporter kept reminding herself to keep the professional distance that was needed to be as objective as possible, but the exuberance, the reverence the nun showed for the act of playing, proved a formidable foe. Amy found herself drawn further and

further into the simple world of a player who would never see a
mutual fund or a limited partnership.

Amy didn't begrudge the players their money. She made quite a
nice living from the daily games played by grown men. But there
seemed to be plenty of money to go around, and she had never
backed away from getting more for herself.

Bernie made her look at things differently, though. When Amy
talked to the nun, she couldn't clear her mind of the images of little
leaguers celebrating the days of summer on ill-kept fields.

Chapter 33

The press conference lasted a long time. Reporters repeated question after question in hopes that she would add some new phrase that they could quote in tomorrow's headlines. Buddy shadowed her the entire time. He made sure she stayed away from any discussion of miracles and the college game when she had "the vision." He led her from TV interview to TV interview, until she finally asked to go to her room and sleep. Buddy consented.

While the world's attention focused on Bernie's debut, the rest of the Memorials found themselves gathered around Dean Larson's locker. His two homers had powered the way for the victory, and nobody had seen Dean throw the lumber like that for years.

"What crawled up your pants tonight?" Tommy Chang asked, as he watched the crowd of reporters throng around the curtain protected by four large security guards.

"I felt comfortable, you know," Dean answered.

"Comfortable? What the hell does that mean?" Tommy asked.

"I don't really know. I seem to have everything in place. Haven't you ever felt that way at the plate?"

"Not this year," Tommy answered. He grabbed a towel and headed for the showers.

Dean sat in front of his locker and thought about the game for a long time. A few reporters stopped by to ask him about the two dingers, but he was just a sidelight.

"I haven't seen that kind of power out of the catcher position for the Memorials in a few summers." Amy stood four feet from him. She was radiant in a slick navy suit with a cream colored blouse and just the right sized golden necklace.

"Wrong story, Lois Lane," he teased. "ERA meets ERA should

be the headline tomorrow, don't you think?"

She stepped toward him and her suit shifted over her hips, then back again. It was a subtle thing, but a ninety-mile-per-hour fastball had looked like slow pitch softball tonight. Dean was seeing everything in vivid detail.

"Don't you have to go to the press conference?" Dean asked her.

"I have my interview. It's an exclusive. I've done enough damage for one day." She enjoyed her special status.

"Sounds like it." He pulled his towel over his shoulder, slid his feet into shower sandals and grabbed a tube of liquid soap. He wanted to make a smooth segue into —

"You still owe me a movie," Amy said softly.

"That I do. I'll have to make good on that soon," he said. Four new reporters rushed through on their way to the press conference. The jostling broke the spell.

"I've got to write my story," Amy said as she turn and walked away.

Dean took a long shower. His thoughts were jumbled, and he tried to focus on the game. He had really been in there tonight. He had seen the ball. He had crushed the ball. It was important to understand the secret to getting to that zone. As much as he hated to admit it to himself, he knew there was only one difference between tonight's game and all the rest. He had gone with Bernie and spent that morning hour thinking of other things, important things. Dean put little stock in religious voodoo and rites and such, but no baseball player worth his salt turned his back on a coincidence like this. Under the hot steam of the shower, he decided to test his theory. He would go with Bernie again for the early morning retreat.

The last person who left the locker room that night was Toby Haynes. He had yet to play in a game. He spent his time pouring through the baseball magazines for any mention of the Memorials' Wilmington farm team and the young prospects. One, a young second baseman, was off to a fast start. Another, this one a shortstop, had hit six home runs in the first ten games. Toby had taken to staying in the locker room longer than everybody else recently. This was partly so he wouldn't have to walk out the front door and see the disappointed faces of the media who waited for someone else. It was also partly because he felt his grip on the dream slipping.

The Memorials lost their next four games, three to the Giants and the opener to the Astros in Houston. The one and eight record failed to put the scare into the other teams that Moss had enjoyed last year. Teams now looked to sweep the Memorials.

The only bright spot during these days was the play of Dean Larson. He went on a power tear and became virtually the only reliable offensive player in the lineup. Moss still didn't change the batting order. He fretted and waited.

The team sat at two and eight when Dean decided to take the reins of leadership firmly into his hands. He called Jon John and Vitamin Vitarello to his locker.

"Why are we here?" Vitamin asked as he downed a large, green pill that resembled compressed salad.

"You know how you've been asking what changed in my swing?" Dean asked.

"Yeah, and so?"

"Something has changed."

"You've been holding out on me." Vitamin eyed the catcher.

"No, it's just it's a little weird. I didn't think you'd understand, so I tested it first. It seems to work," Dean said.

Jon John stared at his battery mate, but made no sign that he would speak.

"So?" Vitamin pressed.

"Every morning at five, I go to the ballpark with Bernie."

"Geez!" Vitamin slapped his head. "Do I want to hear this?"

"Shut up!" Dean slugged Vitamin in the arm. "Now listen, we go to the ballpark and just sit there. She prays, or something, and I — well, I think about what's important."

"What's important?" Vitamin queried.

"Yeah, you know, what's really important."

"So you think about baseball?" Vitamin asked.

"No, idiot. I think about my kid." Dean's sincerity almost moved even Jon John to speak, but neither the pitcher nor the first baseman said a word.

"It's really helped my focus. You two are reasonable guys. I'm simply offering you a chance to participate."

"You want me to haul my butt out of bed at five in the morning to think about what's important to me?" Vitamin asked.

Dean cajoled, "We're two and eight. We can't lose any more by trying it."

Vitamin eyed his friend cautiously. "I think you've hit some kind of weirdness my man, but — you are slamming the crap out of the ball. So what the hey, I'm in."

"Yes." The word fell from Jon John's lips.

The next morning, Bernie found Vitamin and Jon John waiting with Dean. She paused a moment and then smiled. Teammates should share.

For Vitamin and Jon John, the hour began uncomfortably. Jon John's mind wandered to the outfield grass. It reminded him of the hayfields of Montana. That's where he helped his uncle put up hay for the family ranch. He felt the sun and the smell, and his father and uncle egging him on to work faster.

Vitamin looked up into the night sky and at the stars. They were like the ones over the ocean he saw every night for the two weeks he spent on a boat every off season with a couple of childhood buddies. He shook his head after a moment, because he swore he felt the stinging sea breeze. When both men got up to follow Dean and Bernie out of the ballpark, they were confused and calm. Jon John refused to show any outward emotion.

That night, Jon John rediscovered the movement on his fastball. Instead of throwing batting practice to the opposition, he K'ed ten and gave up two earned runs over eight and a third. Vitamin slammed a two-run shot, and Dean scored twice and drove in another.

Vitamin and Jon John hit the sack before ten. Five o'clock would come early and they had tasted just enough of success to try this thing again. Their win gave them new confidence. They remembered that the game was fluid, and now it flowed from them au natural.

Bernie also went to bed early that night. Baseball was wonderful, and now began to resemble the convent in a weird way. After her early problems, she now felt that everything had turned out right. She slept well with no idea of the impending storm about to rain on her parade.

Judge Vincent Black of the district court of Orlando slumped in his chair and stared at his eighth cup of coffee. There were few cases that caused much of a stir in a judge's lifetime, but the one before him now fell into that category.

Johnny LePlant, et. al, vs. the Washington Memorials had charged discrimination against the male reporters who were denied access to the locker facility provided to a new team member, a Catholic nun. The team who had transgressed, the Washington Memorials, thought they'd brokered a deal by allowing a female reporter inside. The team claimed this owned up to its responsibility for media access.

Judge Black was well aware of the case history of female sports-writers suing to gain access to these rooms, the lack of which they proved a legitimate barrier to their ability to compete in the market-place. He had even considered equal access a good idea. No one involved in the original case imagined that some day something like this would come up.

He now faced a more difficult question. There could be no quibbling among people who read the laws. If a female reporter had significant access to a men's locker room because it was fair in the workplace, then a male reporter must be accorded the same rights in a women's locker room. As much as the scales of justice must blind, this core argument was both powerful and difficult for the judge to accept. He took one last sip of coffee and took the first step toward the courtroom.

"All rise. The Honorable Justice Vincent Black now presiding," the bailiff chimed.

The judge walked slowly into the courtroom and took his seat. Attorney Horace Trent sat behind the table on the plaintiff's side of the room. His client, Johnny LePlant et. al, had filed to be granted access to this nun as she now fell into the category of major league baseball player. Tyrone Moore, attorney for the Washington Memorials, sat at the defendants' table. He was here to argue the organization's position that the nun required special considerations.

Judge Vincent Black didn't move. He'd sat in his chair in contemplation for the past few days as the hearing had raged. There had been more briefs from more groups, from the ACLU to New Conservative Motherhood Brigade, that had to be duly noted and given a response. Today, however, Judge Black had finally decided that enough was enough.

He had spent the previous night watching tapes until well past three in the morning. The tapes were a project the judge had given to his clerk, a young man by the name of Reggie Murdoch. Judge Black had directed Murdoch to pull every bit of locker room coverage the young man could get his hands on. The judge was very interested in what was being recorded by the reporters that rushed into the locker room after a game.

The result had been mixed. Much of it was, quite frankly, man at his worst. Reggie defended his collection of video clips by saying that these were the ones that were aired the most.

Black watched as a reporter sidled up to a young man who had just struck out to end a playoff game. The reporter wanted to know if something had been bothering the player during the whole series, considering the man hit only .202, .138 with runners in scoring position. The player erupted and went after the reporter. Only a big third baseman stopped the player from clobbering the scribe.

Another scene featured a coach who had lost his temper with a reporter who had repeated the same question three other men had already asked. A phone flew across the screen, followed by an answering machine and then a tirade of cursing.

The final clip, he remembered vividly, involved no reporter at all. Instead, it was a manager and player locked in combat on the slick floor of a steamy locker room.

Judge Black looked at the two lawyers with a frown. The courtroom was packed. Reporters from every major news service sat with pencils and paper poised for his words. He didn't recognize half the logos on the lapels of jackets, most of which he considered dubious. He knew his decision would be immediately appealed. He cleared his throat and spoke with the certainty of his conviction.

"Ladies and gentlemen, I have reached a decision."

Chapter 34

As the hearing drew to a close in Orlando, the Memorials won an afternoon delight from the Mets. Jon John was spectacular in a two hit shutout that left only Mad Max Standish upset because Jon John pitched the whole game. Dean and Vitarello continued to tear up opposing pitching. The games of Mike Flowers and Tommy Chang picked up as well. The upturn for them began the day they first came across their teammates sitting with the nun, early in the morning, on the infield.

Mike and Tommy had arrived at the ballpark early to play a practical joke on Vitamin. They'd planned to replace the vitamins in his blue bottle with pure sugar pills, but they'd never made it. On their way to the dugout, they'd noticed Vitamin's car. On further investigation, they'd seen the four people out on the pitcher's mound.

After a short explanation from Bernie, the center fielder and the second baseman had both decided that they were up anyway, why not give the stuff a try? It couldn't hurt. The change in their play was a statistical fact.

Their emergence at the top of the batting order provided more opportunities for Dean and Vitarello, who remained hot. This led to more wins, but they still lost more than they won. As Moss told them over and over, pitching wins championships.

After a home game, Mike stopped Bernie on the way to the Winnebago. The famed mobile home held the nun at home games, and on the road they used the curtain for privacy.

"See you tomorrow morning?" Mike asked.

"As always," Bernie replied. She enjoyed the time even more now. She liked the community with her teammates, even if they all were thinking very different thoughts.

Bernie was the second to last to leave that night. Since joining the team, Bernie had moved into a small apartment near the stadium. It was an easy bus ride from the stadium, but there always seemed to be someone to give her a ride, so she rarely rode the bus. Tonight, however, she was alone. She grabbed her bag and left the Winnebago for the bus stop. That's when she saw him.

Toby Haynes leaned against a fence and gazed out over the ballpark. He looked like a lost deer that had just wandered into the New York Stock Exchange. A newspaper lay next to him on the ground. Bernie approached slowly.

"Toby, are you okay?" Bernie asked.

"I'm fine," he said.

"I don't think so."

He sighed. "I don't like to bring people down after a win."

"I see. Well, it just so happens that I'm happy about us winning the ball game today. But right now, I'm concerned about a teammate." Bernie looked at the newspaper. It was opened to the minor league box scores.

"It seems Wilmington is doing well," she said and picked up the paper.

"Very well," Toby commented.

Bernie scanned through the box score and saw the name Howard listed at second base. This Howard had gone four for four with three runs scored and had driven in two. His average was now .341.

"Do you really think this Howard kid is any good?"

"He's very good," Toby answered. "I've seen him play."

"Is he better than you?" she asked.

"I'm afraid we're about to find out," he said. "I've got a bad feeling about how much longer I'll be here."

"Why would they send you down?"

"I'm hitting .153, and I'm only a little better than Howard in the field. It's not enough to keep me here."

"It's early in the year."

"Early quickly becomes late," Toby sighed.

"Do you really think so?"

"When you do what I do in the majors, you're always expendable. Being a good defensive player isn't the easiest thing, but being replaced by a good offensive player is. If I were a general manager, that's what I'd think."

She paused and put a hand on his shoulder. "Toby, what are you doing at five tomorrow morning?"

"What?"

"I lead a kind of morning vigil with a few of the guys, and I'd like you to come." She looked at him seriously.

"Who comes?"

"Vitamin, Dean, Jon John, Mike and Tommy." The names rolled off her tongue easily, like old friends. "Some of them think it helps their game, but it really just gets you thinking about what's most important in your life again."

"Forgive me, Bernie, but it sounds a little strange."

"Yes, it is. It's very strange how so many people get lost when they forget what the important things are. You think about it. It can't hurt," she said with a shrug and turned to leave.

"Where do you do this?"

"The ballpark. Be here tomorrow, if you want to —" She never finished.

"Bernie!" The shout echoed across the length of the parking lot. Amy Springer walked quickly to her. "Have you heard?"

"Heard what?" The nun asked.

"Justice Black just ruled on you."

"What did he say?"

"He ruled that since he cannot make special exceptions for one ballplayer, he would indeed treat everyone the same. Starting tomorrow, reporters will be barred from all locker rooms." Amy took a deep breath.

"Oh my," Bernie said quietly.

"They're going to kill you tomorrow," Amy said.

"The players?" Bernie asked.

"No, the reporters."

"If it's just the reporters then," Bernie began.

"Just the reporters? Just? Who do you think distills everything down for the American viewing public to sit, watch and judge sports every single day? Reporters, that's who." Amy paced.

"What can I do?" Bernie asked.

"Be very careful about everything you do from this moment on.

Don't do anything that might get you in trouble with reporters," Amy stated.

"What could I possibly do that would be so bad?" Bernie asked.

"Trust me. If there was ever a group of people that could find dirt on a nun from Nebraska, these guys can."

Morning arrived earlier than usual for the silent group on the wet grass of Memorial stadium. Toby Haynes did show up for the ritual, but when asked to concentrate on what was important, he found it difficult to lock on any one thing.

At six the group stood. Dean and Vitamin ran out to the first newsstand they found open and got four or five newspapers and divided them between everyone.

"The rawness of the locker room emotion, unmasked by the pioneers of journalism and made equitable by the modern day woman reporter was ripped from the fan by the old-fashioned, outmoded mores of one Judge Vincent Black. Shame, I say, shame!" Phillip Nested, *New York Times*.

"Modesty prevents Judge Black from allowing access to a player. This is about one player on one team that plays in only one city, one night at a time. Judge Black has removed the First Amendment. In the end, we barter away our dignity." Johnny LePlant, syndicated columnist.

This was going better than any of the players had imagined. Dean stepped to the middle of the group and read a portion of Amy Springer's article aloud.

"I do not know how the lack of access will affect the story of the game. Presumably there was a story to report before locker room interviews became the vogue, especially on television. As a reporter, it is my job to get as complete a picture of sports as possible. Nothing has changed that. We know that this verdict will be appealed, and until then our focus will shift back to the drama between the foul lines."

They left the papers in the recycling bin. Bernie led the way to the parking lot. It was now 7:45 a.m., and they decided to go to breakfast. As Tommy pushed the front locker door open, they all saw the glare. It was not pointed at them, though. A small army of reporters was hunkered down, pointing toward the road coming *into* the stadium. They waited and watched for any sign of the nun.

Bernie breathed heavily behind the hastily closed door to the locker room.

"What are they doing?" she asked.

Vitamin peeked out the door and looked over the crowd. "It ain't a celebration party, kid."

"They want you to comment on the verdict," Dean finally said somberly.

"I didn't write it," Bernie answered.

"You're at the center of it," Dean responded.

"I still didn't write it. And I don't want to talk to them about it." The room grew silent, as every man there remembered the agony of answering pointed questions from the press.

"What we need is a diversion," Tommy smiled wickedly.

"Brother Tommy, I couldn't agree more," Mike answered.

"What are you guys talking about?" Dean cautiously asked.

"Play action," Tommy started.

Mike stepped in without breaking rhythm. "We get the good men of the media out there to focus on something long enough to get her free and clear."

"Sounds great," Dean replied. "But those guys out there happen to be a human roadblock to the players' parking lot. Even if we could get to a car, we couldn't get out."

Mike and Tommy cracked the door to survey the situation. Dean was correct. The human wall of waiting questions cut off the cars in the players' lot. Mike and Tommy's attention was drawn to the narrow road that ran up to a large gate at the back of the stadium near the locker room entrance. Vans brought food and souvenirs there for unloading. That road was mostly clear. The cars and vans of the media were lined up, each parked halfway on the curb to leave a fire lane open. There wasn't much room, but there was enough.

"All we need is to get a vehicle on that road," Tommy surmised.

"We can't steal one of the reporter's cars, can we?" Mike teased.

"No, we can't," Dean stated firmly in order to keep this from getting out of hand.

"We don't have to." Tommy turned back to the group and gloated.

"You have it, don't you?" Mike coaxed.

Tommy scanned the group and stopped at Toby. "Toby, do you

play the piano?"

"Some," Toby answered.

"Mike and Toby will come with me. Vitamin, you and Dean prepare for operation hide the habit."

In the players' parking lot outside, one figure walked away from the mass of reporters. He lit a cigarette and played as if he was doing this out of a respect to the non-smokers in the group. He wasn't. Johnny LePlant never did that kind of thing.

Johnny wormed his way over to the Winnebago. He reached into a pocket and took out a key, a gift from an insider in the Memorial organization. Johnny tried the key and it worked. He slid inside the vehicle without being seen.

Vitamin and Dean waited with Bernie. All three paced.

"I really don't think this is a good idea," Dean said for the fourth time.

"It'll work. It'll work," Vitamin assured the catcher. "I have complete trust in those guys. Don't you?"

"I suppose." Dean sighed.

High above the field, in a special booth just to the left of the press box, was the control center for the Jumbotron and music system for Memorials' Stadium. Tommy, Mike and Toby entered quietly and went right to work.

Tommy turned on the electric organ and let it warm up. He offered the bench to Toby. The young utility man felt his heart leap. No one had ever asked him to be a part of a team effort off the field before.

Tommy joined Mike as they switched on the computers necessary for the Jumbotron. All three stopped and gawked as they gazed out of the large windows of the room. The two giant screens flittered and flickered to life.

"All right, boys," Tommy began. "Now we have some fun."

In the Winnebago, Johnny sat in one of the chairs and cursed the coffee he'd drunk that morning. Caffeine worked on his bladder in a hard and cruel way. He knew it was best to remain in the vehicle. No one had seen him enter, and his plan required surprise. He stewed for a moment, before receiving his salvation. He remembered he was in a Winnebago, and mobile homes had their own bathrooms. Johnny opened the little door and stepped inside.

The familiar strains of the charge — dah-dah-dah-dut — dah-dah — was faint at first, only a few of the reporters heard it. The next charge was louder, and by the third rendition every head turned toward the stadium. Their first steps were gradual, but their pace quickened when those in the lead noticed the scoreboard blinking to life. Something strange was happening at the ballpark this morning, and strange meant news.

Dean watched from the doorway as the reporters moved like lemmings toward one of the park's gates. He waited. Finally, the last of the group reached the gate and entered. This was their chance.

"Bernie, Vitamin, we're leaving," Dean called out as he threw open the door.

The scoreboard lit a simple message without pictures or animation. It read, "How many reporters does it take to screw in a light bulb?" Men bristled under their lack of sleep, and then turned red as the answer flashed. "30. One to screw it in, and 29 to second-guess the strategy."

The men took down notes furiously. Whoever was responsible would pay dearly in that day's column. The notes went unfinished, though. Each pen stopped when the roar of a large engine echoed in the empty stadium.

The Winnebago was parked near the vendor entrance, and therefore had access to that narrow road now flanked by cars and vans. Vitamin had been the first to reach the vehicle and slide into the driver's seat. Dean had fallen into the seat next to him, and Bernie had flopped onto a bench in the back.

"Hang on," Vitamin yelled. "This is going to be close."

The mobile home lurched forward and picked its way through the narrow gap. The force almost unseated Johnny LePlant, who had grown tired of waiting and assumed the normal reading position of a man in a bathroom. He silently cursed and pulled his pants up. What were these lunatics doing? The question was rhetorical. He knew. Sister Mary was running. This was the moment he lived for — the exact point in time when the young phenom learned nobody gets away from Johnny LePlant.

The bathroom door banged open, and a blur flew into the mobile home, ranting at the top of his lungs. Bernie jumped four feet off the backbench and almost hit the ceiling.

"AAHHHHHH!!!!" Her voice filled the interior, and then some.

"What the —," Dean's head jerked around to the voice.

"You!" Bernie screamed at Johnny.

"Who?" Vitamin couldn't help himself. "What's wrong?" He turned to see the problem. He saw Johnny. "What's he doing here?" the first baseman asked Dean.

Dean Larson didn't answer. His eyes were wide with horror, and Vitamin briefly wondered why Dean was acting so strangely. The catcher had seen reporters before. That's when the metal started to scrape.

The Winnebago had veered only about two feet when Vitamin had turned around, but that was six inches more than there was clearance. The side of a lovely new Volvo was crushed as the mobile home barreled on. A mini-van followed.

"The brakes!" Johnny screamed.

Vitamin hit the brakes.

"No!!!" Dean pleaded.

The wheels locked up and the mighty recreational vehicle began to slide. The back end slipped off to the left, and what was once the private changing facility for the nun was now a bull dozer taking out the cars, vans and trucks that lined the road. After a few dreadful moments of twisting and wrenching metal, the Winnebago finally stopped.

The reporters descended en masse. Cameras flashed. Microphones were turned on. The reporters all watched and waited for any signs of life from inside the now dented and bruised vehicle. Finally, the door opened.

Vitamin emerged first, followed by Dean and then Bernie. They looked around at the media and frowned.

"Here they are boys." The voice boomed from Johnny as he stepped from the injured mobile home. "I couldn't let them get away. Thank me later."

"I knew this was a bad idea," Dean whispered.

Chapter 35

Dean dropped Bernie off at her apartment building, and she struggled up the stairs to her fourth floor efficiency. Dean asked to come up, but Bernie wanted to be alone. That was not to be, as Bernie found Amy Springer standing at her door, arms crossed, in a running outfit.

"What happened this morning?" Amy didn't even wait for Bernie to get her keys out.

"Good morning to you, too," Bernie offered. "And nothing much happened this morning."

"Nothing much?" Amy scolded with the warmth of a prosecuting attorney. "We have reports that something resembling the Bay of Pigs went down at Memorial Stadium this morning."

"It wasn't that bad."

"The buzz says the parking lot now looks like leftovers from a junk yard."

Bernie sighed and opened the door. She led Amy into the bedroom/dining room/living room and made coffee. Bernie recounted the morning's mishap in detail, mainly because Amy stopped her constantly to question. The reporter remained calm until Bernie described the final moments.

"And then the whole thing turned sideways, skidded and stopped. That was it."

"So everything was fine until Johnny LePlant burst out of the bathroom?"

"Yeah, in fact the plan worked great, except that Vitamin had to turn around and look."

"The cars belonged to the reporters?" Amy asked weakly.

"I think so."

"This isn't good."

"I didn't mean for any of it to happen. It was just an accident."

"I believe you. I really do, but you've just inconvenienced a bunch of reporters. There are no breaks from the media. And Johnny, what was he doing in the Winnebago in the first place?"

"He said it was his protest for freedom of speech."

"I'm going to give you some advice now. Please, take it to heart. When you go to the ballpark tonight, say nothing. Offer absolutely no comment until you speak directly with Buddy Wilson. I'm sure he has a plan."

"Why shouldn't I say anything?" Bernie asked.

"Because no one will hear it the way you tell it. They'll get bits and pieces, and you'll spend the rest of the year explaining yourself."

"That's not the way it should be."

"And maybe the Earth shouldn't be round, but wishing won't change it." Amy turned toward the door.

"Amy?" Bernie asked. "What are you going to write about this?"

Amy felt her heart and her notebook rip her soul in two. "I don't know," she finally answered and left quickly.

Dean stumbled up to his apartment, almost too tired to find the key to unlock the door. He didn't have to worry because help stood there in front of him in the form of Moss Thompson.

"What were you thinking this morning?" Moss glowered as he snatched the keys from Dean and opened the door.

"Well," Dean winced as he led his coach inside, "you just had to be there. You know we had this plan and everything. And the guys all pulled together. It was like a double play, Mike to Tommy to Vitamin. It was close to working."

"About as close as the Grand Canyon." Moss frowned. "You do understand this will cost you?"

"We didn't mean for it to turn it out this way."

"Well that don't exactly matter now, does it?"

"All we'll have to do is stand somewhere and make a public apology for getting out of hand."

"Out of hand? It's one thing for a bunch of wild-eyed young guys to paint the whole city red. It's an entirely different thing for two time-tested vets, a nun and three other players to crash up a bunch of vehicles. Now, what's going on?"

"I don't know, but lately I'm having as much fun as I did my rookie year."

"And it's leading to rookie mistakes," Moss countered. "And just what in the heck were you doing at the park at that hour?"

Dean paused. He wasn't so sure telling Moss about the morning vigil was the best thing, so he hedged. "We were all just getting in a little important work."

"That's commendable, I suppose. Just promise me no more car wrecks."

"I promise," answered Dean as Moss stormed from the apartment.

Dean sat there for moment, truly afraid. In newsrooms all across the country, reporters were sharpening their wit and word processors. There was one in particular that he knew he should call, and not just about a wrecked Winnebago.

"I wanted hot coffee!" Amy yelled at an intern later that afternoon. The young man was too shell-shocked to do anything but run for another cup.

The circle of activity around Amy's desk had a radius of six feet. No one ever crossed that boundary without receiving a verbal tongue lashing for his or her trouble.

Her editor, Russell Harris, wouldn't even speak with her face-to-face. He knew when her temper was not to be tested, and this was one of those times.

As for Amy, the issue wasn't anger. It was frustration. She had toiled too long in the shadow of others for her big inside break to do something this stupid.

"Hello, Amy." The voice cut through the air like a serrated knife.

She spun in her chair to look upon Johnny LePlant.

"Your girl chinked her armor."

"Scratch, nothing more," Amy answered back without emotion. She smirked and said, "I imagine it feels different to be on the outside looking in, Johnny?"

Johnny stared like a high-stakes poker player trying to bluff.

"Not for long. The ruling can't stand."

"By the way, what were you doing in the bathroom of a woman's dressing room?"

"Freedom of the press. I'm righting a terrible wrong."

"I had no idea you were such an idealist."

"I bet you enjoy this. All the boys are talking about you. I offer my congratulations." Johnny fished into a pocket and took out a pack of cigarettes. "I was talking to my editor yesterday, and it seems he would be interested in an insider's book about the nun's rookie frolic. I told him you and I were old friends." Johnny tapped the pack and slid a cigarette out.

"You aren't going to smoke in here, Johnny."

Johnny rolled the cigarette between his fingers. "There's a $50,000 advance for you." Johnny put the cigarette in his mouth.

"And yours is much higher?"

"I do have the track record." Johnny produced a lighter and flicked on a flame.

"I told you, you're not going to smoke in here!"

Johnny put the flame to the cigarette and let the end glow with heat. The coffee splashed first into the lighter, then onto the cigarette and finally onto Johnny's face and shirt.

"What are you doing?" Johnny screamed.

"Don't worry," Amy said. "It wasn't hot, trust me."

"You're crazy."

"Get out of here, Johnny." Amy stood.

Johnny wiped his face and his hands. "You will regret this." He turned and stormed off without further comment.

"Ms. Springer?" the timid voice of the intern whispered.

"What is it?!?" Amy roared.

"Here's your coffee, and — and this came for you." The young man handed her a plain envelope with her name typed on the outside.

She reached inside carefully and retrieved a single item, a ticket to a movie that started at nine o'clock that night.

Chapter 36

Buddy Wilson opened his second bottle of Tums at noon. The Memorials were scheduled for an afternoon delight with the Chicago Cubs and requests for interviews were stacked high on his desk. The season had not started well, and just when it looked like the team had turned a corner and was headed back into the race, a PR nightmare had exploded in his face.

C.W. McDermott demanded that his team be reined in and the perpetrators dealt with severely. Buddy sketched his strategy over coffee that morning. The organization would pay for the cars and vans. The players were docked some pay. Bernie lost the least money. The thought of denying a tiny church in some small town was no way to help the Memorials' public image. His analysis of the situation to the press had been that everyone was under a lot of pressure. Each would apologize in person for their role.

"Buddy, you wanted to see me?" Moss asked as he stood in the doorway.

"What's going on down there, Moss?" Buddy looked out of his office onto right field.

"Well, we started badly," Moss began.

"I don't mean that. I mean what were five players, including the nun, doing at the ballpark before eight in the morning?"

"They told me they had some important work to do. You know, baseball stuff." Moss tried to smile.

"Why are members of this team attacking the press?"
Moss chuckled.

"It's not funny!" Buddy cautioned. "This is serious."

"It was an accident, Buddy."

"There are no accidents," Buddy continued. "Today, each

member of the group will make a public apology, serve a one-game suspension, and be available to the press for questions. I want you there when that happens."

"Me? Why?"

"Damage control."

"I'm no good with reporters," Moss protested.

"You are today." Buddy's commanded.

The TV networks had been on the story non-stop and newspapers were asking other players leading questions. The early angle painted the players as five men who'd never grown up and one fallen religious figure. Professional athletes were basically warped people who lived outside of reality.

The game proved worse than the bad press. The Memorials committed five errors and scored zero runs in a pathetic loss to the Cubs. At the press conference that night, each member of the fiasco was to offer a quick apology. Bernie requested to go last. She stepped to the podium and stared right back at the hungry eyes turned toward her, ready to feast.

"I'm sorry the incident happened. There are no excuses. I accept that," she said flatly.

"What were you trying to do, escape?" Johnny LePlant, smug as ever, piped up from the back.

Bernie started to say something, but she never got that chance.

"I believe, if my information is correct, she was trying to escape you." Amy Springer stood on the other side of the room and spoke loudly so everyone could hear.

"Let's ask her that." Johnny called out.

"I —," Bernie stammered.

"Did Mr. LePlant come barreling out of your private bathroom, where you normally take showers?" Amy jumped in the fray from the back.

"Yes."

"I guess the question is to you, Mr. LePlant. What were you doing in that bathroom?" Amy asked.

"This is not about me," Johnny snipped. "I didn't crash the Winnebago."

"No, you jumped out from a hidden position and frightened everyone aboard, including the driver. When he looked away, he crashed. So you're saying you had nothing to do with this?"

"I was there on a protest of freedom of the press," Johnny roared.

"So interesting that you should bring that up. Are you aware of a ruling barring media from the locker rooms of professional teams?" Amy asked.

"I —," Johnny caught himself.

"Are you?"

"Yes."

"So you were in violation of the court order?"

"That's not the point," Johnny stumbled.

"I see. So you want to crucify these people for being in a Winnebago, legally, while you share none of the blame, even though you were there illegally?" Amy waited for an answer.

"I think that's about enough." The voice was Buddy's. He ended the session, although he almost enjoyed watching a reporter go after a reporter.

Bernie tried to catch Amy's eye as she left the stage. She wanted to show some kind of thanks, but Amy wouldn't meet the nun's gaze. The reporter knew she'd stretched the limit, perhaps broken it. Now was not the time for pleasantries.

Johnny received a three game suspension from the league for breaking into the Winnebago. He couldn't write about or attend a game during that time. It had been the first time a reporter had been issued such a fine. The league would've reduced it to two games if Johnny would have given up the name of his accomplice, but the reporter refused.

Johnny weathered the storm. He turned his attention toward Washington D.C. His syndicated column and appearances on nation-wide TV programs hinted that he had an agenda, something that lay in wait.

Public opinion of the pious pitcher soared. People didn't like the idea of somebody sneaking into a nun's dressing room, and they also bought into her desire to escape the lights. Just when it appeared everything was going to work out, things took a turn for the worse.

Chapter 37

Dean paced in front of the old movie house outside of D.C. where the catcher chose to take his day of suspension before joining the team in St. Louis. He was nervous and that scared him. What was his problem? This was just a friend, right?

Amy sat in her car and tried one more time to open the door without her hand shaking. This was the first time she'd been to a movie with a man alone in almost four years. That is, alone with someone she wanted to be alone with. She repeated in her head that this was nothing more than two people sharing an afternoon — to believe anything more asked for disappointment.

"Hello," Amy managed as she approached Dean in front of the theater.

"Hi," he said. "I see you got my ticket."

"I can honestly say it made my day."

"Good," Dean replied. "Well, shall we go in?"

"Sure."

Dean's cheeks flushed as he held the door open for the reporter. Amy concentrated on walking without shaking. The two somehow found seats in the final row in the back, far from anyone else in the theater.

The lights dimmed. Amy stared ahead at the movie screen. She concentrated on not breaking out in a cold sweat. She wore a white sundress, sleeveless. She breathed unevenly and hoped Dean didn't hear her.

Dean felt his stomach twist and flip, while his right leg kept involuntarily shaking. The opening credits rolled. Maybe he should leave, he thought. He had half a mind to just stand up and walk out without a word.

While half a mind can design such thoughts, it takes a whole brain to act them out. He told himself that he meant to get up, he really did, but her light perfume hung in the air. He stole a glance at the soft skin of her shoulder. His arm rested on the padding, two inches from hers — two inches of mere air.

Amy's heart raced ahead of her breath. His arm rested close to hers, almost near enough to touch it. Would this really happen?

Neither moved much during the movie. Their bodies remained stiff, as if some heavy penalty would be exacted if they fidgeted. The heat on their skin where it almost touched, burned hotter and hotter until the final credits rolled and the lights came up.

As the two left the theater, neither could've told anyone what the movie was about.They walked to Amy's car.

"You know, I could give you a lift to the airport," Amy said and smiled weakly.

"I don't want you to have to park or fight the traffic," Dean stammered back.

"I wouldn't have to," Amy replied. "They have the drop and kiss —"

This brought everything to a standstill. They faced each other at Amy's car. Two people who really wanted nothing more than to be loved and accepted for what they were.

"I —," Dean tried to cut the tension, but Amy cut him off.

She was slow but forceful. She moved in close and her lips found his. She had not felt this good about a man in a very long time.

Dean fought to suck in air as her warm lips connected with his. Ten thousand thoughts, all about touching Amy's body, flooded his mind. This was wonderful. This was great. This was — too long.

Dean pulled away, but not abruptly. "I need to catch a plane."

Amy smiled, "I'll see you in St. Louis?"

Dean nodded, backed away and walked toward his car.

Chapter 38

It was the worst start in Bernie's short career, and the cameras caught every minute of it. She had only spent fifteen minutes praying that morning, but she wouldn't blame it on that. The main culprit was no movement on the knuckleball.

St. Louis Cardinals hitters began licking their chops by the bottom of the second inning. Her bread and butter pitch hung fat like batting practice. Dean mixed in some curves and one or two fastballs in an effort to keep them in the game, but in the third, tragedy struck.

Losing two to zero already, Bernie surrendered back-to-back-to-back homers on three straight pitches. Moss had seen enough. Bernie was lifted after two and a third. Typewriters hummed with the news of the three-pitch, three-homer debacle.

Many labeled her a flash in the pan. It didn't help that Bernie went out and lost the next three starts. The rising star was now the fallen angel and more and more reporters revisited the stadium stunt as more than just an accident. It was an expression of a deeper problem.

Through it all, the morning vigil continued. Not one of them could explain why. Dean and Vitarello enjoyed good power numbers, but solo home runs couldn't carry the team. Tommy and Mike had high on-base percentages, but no two hitters got pokes consecutively. Opposing pitchers scattered the good offensive numbers into losses for the Memorials.

More than anything else, the group enjoyed their hour of silence. It was a reprieve from reporters and call-in shows that shouted the words "underachievers, bums and losers" at them. So long as they took one hour to remember everything else, they could weather the storm. The seams, however, were beginning to unravel.

"I just don't get it, Boney," Moss mused in his office to the pitching coach after another loss.

"They're losing," Boney replied matter-of-factly. "It ain't brain surgery, Moss."

Moss watched in practice as Link Molansky huddled with Lenny and Max. There was a growing division in the team over Bernie. Link even fed Johnny a few choice quotes on how the nun had destroyed the chemistry of the one-time contenders. The comments broke the locker room into two camps.

Despite the problems, the Memorials were a game over .500 and still within shouting distance of the lead. Mad Max Standish became the lone member of the team selected to the NL All Star roster. Everyone else scrambled to make travel plans to visit their families for the long weekend. The game scheduled for that afternoon with Cincinnati became almost an afterthought. They were not a team ready to play, particularly Dean Larson.

The catcher stood next to Amy Springer a few hours before the first pitch. They were quiet, until she turned to him.

"So, you're going home after the game?" Amy asked flatly.

"I have to," Dean replied. "But at least Bernie's going with me." He tried to smile.

"When will you be back?"

"The morning before we start the Giants series."

"Good," she said, and walked away.

Dean thought for a moment about the time they'd spent at the old movie theater. It didn't last long. Soon, the smell of roasting hot dogs filled the air, and Dean turned toward the locker room.

Moss made out his lineup card and rubbed his eyes. He hadn't slept well in a month. His team lacked the desire to reach out and use their abilities. He'd yelled, thrown bats, challenged their manhood. He'd devoured self-help books and even toyed with the notion of hypnosis. He'd caught himself in the mirror last night. He'd looked liked a refugee from an ocean liner accident found after three months at sea. Moss silently promised himself a reprieve. After all, his team was still in it.

A win this afternoon would take them two games up on .500

and Montreal was still in their sights. He hoped that today would be different. His wish came true, but not like he'd planned.

Jon John took the hill and threw five strong innings before the hundred plus degree heat of summer in Ohio began to wilt his strong right arm. The game stood at one a piece, as the tall man of little speech got two hard-hit ground balls right at the shortstop, Flip Toussant.

The next two batters went yard on Jon John. The normally stoic man began to boil. He felt the frustration of the team as the second ball cleared the center field fence by at least ten feet. The first part of the season had disappointed him. The team had disappointed him. This game had disappointed him, and disappointment made him mad!

Matt Terwilleger was a seldom-played member of the Reds, who was in the lineup to give someone an extra day off. He had seen Jon's fastball hit a speed bump and brake to very hittable. Matt stepped in with extra bases on his mind.

Jon John's first pitch never got to ninety miles-per-hour. Officially, it clocked in at eighty-two, but the location was precise. It nailed Matt on his inside shoulder.

Matt was a small, bulldog type guy used to getting dirty to get the job done. He shook off the effects of the impact and walked to first base. The umpire, Melvin Grabbing, warned Jon John, Moss and the Reds' bench for the beaning. The next hit batter, the pitcher and the manager would be tossed out of the game.

Jon John got a deep fly ball to end the sixth. Everyone lumbered off the field. The bench looked more like a wake than a ball team. Link Molansky picked up his bat, swung it twice in deep anger and kicked dirt all the way to home plate.

"Let's go, Link!" Bernie called out as she stood near the front of the dugout charting pitches. The encouragement was lost on Link, and only made him madder.

Link was the kind of batter who never gave ground to a pitcher. That's why the situation turned ugly. Jason Landers, a rookie, wasted nothing on the fastball that caught Link on the inside thigh. It was payback for the plunking of the Reds' player the inning before. A season of frustration broke lose in Link's soul. He kept the bat and charged the mound as the ump threw pitcher and manager of the

Reds from the game.

Link got halfway to the mound before the Reds' first baseman, Tuffy Jackson, took him out with a forearm to the side of the head that knocked Link to the turf.

The bat fell from Link's grasp, as cobwebs filled his head. Tuffy had played linebacker on a college football team and was rumored to be the meanest player in baseball. Tuffy picked up the bat and pointed it at Link's chest. Link tried to get up, hoping his team wasn't far behind. Tuffy bent down and grabbed the front of Link's jersey.

"Now we learn you some manners," Tuffy growled.

Tuffy cocked his big right hand, and Link refused to close his eyes. The punch, however, never landed. Screaming in from the third base line, Bernie threw her entire weight behind her shoulder, and threw that shoulder into Tuffy's gut.

The first baseman fell backwards and turned bright red. Both benches met in front of the mound and punches flew. In the middle of it was Link and Da Bull Ramirez. Da Bull because of his size, Link because of his tenacity.

Right before cooler heads prevailed, Tuffy found the sleeve of the nun who had flattened him. Tommy tried to pull him away, but the one-time linebacker managed to get off half a punch that landed right across Bernie's left eye. The nun snapped to the turf.

Dean and Vitarello, who were trying to separate people, saw the punch. They dropped the fighting players they held and added the rest of the Memorial beef to the fray.

It was a thirty-minute fight the day before the All Star game. Reporters saw blood and smiled. The Winnebago accident faded from memory. Seeing a nun fly across an infield and take out Tuffy would be fodder for at least three columns, and nobody was more pleased than Johnny LePlant.

The locker room was silent after the game. Link threw clothes and combs into his locker. His rage filled the entire space, and then some. There was nothing worse in life than owing someone you despised.

"Hey, Link," Moss said as he sat down next to the third basemen. "That was some brawl out there today."

"Sorry about that, Skip." Link refused to look him in the eye.

"You look a little upset. Is there a problem?" Moss asked.

"I don't want her here. This isn't the place for a woman," Link stated firmly.

"Maybe it is, maybe it isn't. But right now she's better than any arm we've got on this team."

"Then use her for trade bait," Link scowled.

"Link, I've always respected you. But the truth is, she's not what's wrong with this team. You are."

Link planted both feet underneath him with force. Both fists balled up and readied to strike. "You son of a bitch, you take that back. Nobody's more loyal to this team."

"Then you tell me, Link, if some batter had rushed Bernie, would you have been the first out there?" Moss raised an eyebrow and walked slowly to his office.

Link never liked being wrong, so he took pains to make sure he never was. He packed his bag and checked the clock. He had an evening flight to Chicago to catch. He hated All Star weekend. Link needed the game to keep him straight. The confrontation of pitcher and batter kept him sane and alive; in it he found a purpose and a meaning. He looked over at the sheet separating Bernie from the team. He slowly rose and walked over to it.

"Hey, Bernie," Link called out.

"Yeah," the nun responded and pulled back the sheet. She held an ice pack over her right eye.

"I wanted to say, thanks."

"No problem."

Link fidgeted. "I thought nuns didn't fight?"

"I'm a nun, but I'm no saint," Bernie answered.

Link chuckled and left the locker room. His thoughts were deep and troublesome.

"You ready to go to Minnesota?" Dean approached Bernie's sheet a little later.

"What do I say?"

"No comment."

Dean walked in front of Bernie as they made their way through the mass of reporters. He refused to stop, so the group couldn't close the pair off in a circle. Bernie repeated "no comment" like a mantra and stared straight ahead.

"What's a matter Sister Mary? Too ashamed to tell us anything?" The question flew from the lips of Johnny LePlant. He hoped she would explode and prove his new theory that she couldn't handle pressure.

Bernie said nothing. She didn't even look at him. She followed Dean out to his car. The two drove off.

"How's the eye?" Dean asked as the car rolled on into the night.

"Black and blue," she answered.

"Good, maybe you'll think twice before you rush out there next time."

"We do this more than once a year?" she asked.

"Sometimes."

"Nobody told me that."

"Just part of the job," Dean laughed. "We did get 'em pretty good, though, especially ol' Tuffy. Somebody needed to take him down a peg, and you sure did that."

Bernie chuckled at the memory, too, and then she frowned. Nuns aren't supposed to tackle people, but it felt so great. She reveled in the memory of Tuffy splayed out on the field. She whispered a quick prayer and promised that she'd call Father Michael for a phone confessional.

Dean Larson had figured out that Bernie had no place to go for the break except back to the church. He didn't know if she had a preference or not, so as an option, he offered his home. At the very least, it gave his family something to talk about besides him.

Chapter 39

Emily Larson, Dean's wife, stood tall in the doorway of the two-story brick home off a small lake an hour west of Minneapolis. Her skin was wind blown, but not quite tan. She was a woman who spent many daytime hours out in the elements. She was not beauty queen beautiful, but she was devastating. Years ago, Emily Larson swam for the University of Minnesota, and now instead of walking she flowed through the air around her. Her hair hung in a simple ponytail behind her. The jeans and t-shirt she wore seemed made for her.

"Welcome," Emily greeted Bernie and Dean warmly.

"Thank you," Bernie replied.

"I must confess, I'm at a loss," Emily began to the nun. "I know the team calls you Bernie, but I'm not on the team."

"Bernie's fine, or Sister Mary."

"Sister Mary then. I'm not big on nicknames." Emily faced Dean for the first time. "How was the trip?"

"Up and down," he answered.

"Daddy! Daddy!" The ten-year-old shot out from behind Emily and jumped into the arms of her father.

"And how are you?" Dean looked into the face of his tomboy.

"Great!" she chirped.

There were two things Sister Mary knew the moment she saw Becky Larson: Becky was a natural athlete, and both her parents adored her. Sister Mary remembered the night during spring training when Dean confided the rift between his wife and his work. The catcher had never spoken of it after that.

"Do you know who this is?" Dean asked his daughter.

"Bernie!" Becky answered.

"Sister Mary," Emily corrected. "These two are taking a break from baseball, Becky. Let's let them just be people this weekend, okay?"

"Okay," Becky sighed. "But they're not as much fun that way."

Emily tensed, but it was hardly noticeable. "Why don't you help our guest unpack, and then we'll eat dinner."

Everyone was cordial at the table that night. There wasn't a TV in the dining room, and the only sounds were the breeze and Becky's description of how her summer was going. After dinner, Sister Mary offered to help clear the table, but Emily informed her that Dean had volunteered. Becky took the nun outside to show her the place, and Emily helped Dean clean up.

"That's the lake where Mom and me swim," Becky stated as the pair stood on the bank of the small pond on the property. "We race a lot, but she always wins. I'm getting faster, and soon I'll be faster than she is, but don't tell her that. I want it to be a surprise." She had her mother's way of flowing through the air.

"That's the batting cage." Becky walked Sister Mary to a shiny, well-built structure. "Daddy spends a lot of time here. Even in the winter sometimes."

Sister Mary lingered at the place. It was a small shed with a heater off to one side. The inside was well lit by skylights and the pitching machine was well maintained.

"So, you're a nun," Becky sized her up like a trading card.

"Yes, I am."

"Jod Aadland says you can't ever have kids."

Sister Mary blushed. "I can, I just choose not to."

"Why's that?"

"It's a special vow I took."

"Jod says the difference between us Lutherans and you is that if we had nuns, they could get pregnant." Becky repeated the words as if she recited a recipe.

"Has Jod Aadland ever been wrong about anything before?" the nun asked.

"I don't know, I guess so."

"He's wrong this time." Sister Mary's smile seemed to stop the child's line of inquiry.

In truth, it wasn't the smile, but a question that kept popping back into Becky's head and interrupting her thoughts. A question her mother had told her not to ask. But as these things often go, the ban only focused the child more and more on the question until it became too much for her to contain.

"Can you teach me to throw the knuckleball?" It was out before Becky could stop it, or so she claimed.

"Why do you want to learn the knuckleball?" Sister Mary asked.

"I can swim with Mom, and if I can play with the boys like you do, then I can pitch to Daddy."

The logic sounded right, but Sister Mary didn't digest the request easily. Becky could learn to the throw the pitch. Sister Mary felt, however, that baseball was a sore enough subject in this household without any extra help from her. Sister Mary looked back at the house and saw two people through the kitchen window. The woman was animated and angry. The man was stoic, silent, unmoved.

"I'll make you a promise," Sister Mary began. "I'll teach you the pitch next summer."

Becky frowned.

Sister Mary continued, "And just for now, let's not tell your mother."

The girl eyed the nun suspiciously. "How do I know I can trust you?"

"I'm a nun. We're not allowed to lie. Didn't Jod Aadland tell you that?"

"No, he didn't."

The two headed back inside.

"Iced tea?" Emily offered a glass to Sister Mary later that evening.

"Thanks."

The two women sat in comfortable chairs on the porch and watched Dean and Becky play catch out near the lake.

"The tea is good. It's tough to get good iced tea out East, they always want to put sugar in it." Sister Mary took a long drink of tea.

"I've heard that," Emily answered quietly.

Sister Mary studied the woman in the chair. She was not relaxed, but the strain of her feelings was barely visible. The eyes were bright and alert, just like Sister Mary's grandmother, Esther.

Esther had lived a hard life against Mother Nature, cattle and dust. As long as she lived, which was into her nineties, Esther always had eyes just like Emily's.

"The season's not going so well, is it?" Emily asked.

"It could go better, I guess."

"Don't worry too much. Baseball tends to go in spurts. The only way to win is to stay in for the long haul, or so they tell me." Emily's voice trailed off.

"You follow the game closely."

"I try. Sometimes a box score can pass for communication." Emily refilled her glass.

"You want him to quit, don't you?" Sister Mary asked without looking at her host.

"No, I want him to retire," Emily answered, caught off guard at the nun's directness.

Sister Mary felt the break in her voice. She felt Dean and his wife drifting apart in Emily's words. Sister Mary reached for some hope. "Becky is a nice kid."

"She is." Emily stopped and rubbed her eyes.

"Dean tells me you swam for Minnesota."

"That was years ago."

"He says you were good."

"I had my time. I even made the U.S. National team once."

"I bet that was amazing."

"It wasn't an Olympic year or anything, but I got to travel. I remember always feeling great when I walked into the pool house. People were up in the stadium yelling and waving flags. The gun would go off, and I'd race. It was the simplest, easiest thing I ever did. I expect that's what it's like when you take the mound." Emily turned to look at Sister Mary.

"It is pretty amazing when there are thirty thousand people all gathered and hanging on every pitch. Then I look up and see the TV cameras, and I know that millions more are turning on their sets just to see me throw. That's quite a feeling."

Emily shook her head. "I bet it is."

"Sometimes," Sister Mary confided, "I even forget who I am for a second and there's this feeling that life between the baselines will go on forever."

Emily sighed deeply.

Chapter 40

"I told you we stink! We're so bad women and children could take two out of three from us on a home stand." C.W. McDermott faced Buddy and Moss in his office in D.C. "Pennant, you told me! Just one pitcher away from going all the way! Hell, we're one pitcher away from having one pitcher."

"There's half a season to go, sir," Buddy cautioned.

"Half a season wasted. I'm not even going to the All Star game this year to see our mercy pick, Max, watch from the bullpen," C.W. fumed.

"I'll give the other owners your regards," Buddy said.

"Then listen to them laugh at me? No!" C.W. considered the empty glass in his hand. "You are not going."

"I'm not?" Buddy asked.

"No, you are going to clean house. I want trades, new blood. I want a sense out there that the Washington Memorials do not let defeat ferment here."

Buddy cleared his throat. He was stalling for time when he said, "I'll see what I can do, but do you think it's wise to bust up the team?"

"They're already busted," C.W. stewed.

"I'll try and find out what's available," Buddy said slowly.

"No mister, you will do more than try. If you can't handle it, then I'll find someone who can!" C.W. poured himself a drink. "You can start by sending that nun down. Some religious icon. She's been suspended once, one more pending. At least she didn't hit the guy."

"I don't think that's wise." The room went silent. The voice belonged to Moss. He never spoke in these meetings unless C.W. asked him a question.

"Excuse me?" C.W. stepped from behind the bar like a pit bull eyeing a bone.

"Well — I," stuttered Moss. "I mean, she's second on the team in ERA, second in innings pitched, and the only starter with a winning record."

"Is that true?" C.W. shouted at Buddy.

"Yes," Buddy croaked, still shocked that Moss would speak up in her defense.

C.W. was riling himself up into a good yell. "Okay, Coach Thompson, you tell me what to do."

Moss's internal thermometer leapt from ninety-eight point six to a hundred and twenty in two seconds. He was more comfortable with two gone, a runner on first and a light-hitting second baseman at the plate in the bottom of the ninth trailing by a run.

"Well," he started. "I think they need a team meeting to air out their problems. You know, refocus."

"Team meeting?" C.W. snarled. "We're .500 and you think some team love fest where we get in touch with our feelings will take us from Clark Kent to Superman?!?"

"It's worked for other teams," Buddy inserted.

"I want results, not psychobabble," C.W. spewed.

"Okay, you want results?" Moss asked.

"You bet your sweet butt."

"We bring the team back a day early, have the meeting, and if we win the series with Philly then the team stays intact," Moss stammered quickly.

Buddy almost fell over. Moss had never done something like this before, ever. Buddy also reminded himself that Moss was a lousy gambler.

C.W. thought about this carefully. He loved to gamble. Dramatic wages like this especially tempted him, but the wager was not sweet enough. He rolled it over in his mind a few times then turned to the pair with his answer.

"You can have the meeting of the minds, but you only have one game to show me progress. If they win their first game against Philly, you can keep this group together and we play out the string."

"If we lose?" Moss asked.

"You resign, telling the press boys you consider this debacle your fault, and I bring in new blood to take this thing apart." C.W. slammed his empty glass to the table to emphasize the point.

Buddy stepped between Moss and C.W. "I already said I didn't think breaking up the team was the best idea."

"Then I guess you can leave, too." C.W. glared at Buddy.

Buddy looked at Moss and the two nodded.

"Okay, I accept," Moss managed to get out.

"There is just one last item," C.W. continued.

Moss stammered, "But we already agreed."

C.W. shook his head. "We didn't shake on it, and no deal is finished until we shake."

Moss asked, "What is it?"

C.W. swished his drink around in his glass before he said, "I want a message sent. Someone goes down on the first day of the second half."

"But you said —" Buddy never finished.

"If you lose, I don't want people screaming about how they didn't see it coming," C.W. said.

"I don't think it's necessary." Buddy tried to control his temper.

"This way or no way,"

"This isn't right," Moss responded.

"When has this ever been about right? This is about winning." C.W. went to the door and opened it. Moss and Buddy turned to leave.

"We have a deal?" C.W. asked.

"We do," Buddy and Moss answered together and then left to make the necessary phone calls.

On a phone in a kitchen halfway across the country, Dean Larson listened intently. "I understand."

Sister Mary and Becky finished dessert. Dean turned to the three and slowly walked to the table.

"Becky, could you get the TV room ready for us?" Dean asked.

Becky's eyebrow went up. "Dad?"

"Please," Dean commanded. Becky slid from her chair and walked slowly into the next room.

"What's up?" Emily asked with hesitation.

"Buddy's calling the team back a day early, something about a team meeting. We leave in the morning," Dean mumbled.

"Why?" Sister Mary queried.

"I don't know," Dean answered truthfully.

Emily threw her fork into the small dish in front of her on the table. Sister Mary quickly stood.

"I'll go help Becky." The nun left the room.

"I — I'm sorry," Dean said.

"Not acceptable," Emily seethed.

"It's my job."

"No, it's what you do. Being a father and a husband, that's your job."

"You see this house, this kitchen, the car you drive? That's all baseball."

"I know. I've been there for baseball. I lived through the minors. Baseball has been the last eighteen years. I want the next eighteen."

"I can't just quit in the middle of the season," Dean's voice intensified.

"No, but you can quit at the end."

"We'll talk about it then."

"No!" Emily rose, her chair tipping back and clattering to the floor. "We always put it off. This time I want a decision."

"It isn't that easy."

Emily shook her head. "You've had two years to think about it."

"I need longer."

"So you can what, get more distant?"

"That's unfair," Dean roared as he stood.

"Is it? When was the last time you, I mean all of you, spent the night with me?"

"You knew when we got married that I was a ballplayer, okay? That's all I have ever been. It is what I am. To give it up is to get rid of me!"

"Bull!! You are a husband and father. That's what you are. For eighteen years baseball is what you've done. Sooner or later it's going to end. All that you have to decide is whether or not you want to lose what you do and what you are!"

Chapter 41

The day before the start of the second half of the baseball season, Toby Haynes walked slowly into Moss Thompson's office.

"You wanted to see me, coach?" Toby asked.

"How are you, Toby?" Moss eyed Toby sadly.

"Short weekend," Toby mustered. "If you'll pardon me, I need to get to the meeting."

Moss shook his head. "You don't need to go the meeting, Toby. You're being sent to Wilmington. You report tomorrow."

Toby didn't say anything for a second, and then he asked, "Was it something I did? I was hitting better. I made one lousy error, why?"

"We're shaking things up a little," Moss stated coolly.

Toby finally stood and walked to the door. "Am I coming back?"

"I don't know," Moss answered truthfully.

Toby left. A full minute later, Buddy entered the office.

"What do we tell the team?" Moss asked.

"We tell them the truth," Buddy responded. The two men walked somberly down an inside hallway and into a large conference room. The rest of the Memorials' players were sitting and waiting as Moss and Buddy moved to the front.

"We're all here, so we can begin," Moss said.

"No, we're not," Bernie piped up. "Toby isn't here."

"As I said," Moss repeated, "we're all here so we can begin." The comment had the desired effect. The room lapsed into silence. "We've got to face a hard reality, people. Management has determined you guys aren't a .500 club. Management will not wait for a slow turn around."

The players sat up in horror, struck hard with the reality that baseball was sometimes more than just a game. It could be a brutal way to make a living.

"Some people who participated in the first half fiasco, are not here," Buddy jumped in. "This is a message and a warning."

"You sent Toby down 'cause we went .500?" Link snarled from a corner.

"Partially, and partially it was the first step toward breaking up this team. Ownership has given us one game to prove this team can win. That game is tomorrow. If we lose, we all end up like Toby." Buddy's words echoed over the team.

"That's crap." Link kicked a chair.

"This team is crap. We put the best group of people together we could. You have a chance to be special. This is your last shot. We lose this game, and everything we built is gone." Buddy stared around the room, meeting every eye he could.

"Hey, coach?" Vitarello shouted. "Who takes the hill tomorrow?"

"Bernie," Moss said firmly and then quickly left the room. Buddy followed.

A few members of the team stood up to leave, but sat back down. In front of the only door out of the room, blocking the entrance with his massive arms crossed over a wide chest, stood Dean Larson.

"And now we have our meeting," Dean announced. "Any thoughts to begin with?"

"We're not going to let the nun pitch!" Mad Max Standish crowed from the back of the room.

"I don't think that's our choice," Dean responded.

"Not our choice?" Max stood. "It sure is our choice. This is our team, guys. We aren't talking about an experiment here. We're talking about one game for the future of this team."

"I think Max is right," Lenny de Haven piped up from the back. "She's just a rookie, Dean."

"Moss is the coach. The coach's job is to field the best team he can. She's got the best stats, Max. Look them up yourself," Dean replied coolly.

"You're only as good as your last outing. Everything else is ancient history," Max replied.

"I think I should be starting," Jose Martinez shouted from the left side. "I'd rather die by my heat than suffer death under her floater."

"She can throw the pitch. We've all seen that," Vitarello said as he rose to his feet. "This is the problem right here, guys. Instead of realizing that she's going to be out there pitching for the future of this group and making sure she can do the best job she can, we sit around and whine about the choice."

"Hey, Vitamin boy, did you ever notice that most of our arguments are over the nun?" Max continued.

"That's your problem," Vitamin snapped back.

"No, it's our problem. You want team unity, how's this for team unity? Bernie, I don't think most of the team wants to bet their future on you. You should go to coach and tell him you'd rather not pitch." Max eyed the sister carefully, as she considered his suggestion.

The scrape of a chair against the floor caught everyone's attention. Link Molansky stood up and kicked his chair to the side with his right boot. He walked slowly to the door, letting the hard soles of his boots click against the tile of the floor. He stopped near Dean, turned to face the room, and crossed his arms over his muscular chest.

"The nun pitches," Link said flatly. "Anybody got a problem with that can take it up with me — outside."

The words landed on the group like wet blankets on a fire. Most of the followers like Day, Pierce and Flip backed down. Max and Lenny remained firm, though, and their gaze landed on the hulking form of Jorge Da Bull Ramirez.

Jorge wanted to escape the whole argument. He didn't want the nun to pitch. He felt it was too big a risk to start the nun, but what about his childhood? How could he stand against a nun after all the nuns had done for him in the past? Da Bull didn't attend church that often or think about it enough to call himself devout, but certain things gnawed at his insides. He sat there and fought the silent battle between his mind and his past.

Link never wavered. His attention rested on Da Bull. If bat speed were the judge of hand speed, then this Da Bull would be tough to face. Link knew that if Jorge walked into the hall, he would follow. He hoped that it wouldn't come to that, because Da Bull could probably take him.

Max and Lenny glared at Da Bull. They goaded him silently toward taking himself out into the hall and ending what they considered to be the problem with this team's pennant drive. They both smirked when Da Bull rose to his feet.

He took a few steps and stopped in front of Bernie. He looked her up and down then looked at Link, who glared back. Jorge turned back to Max and Lenny, then returned to the nun. His eyes narrowed and he spoke.

"Don't screw up tomorrow," Da Bull said and strode out of the room. The rest of the team disbanded soon after.

The first place Bernie went after the meeting was Toby Haynes's locker. Toby had believed in her, and now he was gone. She'd always believed in her knuckleball. She believed she was a good pitcher, but it was clear half the team had doubts. There's usually a bit of truth in doubts.

"Don't think about it," Link suggested from somewhere behind her.

"I can't help it," Bernie replied.

"The guy down in Wilmington was whacking it pretty good. Only a matter of time." Link shook his head slowly.

Bernie asked, "Would they have sent him down if we were winning?"

"Tough to say. Hitting .250 without power is a tough way to earn a living at the plate."

"Thanks for what you did back there." Bernie turned to Link.

"There's only two things worth anything on a baseball diamond: concentration on the game and loyalty to the team. I take both seriously. You proved to me the team means something to you." Link looked away, as if his words physically hurt him. "Coach made his call. I respect that. Everything else is just whining. I hate whining." Link left.

Chapter 42

The bar held almost no one at five o'clock in the early evening. The dark wood and mahogany-colored leather bar stools foretold of crowds that arrived no earlier than ten. Dean sat with a draft beer in front of him, deep in thought.

"Buy me a drink?"

Dean looked up to see Amy Springer in a casual shirt and jeans. "What's your poison?" he asked.

"A draft — whatever you've got." Amy slid easily onto the stool next to the catcher.

Dean signaled the bartender for another beer.

Amy took stock on Dean's tired eyes and sullen face. "So why the long face?

"Off the record," Dean began. The comment stung a little, but she hid it well in a sip of lager. "If we don't win the game tomorrow, McDermott holds a team garage sale."

"No!"

"Yeah, and I don't think too many of us will be here after the dust clears."

Amy took a longer sip. "You know that for a fact?"

Dean shook his head. "Just a feeling."

"All on one game?"

"Yep." Dean took a long draw of his beer.

Amy set her mug down and pondered the bubbles rising up in the beer. "Who's taking the mound? Jon John? Day?"

"Bernie."

The name froze the reporter in mid-sip. "She knows about the deal?"

"Yep."

"How's she taking it?"

"Fifty-fifty her nerves get the best of her."

"I see." Amy downed the rest of her beer and stood up.

"Where are you going?" Dean asked, disappointed.

"I have two choices," Amy told him. "I can sit here and listen to stories about Minnesota, which I'm sure I'll love, or I can talk to Bernie."

"It's probably best," Dean answered. "I didn't have much to say about Minnesota anyway."

Amy bent down, close to Dean's ear and whispered, "That's good." She rested a hand on Dean's shoulder, let it slip off, then left without saying anything more.

"Forgive me, Father, for I have sinned," Sister Mary whispered into the phone receiver.

"What is the problem, Sister?" Father Michael's voice was hard to make out.

"Father, I'm having a hard time hearing you," Sister Mary said louder into the phone.

"Oh that," Father Michael answered. "The contractors are here. They're ripping up the floor to put a new one in. You wouldn't believe the rot, but the new one is going to be great. I just saw the — oh my, Sister Mary, you didn't call to ask about the repairs did you?"

"No," Sister Mary confessed. "I called to say, I haven't acted like a nun should."

"Oh, you mean the fight. I saw, but I don't think protecting a teammate is such a terrible act."

"Father!"

"Okay, so — so we who wear the cross aren't supposed to tackle first basemen on national TV," Father Michael said quickly, then added, "say three Hail Mary's and —"

"There's more." The nun's voice quavered.

"There's more?"

"Father, I enjoyed the fight. Deep down, when I saw him flat on his back, I liked it. I know that's wrong, and I hate myself for it."

"Sister Mary —"

"I tried not to let the fame get to me, but I like people cheering for me. I like being a professional baseball player."

Father Michael waited as a rotary saw whined in the background. "But that's what you are."

"No. I'm a nun who can pitch. I was supposed to stay that way. Pitching wasn't meant to be more important than my vows. Well — I'm afraid that may have happened."

"Are you considering leaving the church?" Father Michael asked.

After a long silence, she answered, "No."

"You sound as though you might be."

"Well, I think God sent me a message." She told him about what would happen if the team lost the next game. "And I can't help but think this is all my fault for losing sight of what this whole thing is about. My vanity destroyed this team."

The priest allowed a measured silence to pass. "Sister Mary, I don't mean to doubt your interpretation of things, but do you really think God is punishing you?"

"I haven't won in my last three starts, and the team is only .500 with me as a member."

"It's very possible they could be worse without you," Father Michael offered.

"Or better. You see, there's no way of knowing for sure. And now I'm the one who has to pitch the game tomorrow."

Father Michael's voice was lower and deeper than before. "That's why we have faith."

"Well, Father, to be honest, I'm having a little difficulty with that right now. If my faith is so good, why am I poised to be the instrument of destruction for this team?"

"Have you ever considered," Father Michael asked, "that perhaps you are their salvation?"

The doorbell rang.

"I have to go," Bernie said.

"Remember your faith, Sister Mary Bernadette. No matter what, it will always be there for you," Father Michael assured her. "And good luck tomorrow." The pounding of hammers drowned out the last of his words.

"Thank you, Father," she yelled and hung up the phone. She then answered the door.

"Congratulations," Amy said and rushed past her into the apartment with a bottle of something that looked like wine. "Do you have a couple of glasses?"

"Excuse me?" Bernie asked.

"This is sparkling apple cider. I thought wine before the big start wouldn't be appropriate," Amy went on as she blew into the tiny kitchen and rifled through a cupboard looking for glasses. She found two and set them on a counter.

"So you've heard," Bernie said.

"I am a reporter." Amy poured the cider and held out a glass to Bernie. "To your health and your knuckleball." They both swigged.

"The team doesn't want me to pitch tomorrow," Bernie confessed. "If you were them, would you want a rookie with a knuckleball to decide your future?"

"If she's the best pitcher I've got, then yes. Yes, I would."

"And if I blow it?" Bernie asked.

"I suggest you don't."

Amy set her glass purposefully down on the table and stood facing Bernie. "You can do so much tomorrow, half of which I don't even think you understand. I won't tell you things will work out. We both know that doesn't always happen. But I do know one thing, you will have to live with your effort for the rest of your life. So I guess your choice is simple. You can pitch nervous, or you can pitch with everything you've got."

Five o'clock seemed to come earlier than it ever had in the history of Bernie's life. She sat alone on the pitcher's mound deep in prayer. The regulars had made other plans. Some called agents to check on interest from other teams. A few took batting practice at the twenty-four hour batting cages. The balance of the team took sleeping pills to force rest upon themselves and slept through their alarm clocks. Bernie fought to keep her disappointment at being alone from her thoughts and prayers. In truth, she wasn't entirely alone.

High in the stands, Link Molansky watched with an extra large Styrofoam cup of coffee in his hand. His stare did not waver. In his own way, he tried to make peace with the first half of the season, but making peace wasn't something Link did well. For an hour, all he did was sip the coffee. He raised his eyebrows the one time he saw the nun's lips move.

"I didn't ask for this, and I'm not sure I want it," she whispered down on the field. "But I'll do it." She crossed herself then stood and walked away.

Link couldn't hear her words, but he could tell they were difficult for her say. He finished his coffee, alone high up in the cheap seats. He considered the field from that vantage point and tried to understand the events that had brought him to this moment. He found no answers, but the call of the infield dirt and some unseen umpire calling out on the wind, "Play ball!"

Chapter 43

Bernie knelt on the floor of her Winnebago that afternoon. She fought the temptation to pray for her baseball game today. Her prayer was for the comfort of those whose future was on the line. Then Bernie sat in a chair and pulled on her cleats.

"Are you ready?" Moss's voice called from the other side of the door.

"Yes." Bernie opened the door and let her manager in.

"That's good to hear, because this is a big game," Moss offered as he stepped inside and closed the door behind him.

"Why me, coach?" Bernie asked earnestly.

"Why?" Moss thought a minute. "I admit that if you'd have told me I had to pick a pitcher on opening day to save my butt, I would've never guessed you. But you've earned it. Right now, you're the best chance we have to win this game today. I really believe that."

The afternoon glowed as the teams took the field for the first game of the season's second half. The Phillies looked sharp, and the Memorials looked as if their nickname should be changed to Dead Men Walking.

"Whatever happens tonight," C.W. McDermott declared to Buddy as the two sat in the owner's box high in the stands. "It's been a pleasure working with you."

Buddy smiled at the owner. He glanced from C.W. to the phone that sat on the table. Every team's general manager's phone number had been programmed into it for speed dialing. C.W. didn't want to waste any time. Buddy sighed and looked down at his feet as the Memorials took the field for the first inning of play.

Bernie tossed her warm-ups and fought to get loose. She had

never played baseball as anything but a game. The winning and the losing were always confined to the field. In the last few days, the losing had spilled over the sides of the diamond and flooded the lives of her friends and teammates. She had no room for error. Every pitch had to be perfect. She sized up the plate and knew the corners were the key. If she could hit the corners with her pitches, they would win.

The Memorials nervously moved their feet and kicked the dirt behind their pitcher as Len Driver stepped into the batter's box. Bernie's first pitch missed just outside the right corner. Her next missed high. Her third pitch missed inside. She felt the guys deflating behind her.

"Time," Dean said to the home plate ump. The catcher jogged out to the pitcher's mound.

"How are you doing?" Dean asked Bernie.

Bernie kicked the rubber. "I just missed with three straight pitches, didn't I?"

"Yeah, you sure did. You wouldn't be trying to paint some corners would you?" Dean stared at her somberly.

Bernie couldn't lie. "Yes, I am."

"Well, stop it! You know that's not the way you throw."

"But I have to be perfect today."

"You can't be perfect with a flaw in your delivery. I know you feel the pressure, but I will not go down like this. Either you tell me that you can throw the knuckleball like you usually do, or I'm going to get Moss out here and yank you off the mound."

The words stung. "You don't think I care?"

"Yeah, I think you care. You care enough to throw it right. What's it going to be?" Dean's voice was flat and unforgiving.

"Why don't we go one batter at a time," Bernie answered slowly. "If I can't do it, you can call Moss."

"All right." Dean turned and walked back to the plate.

Dean squatted behind the plate. He put five fingers down between his legs.

Bernie nodded and came set. Her mind briefly flashed on the outside corner, but she fought that desire. Her fingernails dug into the seams of the baseball. She felt the power of the leather ball grow in her hand. Her front leg lifted. She closed her eyes and relaxed her tight grip on the ball. The front leg came down and the back one pushed off. Her right hand cocked behind her head, and the arm motion started. At the last possible moment, she stopped the arm and flicked the fingers. The pitch was away.

The knuckleball arced toward the plate and hung out fat in front of the hitter. Driver's eyes grew wide. He swung. The ball dove and the bat chopped down on it. The weak grounder rolled to Bernie's feet. She threw to first for out number one.

As the crowd watched excitedly, Bernie retired the next seventeen men she faced quickly and efficiently. In the seventh, the Philadelphia catcher drove a ball to deep center field, but Mike Flowers got to the wall and hauled in the shot. That was the last serious threat to the perfect game until the ninth.

Bernie entered the inning soaked with sweat and bubbling with nerves. The first man grounded to short. The second batter sent a high chopper to the right side, which Tommy Chang handled nicely for out number two.

Huey Morris, a young left-hander with power, came up as a pinch hitter. Nobody knew much about the kid except that he hit the ball really hard.

Dean started off Morris with two straight knuckleball strikes. Morris missed badly. Dean called for another knuckleball. Bernie kicked and threw. Huey held as the ball dipped outside for ball one. Dean settled in and called for another knuckler. Again the pitch missed outside. Dean Larson lifted his mask and spat.

He knew the kid was waiting for a big fat pitch, something he could hit. Dean called time and walked out to the mound. He took the ball with him.

"How are you doing, kid?" he asked.

"Nervous," she said back to him.

"Good, keeps you sharp. Now look. I wanted to come out here and talk to you myself because I don't think you're going to like the next call."

"Why?"

Dean smiled and said, "I want you to throw the curveball."

"Are you crazy?" Bernie stared into the eyes of her catcher.

"He's looking for something to hit. This guy is thinking about the bleachers, not the strike zone. You throw him a curve outside.

The man will go for it. I promise."

"I want to throw the knuckleball."

"If he doesn't swing at this pitch, you can throw the knuckleball."

"I want to throw it now."

"Throw the curve. Trust me." Dean's glare was strong, but
Bernie wasn't the kind to be intimidated.

"Hey!" The umpire came out to break the meeting up.

"Throw it," Dean ordered, as he backed away.

Bernie stood there on the mound, letting the anger subside. Dean
had never led her astray before, but this was her chance at a perfect
game. She had come so far for this. This was her moment. She
kicked the dirt and stepped off the rubber.

She walked behind the mound and picked up the rosin bag. She
kicked herself silently. This wasn't about her. It was about the team.
Bernie whispered a prayer and stepped back onto the rubber. She
threw her curve. It spun toward the plate. Huey Morris's eyes almost
jumped out of his skull. He'd seen this pitch before. Never this slow,
but the fences loomed large in his mind. His massive right leg strode
into the pitch. The bat cocked.

The pitch spun down and toward the outside corner and beyond.
Huey's mouth dropped opened as he realized the pitch was outside.
He tried to stop. He wanted to stop, but the baseball fates would
have none of that. His bat reached for the ball and connected.

The ball ricocheted off the end of the barrel and rocketed down
the third base line. The crack of the bat stopped the hearts and lungs
of the thirty thousand gathered in the stadium, and most of the
necessary body functions of a nun who stood alone on the pitcher's
mound.

As the crowd watched the ball scream past the bag, a man dove
full out and led with the mitt. The ball hopped off the dirt and ran
for the outfield, but it never got there. Link Molansky plucked the
ball out of mid-air, then scrambled to his feet. He set his back foot
solidly and threw straight, true and hard.

If Huey Morris had been fast, he might have beat out the throw.
He wasn't, and he didn't. The play preserved nine complete innings
of perfect ball for the nun. Unfortunately, it hadn't secured the win.

Carl Snelling had scattered six hits over his eight innings of

work to keep the game a scoreless tie. He opened the ninth by
striking out Dean and Vitarello. He was sharp—not perfect sharp,
but sharp enough to give his team a chance to win this ball game, if
he could nurse the game into the tenth.

Moss stood on the top step of the dugout trying to figure out
how many antacids would calm his stomach if they actually ever
worked. He felt like a victim. He'd chosen the best pitcher he had,
or at least he felt he had. His gamble had paid off with a perfect
game, and now they still could lose this sucker. He knew that if his
team lost a game like this, it would be crushing.

Link Molansky stepped into the batter's box. His eyes glowed
with a fire that could only be stoked deep within his soul. He liked
his team. He could even live with the nun, especially after a perfect
game. He knew this game was for everything, and that's just the way
he liked it.

The first pitch was a fastball. The swing was powerful and the
connection produced the sweetest smack an ear could find in any
ballpark. The ball shot out into the night climbing higher and higher
toward the center field fence. It refused to come down until it
cleared the wall by a full eight feet.

Link trotted around the bases, and a cool breeze swept over the
field. The whole team lined up at home to bring the third baseman
in. He found the nun, and the two exchanged a smile. He was careful
not to let it last too long.

Up in the owner's box, C.W. McDermott crushed a cigar onto a
table as he turned to Buddy Wilson. "Well, I hope you know what
you're doing." C.W. left.

Buddy Wilson gloated. He hadn't wanted to do that in front of
his boss. He left the box and quickly ran down to see the team.

The locker room exploded with big bear hugs, cigars and beer.
Link shook everyone's hand, and the smile he wore, though small,
was the biggest of his life.

"Hey, boys, get decent," Buddy called at the front door to the
locker room. "I got a visitor."

The largest roar of the night exploded as Bernie stepped into the
room. The team jumped and bobbed like they were ice cubes
floating in a fizzy drink.

"Hey!" Moss yelled from the far end of the locker room. "What is this?"

The guys turned and looked at the coach.

"This is a celebration!" Tommy Chang roared.

"We won one game, people, one lousy game. There's half a season left. Do you remember the post season? We ain't going to get there by doing this after every win." Moss walked into the middle of the room. "This game proved one thing, and one thing only. We can beat anybody out there between the foul lines, anybody! Now it's your job to go out and prove that for the rest of the season." The team roared. "Remember that you guys are this good." Moss let his words sink in. "Bernie, the press wants to see you. The rest of you, remember you got a game tomorrow." Moss walked Bernie to the door.

"Give 'em hell, Bernie," Mike Flowers called out from the back.

Bernie turned, a stern look on her face. The guys pushed the center fielder to the front. Bernie eyed Mike.

"This time, I forgive you." She turned and floated out of the room and down the hall to a room full of questions.

"So how does it feel to be the first woman to throw a perfect game in the majors?" Amy Springer called from the back of the pressroom.

"It feels great. But I must be honest, I had a lot of help."

"So when will you serve your one game suspension?" Johnny LePlant called from the front row.

"That'll be coach's decision," Bernie answered.

"Are you proud of that fight?" Johnny asked.

"No."

"Do you consider yourself a role model?" Johnny's tone changed to that of a prosecuting attorney.

"Do you?" Bernie responded.

"I don't get paid millions of dollars," Johnny countered.

"I make the minimum," Bernie answered. "Almost all of it goes to St. Francis Church in Wanuga, Nebraska. And now, since you seem intent on giving an economics lesson, how much do you make and where do you spend it?"

"I'm not on trial here," Johnny smirked.

"Neither am I." Bernie turned to take more questions from other reporters.

"I'M NOT FINISHED YET!" Johnny roared.

"Mr. LePlant," Bernie's voice went low as she turned to face the reporter. "I was taught at a very young age that monopolizing the conversation was rude."

"I'm just after the truth," Johnny continued.

"No, you're not," Bernie countered. "A miracle happened tonight — a perfect game. Do you know how often that occurs? Do you? And when something that great, that tremendous, plays out before your eyes all you seem to want to do is try and soil it."

"I ask the tough questions."

"Here's one for you," Bernie put her hands on her hips. "Is there anything left in this world for you to completely and hopelessly lose yourself in the celebration of? Because if there isn't, your world must be very difficult to live in. I know it sure crashes in on mine." With that, Bernie left the room.

The guys stayed in the locker room later that night to soak up the feeling of winning when everything was on the line.

"She was something tonight," Richard Day said to his fellow pitcher, Jose Martinez.

"That she was," Jose answered. "I wonder what she does to prepare for a game like this. She's a rookie for Pete's sake."

"She prays." Link Molanksy walked in on their conversation.

"She what?" Richard asked.

"Every morning she goes out to the mound at five or so, and sits there praying for an hour," Link said as if it were the most natural thing in the world.

"Yeah, but that only works for nuns," Richard answered, as a few more guys from the team listened in.

"Vitamin, Dean, Tommy and Mike all go. Look what they did in the first half." Link whistled.

"They didn't show tonight," Richard argued.

"They weren't there this morning." Link let that settle on the small group and walked away.

Richard quizzed Dean about the morning vigil a few minutes later. He confirmed Link's story. He also said he planned to be there tomorrow.

As the guys filed out, they began to ponder the hour of five in the morning, something none of them had seen in a long time.

"You going tomorrow?" Richard asked Link.

"Not my thing," the third baseman answered.

Later that night, Bernie sat with a bottle of wine and listened to the all-talk radio station. Amy had brought the bottle over on her way to the paper. Bernie thanked her friend for the gift and asked her to stay, but the reporter had a story to write. Bernie was half glad. She didn't think it was right for someone to watch you enjoy listening to other people talk about how good you were. She knew it was vain, and that it was wrong. But she felt this one time, God would let her enjoy the gift she had been given.

The morning dawned too early for the nun. Wine still sloshed in her head and her stomach was slightly upset. She brushed her teeth, but didn't hazard a shower and dragged herself out to the corner to catch the bus to the stadium.

The air still smelled sweet with victory as she rode the short distance to the park. Everything seemed right in the world, and she had a lot to pray about that morning.

She reached the clubhouse at five after five. She pushed through the locker room and out into the dugout. When she crested the steps, she stopped in awe.

"Where ya' been, sister?" Mike called. Behind him stood the entire Memorials team — well, almost. All of them were bleary eyed, but willing. Willing to try whatever experience had led a rookie to toss a perfect game against the toughest competition in the world.

She walked through the group to the mound where she stood and spoke softly. "Just think about what's really important."

They all nodded and sat down. Only the veterans really understood what to do, the rest began to muddle through. Bernie surveyed the lot and sighed with delight at their effort. She looked at each one before she knelt. Her first prayer was of thanks for her new friend, Link Molansky, the only member of the team not there.

In truth, he was there, high in the bleachers where he had sat for the past month and watched the proceedings. In some ways he wanted to go down and join them, but he knew he wouldn't. Some people needed to be alone, he reasoned, and he was one of those people.

Chapter 44

Johnny LePlant tried for the next month to discredit Bernie and company, but he faced one huge problem. The Memorials were unbeatable. They won ten straight out of the gate, and then twelve of the next fifteen. They rolled into August one game out and the hottest team in baseball. Johnny's attacks led to criticism among journalists, championed by Amy Springer.

Johnny's phone was silent. Now christened a bully, and a reporter who couldn't see the game if a foul ball cracked him on the side of the skull, he fell from favor and soon stopped his onslaught. His star stopped just short of falling completely from the sky. He woke up one morning, had a cup of coffee and vowed to do a preview of the upcoming football season. He'd step away from baseball for a while. That meant he wouldn't write about it, but he would still watch. It wasn't the games he kept tabs on, but the time between the games. This was where he would find redemption for himself, and damnation for his enemies.

Summer yielded to early fall, and the days of September became heady ones in the National League East. Montreal refused to fold and Washington refused to yield. There was no wild card spot in '94, only those who won the division got a shot at the ring.

Dean continued to hit well, but he became an afterthought compared to the turnaround the rest of the team experienced after they began to attend the morning meetings religiously. Da Bull and Lenny slugged twenty home runs each in the second half while the pitching staff's ERA hovered around 3.00.

Soon after, Amy fell into a more normal work routine. The TV interviews were less and less frequent. During her free moments, she began notes for the possible book about the nun's rookie year. She also saw more movies. But it wasn't until late September at a little bistro beyond the beltway of D.C., and well into the countryside of Virginia, when Amy's personal life picked up again.

She sat at the bar and tried to sip red wine from a glass with a long, delicate stem. Her dress was white satin. That morning she had had her hair done, and picked up a bottle of her favorite perfume. Tonight would be special, because it would be just Dean and her, alone.

Dean had been focused on baseball. Amy had been focused on the burgeoning career of her favorite woman pitcher. Offers to be on sports programs had poured in, as it was widely known that Amy Springer was a confidant of the new phenom. In short, her career had done precisely what it always had: made her sacrifice personal time. Tonight, she would get a little of that time back.

Dean Larson spent an hour shining his only pair of dress shoes before he entered the old plantation, wearing the only suit he owned and feeling really out of place. Dean was not a man who ate at nice restaurants. Even though he'd been told a million times which fork was for the salad, it was always a fifty-fifty chance he'd get it right. He worried about that as had and Amy sat down to eat at a corner table in the restaurant adorned with fine china and a candle.

"You look very — pretty tonight," Dean complimented Amy.

"Thank you." She slipped into her chair.

They talked mostly about baseball. It was something they had in common. Amy liked rock music, contemporary theater and mysteries. Dean preferred fishing and landscaping. But in baseball, they communicated. It was a passion for both. In fact, they were so lost in the conversation and the wine that they failed to notice a familiar figure at the bar.

Johnny LePlant sat in a dark corner and drank a Manhattan. He tried his best to watch the corner table and not be seen. Inside, his stomach swam in the warmth of the drink and the excitement of discovery. He'd had no idea this day would turn out to be so fruitful.

Johnny had eaten earlier that evening at the diner across from the nun's apartment, something he usually did once a week, just to keep up tabs. She rarely left, except for two day-trips to somewhere in the Carolinas. He knew this because he'd tracked her travel, but hadn't been able to crack what she was doing there, and that led to more watching. Unfortunately, she wasn't going anywhere that night. And like most nights, as Johnny had learned from watching her, she stayed up and sorted clothes.

Bernie staged a daily clothing drive at the ballpark, which included the now famous slogan, "Show how much you support the Memorials by giving us the shirt off your back."

At a recent home game, any guy could get in by removing his shirt at the gate and donating it to the drive. It was hugely success-ful, save for a few rogue dermatologists who protested the event on the grounds it was unhealthy. After that, bins stood at all entrances, and the amount of clothes taken in was substantial. Bernie took the collection home every night she was in town and bagged it for donation to a local church.

Johnny had quickly tired of watching and waiting on the nun to do something, anything he could use to bring her down, so he had driven to the ballpark. He often went there to wallow in disbelief that this season, this expansion baseball team was bigger news than his beloved Redskins. He hated that for many reasons, the top one being that it had almost been his Waterloo. As he had looked at the stadium from his car, he had seen something out of place. Dean Larson had emerged from the locker room in a suit.

It was well known in baseball circles that Dean Larson did not wear suits. He hated them, and as far as Johnny knew he'd never been seen in one. That's why Johnny had decided to follow him.

The reporter now watched Amy and Dean and speculated on how this scene would play out on the front page, or the feature segment of a broadcast. He knew this kind of scoop required strategy. All he had so far were two people sharing a nice dinner, which could be easily explained despite the subtext he might pick up from his vantage point. This required something special, a particular question based on a specific fact that would catch the reporter and the catcher in the headlight glare of the public press. That would be wonderful, especially if the timing was right. Johnny nursed his Manhattan and wished he could hear the conversation.

"The mousse was excellent," Amy remarked as they sipped coffee and the dessert dishes were removed.

"Best I've ever had," Dean agreed. It was true, but it was only the second time he'd tasted the dish.

"You know, it's a long drive back into D.C.," Amy observed.

Dean's body tingled, and he fought the rushing warmth that landed on his face.

"They have rooms here, and it's usually not crowded this time of year," she breathed. She tried to sound casual, even disaffected. She came close.

Dean fought the urge to fidget in the worst way and loosen his tie. He just couldn't seem to get enough oxygen. He reached for his coffee and sipped it to kill a few seconds.

"I wish I could," he finally said.

"But?"

"We have the morning thing. I told you about it, and it's tough enough getting to the park at five when you're sleeping in D.C."

"You could miss one, couldn't you?" she asked.

"I —" he hesitated. "This streak's the best thing the team's ever had. You know how superstitious ballplayers are, and I just don't want to be the one who messes it up."

She retreated inside the fine white dress and strong black coffee. The silence quickly became more than Dean could take.

"I would stay. It's just the streak." The bill came. He paid soon after, and they left.

Johnny left the bar when he saw Dean sign the credit card slip. He stayed in the bathroom for ten minutes. He thought that was long enough for the pair to walk past the bar.

Dean waited with Amy outside the restaurant, as the valet brought her car around. He reached out suddenly, and took her hand.

"I'm sorry it didn't work out the way you planned." He only half meant that, and that scared him deeply, but not deeply enough to stop the good-bye kiss from happening.

Amy slipped into her car without a word. Only after turning out of the parking lot did she gather herself. She'd believed him when he'd said his only reason for going back was the streak. It was a baseball thing, and she knew how important baseball streaks were. She'd also believed him when he'd said he would've stayed. Why did baseball players have to be so superstitious? She thought of him often on the drive back, as the night stretched out forever ahead of her.

Johnny got to the door a few minutes after Amy left. He caught a glimpse of Dean tipping the valet a dollar and driving away.

Johnny planned to continue tailing Dean, but two elderly ladies beat him to the valet stand. After each of their cars arrived, Johnny knew the catcher was too far ahead. As he waited for his own car, a long slender smile cracked his face. It was the smile of past glory resurrected.

Chapter 45

"Gentlemen, the chase is on. This team's time is now. We have to catch Montreal." C.W. McDermott addressed Buddy and Moss in his office. "I want the pennant this year!"

"We'll do everything in our power, sir," Buddy answered, knowing full well the only effort that truly counted happened between the foul lines.

"That takes care of the present," C.W. continued. "Now let's talk future."

"Future?" Buddy asked.

"Yeah, that nun is a young arm who quite possibly might win the Cy Young this year. She's set to be a free agent. Don't you think we should get a contract extension?" the owner asked.

"I thought you weren't that impressed with Bernie," Buddy countered.

"That's when we were losers. Now we're winners. She threw a perfect game and she's young. Besides, I signed her to a contract in the first place. I just needed something to remind me why I did that. Now, I want you to get this deal done." C.W. walked abruptly out of the room, as was his habit after giving an order.

Buddy didn't move for a few seconds. Finally, he turned to Moss. "I have a question for you."

"Go ahead."

"I'm not Catholic, so you tell me. What do you offer a nun as a signing bonus?"

On September 23rd, the Washington Memorials did something they had failed to do all year. They moved into a tie for first place in the NL East. Atlanta had beaten Montreal two to one the previous night, while Washington dumped Chicago seven to five in the

afternoon at Wrigley. The whole city became swept up in the drive
as the season now headed into the final three days of September,
when Montreal and Washington had a series in D.C. to decide the
division.

Bernie's clothing drive remained an institution at the ballpark.
During an afternoon pickup of the latest load, she was called into
Buddy Wilson's office.

"How are you doing today?" Buddy rose and shook her hand
when she entered.

"I'm fine," Bernie replied.

"That's good. That's great. Look, I want to talk to you about a
contract extension." Buddy leaned back. Usually, when he said this
kind of thing to a young kid, the player could hardly contain himself.
But the nun sat quietly for a long time.

Finally, Buddy had to speak. "So what do you think?"

"Well —," she began, "to be honest, I never really considered
much beyond this year."

"But you like playing ball, don't you?"

"I do, but as a person of my profession you aren't always given
this kind of choice."

"Is there any rule against you playing for us next year, and the
next, and so on?" Buddy asked.

Bernie's blood raced. Was the general manager of the Memorials
really offering her more years of baseball? This was better than a
dream. "No, there isn't any rule I know about."

"If it's a money issue, then I can reasonably assure you that your
salary will go up substantially next year."

Afternoons spent on the ranch with her father playing baseball
flooded her mind. He had always believed this was possible. There
was so much she thought she'd given up when she'd gotten her call.
Fame, fortune and baseball were now within her grasp.

"Why don't you tell me what kind of figure you're thinking
about?" Buddy prodded, "then I'll see if it's close to mine."

"To tell you the truth, I don't know." Bernie knew she had to be
up front with Buddy. "I guess there is a small matter I have to
address first. You see, I've got a contract offer with someone else at
the moment."

"We'll match any offer," Buddy stated confidently.

"That would be difficult."

"Who is it?" Buddy asked, a little peeved that another team had already contacted his pitcher.

"Him." Bernie pointed skyward, and Buddy understood.

"I take back my promise that we can match any offer." Buddy had negotiated many things in his life, but this was the first time he'd ever tried to negotiate with the Almighty. Buddy tried another tact. "This is just a question, but don't you think baseball may be your calling? Isn't that a little bit possible?"

"I don't know."

"Is there any way to find out?"

"First, I should ask Father Michael. I'm assigned to his parish after all."

"Then we'll wait for now. I respect your need to put everything in order, but this is the opportunity of a lifetime."

"I've got to get back to the clothes," she said and left his office.

Buddy sat in his office and worried about what he would say to C.W. How did you tell an owner that his prize young arm wouldn't re-up until she gets the high sign from God?

On the walk down, Bernie thought about Buddy's offer and her promise to ask Father Michael. That conversation was the second scariest thing she faced. She dearly loved the game and loved to play, and she was primarily worried about what would happen if the answer came back, "no."

"I heard a couple of guys talking today. You win out impressive-ly, and the Cy Young may be yours," Amy Springer commented over pasta salad and red wine that evening.

"I don't care," the nun said, perhaps a bit too quickly.

"You do care."

"Okay, maybe I do." Bernie bit into a hamburger. "But I try not to, because I don't think a person should care that much about it, right?"

"Sure you can care," Amy teased. "After all, you're only human."

"I suppose I am." Bernie smiled at that.

Amy dug into her pasta salad and chomped away. Bernie could tell by the way Amy attacked the lettuce that something was on her mind. Something Amy couldn't quite bring herself to talk about.

"Is everything okay?" Bernie inquired between bites of salad.

Amy took a long draw of red wine. Was everything okay? Of course, everything was okay because she had met someone. Right? What was the possible harm in having finally connected with someone? The red wine curdled in Amy's stomach. She knew very well that there was right and wrong, but what about how she felt when she was with Dean? Didn't that count for something?

Amy put her wine glass down and looked directly at Bernie. "You know, I want to ask something. I know sinning is bad, but are some sins better than others?"

The question stopped Bernie from taking another bite. "There aren't really any good sins."

"What about lying to someone to get someone to come to a surprise birthday party?"

"I suppose technically that's a sin, but no one's hurt by it."

"So it's only a sin if it hurts someone?" Amy reasoned.

"Or yourself, or God," Bernie quickly added.

"That's pretty rough."

"That's why none of us are without sin. It's pretty easy to mess up."

"So it's expected?"

"God forgives us our sins. Yet, I think we are supposed at least make an effort to live better lives." Bernie sipped her drink. "Why the sudden interest in sin?"

"Just thinking," Amy offered. "Don't you believe that something can be right, I mean really right in the end, even if in the short term it might be considered wrong?"

"That sounds like a country song," Bernie laughed.

"I'm serious." Amy frowned.

Bernie considered her friend. "Do you want to talk about it?"

Amy picked at her salad. "There's nothing to talk about."

"Is it bad?" Bernie said in gentle tones, hoping to make Amy more comfortable with something that was obviously stressing her greatly.

"Depends on how you look at it, I guess."

"How do you look at it?"

"It's something I've wanted for a long, long time. It's so perfect, except for one thing."

"Is that thing a major problem?"

"Very major, but I can't stop. Not now. I'm so close to getting it."

Sister Mary Bernadette thought about her friend and the world she lived in. She wanted to say something that would comfort Amy, but the words were hard to come by. Finally, she looked up and said, "Moths spend their whole lives thinking what they really want is to get closer and closer to the flame."

"I'm not a moth."

"I know, I'm just saying that I hope you know what you're doing."

Amy answered, "That's the problem. I know exactly what I'm doing."

Chapter 46

Emily Larson struggled into the house and caught the phone on the sixth ring. She removed her gardening gloves as she talked.

"Hello?"

"Hi Emily, this is Verna." Verna Lindquist owned and operated the grocery store in the small hamlet of Winnetonka, Minnesota. The whole community passed through her door at least twice a month. She functioned as the walking, talking local newspaper and most informed gossip. "I just got a peculiar call."

Verna explained that a reporter from back east had phoned to ask her questions about Emily and Dean. How often did Verna see them together? Had the citizens of Winnetonka noticed any friction in the marriage? Generally trying to lead the shopkeeper into some confession about the state of the Larson's marriage.

"What did you tell him?" Emily asked.

"Told him to mind his own business. I hope I didn't step over my bounds."

"No, you did just fine," Emily told Verna. Emily said good-bye and hung up the phone.

Being the last person to know something horrible was the worst feeling in the world. Emily sat down on a kitchen chair and cried into a dishtowel. She was thankful that Becky was over at a friend's house playing. After almost thirty minutes, the crying stopped and the anger began. She grabbed the phone and dialed. By the time Dean answered, she boiled.

"Hello."

"You tell me what's going on in D.C. right now, Dean!" Her voice knifed into his brain.

"What?" Dean's mind spun.

"Don't even try to play dumb. A reporter called the general store asking about our marriage. So?!?"

"Honey, don't get worked up. It's just a reporter fishing for something that's not there."

"Not there? Our marriage is collapsing. A reporter calls Verna Lindquist. Why?"

"How should I know?" Dean's voice rose.

"I think you do."

"I don't." Sweat poured down his face. The lies burnt the air around him into a thick, hot, choking mass.

"I only want to know one thing. You promised me when we were going to be apart for months at a time that I was the only one. Is that still true?"

Dean turned away from the receiver. The lying physically pained him. It made him nauseous, but he saw no other way out. "I told you, there's nothing to the story."

"That's not what I asked you."

"Nothing has happened."

"That's not what I asked you."

"It's what I'm telling you."

"Then tell me this. Is something going to happen?"

Dean didn't respond immediately. The lack of response answered all questions for Emily. He heard her slam the phone down and something broke deep inside of him.

Miles away from Dean, in the woods of Minnesota, Emily sat by herself and faced her imagination as it conjured up images of what it would be like to be alone.

For a long time after the call, Dean didn't move. When he did, it was to hang up the phone, and then pick it up again. He called the only person he could think of to talk to.

Dean sat across from Bernie at the Pancake House less than an hour later, as the two surveyed the menus.

"What are you getting?" Dean asked.

"Pigs in a blanket. These diners always seem to make them best."

The waitress came and took their order and refilled the coffee cups already on the table. After she left, Dean leaned forward and spoke softly.

"Bernie, I need some advice."

Bernie smiled. "Don't drop your shoulder when you swing."

"It's not about baseball." Dean sipped his coffee. "I'm having trouble at home."

"What's wrong?"

"You know how two people meet, fall in love and then marry." He stopped when he realized whom he was talking to.

"I've heard about it," Bernie offered.

"Well, there's a lot of life after those vows, and people change, right?"

"It's been known to happen."

"I don't know, maybe it's me that's changed, maybe it's her, but we don't get along so well any more."

"Is this about her wanting you to retire?"

"It's about a lot of things. I'm not saying I want a perfect wife. I'm not without fault myself. But don't you think a guy should look forward to talking to his wife on the phone?"

"You're under a lot of pressure, Dean. The three games with Montreal start tomorrow. Don't you think you're being just a little over the top? Deep down, you want to call her, don't you?"

"I'm not so sure anymore." Dean dropped his eyes.

"What exactly do you mean by that?"

"I mean I'm confused."

"About?"

"A lot of things."

"Things like what?"

"I'm not sure Emily and I are— are the right thing, right now."

Bernie bit her bottom lip. "You're thinking of leaving?"

"I don't know."

"Emily is a wonderful person."

"I know that. I married her, didn't I?"

"That was supposed to be forever."

"It hasn't ended yet. That's why I'm talking to you."

"I'm a nun. My views on divorce are fairly public."

"I'm asking if it's possible for people to move beyond each other?"

"Why? Why do you want to know now? This is a pennant race.

This is not the time to decide whether or not to leave your wife."

"Things happen at their own speed, usually with lousy timing."

"I want you to be honest with me. Is there someone else?"

"No." The lie hit him hard. He had to continue. "Not yet."

"I wouldn't recommend that path."

"I'm not looking for recommendations."

"Then why tell me? I've got more opinions than anybody on this team except maybe Link."

"Because you'd listen and you'd care. Because I trust you, and —, because if I could tell you, then maybe I could tell her."

"I guess you've answered your question then."

"Guess I have."

"Do me a favor. Wait until the season ends. You can do it right then."

Dean nodded.

The food arrived, and both dug in immediately to avoid talking about the problem anymore. Dean noted that the pigs in the blanket were good. The nun had been right about that. He took another bite and tried to focus on baseball. He knew that baseball would show him the path to take.

Chapter 47

Game one of the Montreal series swelled with the excitement of a playoff match-up. The three games would determine Atlanta's opponent for the National League pennant.

Bernie took the hill for the Washington Memorials to oppose the ace of the Expo staff, Kade Hilton. ESPN decided to carry all three games. The world watched as a huge grin broke out across the nun's face when the breeze inexplicably picked up just prior to game time.

She worked the first five innings, giving up one hit and two walks. The movement on her knuckleball drew comparisons to John Travolta's gyrations of the seventies.

Hilton proved equal. He walked none and struck out five through five. That left the Memorials in a scoreless tie. It was in the top of sixth, while Hilton sat on the bench, that the thrill of strategic possibilities first tempted Dean.

With two outs and the nun in a groove, Manny Alvarez fouled off a knuckleball and a curve that surprised him. Dean called for consecutive curveballs that missed. The catcher grew nervous about falling behind Alvarez. Dean's mind kept drifting as he considered his next call. There were images of Emily crying and Amy beaming. He fought to focus, but he never got completely back.

"Two and two!" roared the ump.

Instinctively, Dean put down one finger for the fastball. Bernie's eyes popped. She shook her head. Dean growled behind the mask and made the one finger straighter and sterner.

Bernie pondered the call just for a moment longer. Dean had made weird calls before, calls she hadn't understood, and they had worked. She took a deep breath and set herself. She kicked and fired a seventy-mile-per-hour pitch toward the outside corner.

It took all of two seconds for the line drive to clear the center field fence. Bernie hung her head while Dean shook his. She got the third out quickly, and the team walked off the field down one to nothing.

"Hustle, hustle," Moss called to his team as they drooped into the dugout. Boney stood near the manager and kicked at the step.

Bernie went off and got something to drink, still upset over the homer. Moss turned and walked down the dugout as Link took his practice swings. The manager stopped in front of Dean. The catcher was still in his gear, sweaty and confused. Bernie stood nearby, drinking some water.

"Play ball!" the ump called and Link strode up to the plate.

"What was that fastball call out there for?" Moss asked his catcher, as he sent signals to the third base coach.

"He was looking for the knuckler," Dean answered distantly.

"Strike one!" Link missed the first fastball.

"That's the point about the knuckleball. Even when you know it's coming, it's tough to hit." Moss was punchy.

"She'd missed the last two pitches. She was wild," Dean offered.

"Ball one!" Link watched a pitch sail high and outside.

"She's only walked two," Moss glared, "which is some kind of record for a knuckleball pitcher!"

Dean stood quickly and turned red. "You want to call the game?"

"Strike two!" Link watched a big curve break late across the strike zone.

"All I know is that Dean Larson doesn't normally serve up a batting practice fastball to a power hitter with two out and first open. Now, what is going on?!?" Moss pressed his captain.

"I've been doing this for eighteen years. Mistakes happen," Dean countered.

"Not like this, they don't. Now, what's wrong?"

"People yelling at me. That's what's wrong."

"Fine! Don't tell me, but either you get your act straight, or I sit you down." Moss never bluffed about the pine.

Dean looked at his teammates as they waited for him to make his move.

"It was my fault," Bernie piped up. "I shook off the knuckleball. He's just protecting me."

"Strike three!!!" Link missed the fastball again.

Moss considered Dean and Bernie for a full second, then bellowed, "Don't do that again! Bernie get in that on-deck circle!" Moss kicked the floor and paced to the end of the dugout, muttering something about retirement.

Bernie grabbed a bat and got one practice cut in before Flip flied out to second base. She muttered to herself all the way to the plate.

Bernie had gone .000 for the season, with a few sacrifice bunts scattered here and there. She planted herself in the batter's box, still fuming over Dean's call. She knew taking the blame was the right thing to do, but she hated being yelled at for things she did right.

She stood in the box and vowed to just swing. It would make the strikeout come faster, and her time of looking foolish would be over quicker. It was during these moments when she really wished that God had sent her to the American League, where the designated hitter batted for the pitcher.

What happened next was dubbed the clunk heard 'round the ballpark. Bernie's bat nicked Hilton's first fastball and blooped it into the air toward the shortstop. It stayed up as the fielder leaped to catch. He missed, and the ball sailed on into the outfield. It landed softly on the grass for a base hit.

Bernie ran past first and turned around. Her heart raced. The scoreboard flashed history. The first hit by a woman in modern major league play. Now Bernie was nervous. She'd never run the base paths before.

Pitchers were trained on how to decode the signals flashed by managers for just this reason. Bernie looked over at the third base coach. She decided that he wanted her to hold.

Mike Flowers took the very next pitch and lined a single into right field. Bernie was off with the crack of the bat. She dug her cleats into second base and looked up to see the third base coach windmilling his arm. She sprinted for third.

Lonny Watcher caught the ball cleanly on one bounce as he charged it. He planted his back foot and used one of the strongest outfield arms in baseball to uncork a zinger.

Moss and the bench watched as Bernie raced the ball to third.

Two steps from the bag, Bernie laid out face first into the air, clutching for the bag. A cloud of dust flew as ball and nun got to third at the same moment.

"SAFE!!" The call brought thousands of fans and the entire bench to their feet.

"She can run," Moss mumbled to Boney, who nodded.

Tommy Chang almost missed the curve. Instead, he nubbed it out past the pitcher. The ball stopped well short of the shortstop, who was playing deep.

Bernie broke for home on contact. The jump was tremendous. The shortstop immediately knew he had no shot at the nun. His thoughts flashed briefly to Mike, now tearing for second, but his only play was Tommy at first.

Tommy didn't have world-class speed, but he had stolen twenty five bases that year. The stadium held its breath as Tommy breached the bag before the ball arrived. Bernie crossed the plate standing and jogged to the dugout. Her teammates hugged her and celebrated her first run. The game was tied. It stayed that way as Lenny de Haven grounded out to end the inning.

The top of the seventh didn't start on time. Before the first official pitch, Dean called time and walked to the mound.

"Thank you for getting me out of that back there," he said quietly.

"Hanging out dirty laundry won't help this game."

"I'm sorry about the fastball."

"You should be." She paused and saw the ump look at his watch. "But you've been right more than wrong. Just don't make it a habit." Dean trotted back to his place.

Bernie gave up no hits in the seventh, eighth or ninth. Hilton gave up only one. In the bottom of the eighth, Link Molansky finally caught that fastball and drilled it into the left field bleachers. The final score read two to one.

As the team left the field that night, Boney stopped Bernie. "You didn't shake off any called knuckleball."

"I said I did."

"Nuns ain't supposed to lie. I watched it again from the center field camera. He called for the heat."

"I'll stick by my story." She never met Boney's eyes.

"It takes guts to take blame for that. Maybe that's why I like you," Boney said. "Now you mind telling me what's wrong with Dean?"

"Nothing's wrong." It was a half-truth and she knew it.

"You know you can protect a teammate too much."

"We'll find out." She walked off, knowing full well that her next confession was going to be a doozy. For now, she focused on the series. The one game advantage the Memorials enjoyed vanished the next day in a five to four loss. It brought the series down to a one game winner-take-all meeting the next afternoon.

Game three proved to be a test of endurance. The starting pitchers lasted into the seventh, as the lead seesawed to a tie at five. The game drove on through the ninth. Pitchers and pinch hitters played out the chess match between managers on the diamond. It finally reached ten to ten as the game crested the top of the eighteenth inning.

Montreal stranded two as Mad Max Standish pitched out of a runners-on-the-corners jam. No one left the stadium as Da Bull Ramirez strode to the plate late into the night, ready to end the game with one swing of the bat. His first swing made contact. It wasn't solid, but the man was so strong that the poke cleared the infield and landed in front of the right fielder for a base hit.

Da Bull was not a quick individual. In fact, many people referred to the slower players in the league as being gifted with the quickness of Da Bull. Moss scanned his bench and then his lineup card. There were no regular players left. Moss rubbed his eyes and grabbed for a bottle of antacids that wasn't there. An idea had come into his mind two days ago. He'd toyed with the concept at night when he'd played mock games in his head. This was just one of those calls that reminded fans why managers always got the axe first.

"Bernie!" Moss barked, trying to hide his anxiety.

"Coach?" the pitcher asked.

"Run for Da Bull."

Bernie almost fell off the bench as she jumped to her feet. She was a pitcher, not a base runner. The only time she'd been out there on the base paths, she had not been comfortable.

"Bernie, we're waiting," Moss commanded.

Bernie found a batting helmet and trotted out to first base. The crowd gasped when they realized the nun would be the pinch runner.

Boney walked up behind Moss and whispered, "Are you sure about this?"

Moss never answered. He flashed the signs out to Coach Richards at third. Richards was a good poker player, but even he almost lost the blank expression on his face as he translated the call. He didn't understand, but he signaled it across the diamond anyway.

Bernie almost fell over as Richards tapped his brim, rubbed his belly and swept his right arm. She took her lead. On the pitcher's first move, she sprinted toward second.

The whole stadium stopped as the big curveball looped toward the plate. Bernie never looked at home, even though she was supposed to. The second baseman almost lost his cleats when he saw the nun go. His jump was late.

Vitamin swung at the pitch and missed. This effectively blew the hit and run that Moss had called, and hung Bernie out there closer to second than first, and now in the sights of the Montreal catcher, Davis Flint.

The whiff and the late jump slowed the whole relay down, but Flint shot a bullet off toward the base.

Baseball is a game of inches. Had the throw been to the right side instead of high, had Bernie slid for the front corner instead of the back, all might have been different. Bernie stole second.

On the next pitch, Vitamin hit a deep fly ball out to right field. Bernie tagged and sprinted to third. She arrived safely. Dean Larson then played hero, as his drive to deep center field fell two feet short of a two run homer, but scored Bernie. The Memorials claimed the National League East.

Moss's call drew comparisons to a high stakes poker move the next day in all the papers. Sleep came hard for the manager of the Memorials. It wasn't every day that a person tempted fate and won, especially with everything on the line. He promised himself that in the morning he would start thinking about Atlanta. Tonight, he reveled. After all, had it worked differently he would be the one facing the questions and the axe.

"Moss," Buddy called from the end of the locker. "I've got a phone call for Bernie from a Father Michael. Have you seen her?"

Moss quickly crossed to the curtain that separated Bernie from the rest of the team. "Heyt kid, you've got a phone call."

Bernie emerged beaming brighter than the chorus of flashbulbs that went off when she slid safely home. "Who is it?"

"It's Father Michael."

"Oh," she answered softly. She quickly dressed in street clothes and went to the small office where the phone waited for her.

"Sister Mary," the priest's voice cracked in excitement, "that was a tremendous game for you."

"Yes, it was." Bernie became uncomfortable. It was much easier being here when she wasn't talking to the padre regularly.

"I haven't heard from you in such a long time. Is everything all right?"

"It's fine, never been better. I've just been so busy," she answered.

"I see that, and we're all very proud."

"Thank you." She let the conversation go, and there was a long silence.

"I know it's late there, so I won't keep you. I just wanted to call and check in. And tell you the whole town keeps talking about you. The stories you'll have to tell when you come back to us. I can hardly wait."

"How are the repairs going?" Bernie managed to get out.

"Everything is really going well here," Father Michael's voice was filled with enthusiasm. "It really will look beautiful again. You have done a tremendous thing, Sister Mary."

"I'm glad it's all working out," Bernie's voice cracked. "I need to go. It will be an early morning." With that, Bernie hung up the phone and left for the night.

Boney saw her go. He could tell something wasn't right. She wasn't walking like the same pitcher he had watched throughout the season. That made Boney nervous.

Chapter 48

The night after the big win, Amy Springer arrived at Dean's hotel room door with a bottle of wine and two glasses. He was alone.

"Nice sacrifice," Amy said as she walked tentatively into the room.

"Should've been a homer."

"Don't get greedy."

Dean stretched and the joints in his knees and his shoulders cracked under his t-shirt and shorts. "I am so sore. Part of getting old I guess."

Dean collapsed into a chair as Amy opened the wine and poured. "So, you're a hero," Amy teased.

"Almost, maybe." He wanted to talk about other things. He wanted to launch into his thoughts on the subject of them, but he was lost on how to start.

"Here." She gave him the glass and walked behind him. The startled feeling lasted only a second as her fingers dug deeply into the muscles in his neck. His next emotion was relief, as two months of stress from fighting to win the East started to drain away. His eyes closed and his breathing slowed. Amy felt him relax and kept working.

Outside the hotel in the fair Atlanta night, Johnny LePlant sat in his car and watched. He perked up when he saw the woman walk quickly up to the lobby and fly into the door. He smiled at the thought of the pending confrontation. He'd love to hear that one. He counted off the seconds it would take her to get to the elevator, take the short ride to Dean's floor, trudge to the door and finally knock.

The rapping woke Dean from the pleasant numbness of Amy's fingers. It also sent chills down his spine. Who would knock on his door at this hour?

"Who is it?" Dean asked as he got to the door.

"Bernie," the voice called back. "I really need to talk to you."

Dean's first reaction was to hide Amy. He didn't realize she had already sized up the closets. He briefly thought it might be better if Bernie found Amy here. Then the nun would understand his dilemma, but he quickly put that idea away. Now wasn't the time.

"She can't find me here," Amy whispered.

"I know. I know." Dean scanned the room frantically, then offered Amy a large closet in a far corner. She jumped inside as Dean went back to the door.

"We have to go to the ballpark, now," Bernie said with the gravity reserved for morticians.

"What?"

"I'll explain on the way. We have to go."

Dean shook his head and then realized his salvation. "Okay, you want to go to the ballpark, we'll go to the ballpark." He grabbed an old pair of sneakers and followed her out the door.

On the street below, Johnny's interest peaked. First the nun and the catcher emerged and left quickly in Dean's car. Two minutes later, the reporter cautiously exited the hotel and hopped in her car and sped away. Johnny recorded all these items and wondered, hopefully, if somehow the nun might just be involved.

"Do you mind telling me why we're headed to the ballpark at midnight before the start of the playoffs?" Dean was punchy as he drove.

"I've done a terrible thing, and I need to tell someone," Bernie said.

"I thought you always called Father Michael for these kinds of things."

"He's part of the problem," she answered, then waited to speak again until they stood on the infield of Fulton County stadium.

"Okay, now we're here," Dean stated.

"I've purposefully not called Father Michael for a month."

"Excuse me?" Dean's patience ran thin, as he remembered Amy's caressing fingers. "You drag me out here to tell me you haven't talked to your priest?"

"Buddy asked me to sign a contract extension."

"That's great news, but not drag-me-out-to-the-old-ballpark news."

"I don't know if I can take not talking about it anymore."

Dean finally stopped being upset and started hearing for the first time since they'd left the hotel. "What do you mean, you don't know?"

"My life isn't exactly my own. I took these vows when I got the position. You know, gave my life to God."

"And you don't think God wants you to pitch?"

"Right now He does. I know that much."

"But next season is too far ahead for Him to plan?"

"I'm sure He knows what I'm meant to do, but He hasn't filled me in yet."

"So there's a chance you will get to stay, right?"

"Right," her voice wavered. "But there's a chance I'll have to go." She walked across the infield and onto the pitcher's mound. "Do you know who Saint Bernadette, my namesake, was?" She didn't wait for a reply. "She was a young French woman who tended sheep, and one day the Virgin Mother appeared to her. It changed her life completely. Of course, the biggest thing revealed was this hidden spring Bernadette was shown. It has healing powers."

"I saw the movie."

"You've heard me talk about seeing the Blessed Virgin, and it's true. I know it's hard to believe; people are skeptical by nature. Bernadette, as a name, was considered a joke in my order when I took it. They all thought I was grandstanding. The other nuns never believed I had a vision. I ended up an outsider in my own order. But the name just seemed right to me. Then, when Father Michael had his vision and I ended up here, I thought this was the hidden spring I was supposed to uncover. Baseball was everything to me, and I'm just now remembering how wonderful it is, but I have this fear that this isn't my hidden spring. Then tonight, Father Michael called after the game. He told me I would surely have wonderful stories when I returned. That scared me completely. I know I was supposed to ask for guidance. But I don't want to, because I'm afraid of what the answer will be." She knelt and picked up a handful of dirt. She opened her fingers and let it sift back to the ground.

"Bernie, tomorrow you start game one of the pennant. You've been offered this contract, which you weren't expecting. That's a lot for anybody to handle. My advice is to just focus on the game. Everything else will take care of itself."

"I've tried, but I can't stop thinking about giving up baseball again."

"I don't know what to say," Dean said. "I don't have a lot of experience with nuns and that kind of thing."

"But you do."

"I think you need more sleep."

"You may lose a marriage because of the game. You took vows for that, but you told me you and Emily had grown apart. It's because of baseball, isn't it?"

"I wish I could say it wasn't."

"You see. You know how it feels to face losing everything to keep a dream. That's why I had to talk to you."

It dawned on Dean then. He had led by example, and this was the living proof in front of him. "Bernie, are you considering leaving the church?"

She said nothing for a long time and stared out into the outfield.

"Maybe," she finally answered.

Dean let out a deep breath. "I'm going to give you some advice a friend of mine gave me. Don't do anything until after the season is over. If you do it, you can do it right then."

"Dean," Bernie began, "how do you live with yourself if you make the decision before the games stop?"

"Day-to-day," Dean answered. "Day-to-day."

Chapter 49

Bernie drew the start in game one of the NL Pennant race. While her performance was not a thing of beauty, it was effective. Bernie out dueled Greg Hadley and won a two to nothing affair. The Atlanta Braves, however, out hit their opponents ten to two. The Memorials prevailed because they followed their first hit, a single by Tommy Chang, with their second, a homer by Vitamin Vitarello. The Braves followed most of their hits with hard shots right at Flip Toussant, which started four double plays.

"Any problems out there tonight?" Moss asked Dean, as the catcher dressed after the game.

"What do you mean?" Dean asked.

"Ten hits is a lot of hits," Moss pondered.

"Four double plays is a lot of double plays."

"Yeah, and I'm not sure we can count on four doubles per game in this series. I'm worried about ten hits." Moss sat down next to Dean.

"You're the only man I know who worries about what went wrong in a shutout." Dean buttoned his shirt. "If anything, it's one of those team of destiny things. You have to admit when Bernie's on the mound, you never know what's going to happen next."

"You're right. I'm overreacting." Moss blew a deep breath out. "A shutout is a shutout." Moss pulled out a bottle of antacids and chugged a handful.

"I thought you said those things don't work anymore." Dean pointed out.

"I don't believe they do, but then I never believed that I'd be starting a woman pitcher either. If there's one thing that's been constant this year, it's the unexpected."

In an Atlanta hotel room that night, Bernie sat in a chair and reviewed the entire game in her head. She was happy with the shutout, particularly against the Braves, but ten hits was a lot. Every time she'd needed a double play ground ball, she'd gotten it. It was almost like a miracle. That bothered her more than anything else. Maybe this was His way of saying it was okay to stay in baseball, or maybe it meant something else, something she didn't want to think about.

Jon John got the win in game two, with a score of five to three. The runs all came on homeruns from Da Bull and Dean. Marion Pierce took the win in game three, a wild eight to seven affair in which both teams combined for six dingers.

Game four brought Bernie back to the mound, with a sweep of the celebrated Braves a real possibility. The dreams of an entire city and a team rested on the shoulders of the nun. She took dreams very seriously and was determined to succeed, but the Braves were not ready to go quietly.

Bernie struggled in the first five innings. She yielded three runs, two via a homer, and fought her knuckleball the entire time. The pitch was dancing, but not enough to baffle major league hitters. She closed her eyes and tried to feel the ball, but the zone she had visited so often during the season seemed to be just out of her reach.

Dean did his best to keep the team in the game. While the knuckleball faltered, she had more control over the curve than she'd had all season. It took the Braves batting order two innings to realize that Dean was purposely calling for the big curve outside the strike zone. Several of the NL West champions went fishing and came up empty.

Atlanta's three runs fell short of the four provided courtesy of Link Molansky. He doubled in two in the second, then homered with a man aboard in the bottom of the fifth. The gritty third baseman carried the Memorials into the sixth with the lead, and within nine outs of the World Series.

"Bernie," Moss approached the nun before she took the field. "How are you doing?"

"I'm okay," Bernie answered and picked up her mitt.

"I'm bringing in a reliever," Moss stated firmly.

"I can go," Bernie said.

He looked into her eyes and remembered that far away night, years ago, when he'd had to watch defeat unfold. Then he remembered Day's final start last year, and the pain of losing by using a pitcher one pitch too long. "I know you can, but this is why they call me coach." Moss picked up the phone and spoke briefly with the bullpen. He sat back on the bench and felt his stomach's churning go into overdrive.

Three relievers got the Memorials through the sixth, seventh and eighth innings without yielding a run. Mad Max Standish topped the drama by retiring the Braves in order, two by strikeout, to end the game and launch the Washington Memorials into the World Championship of baseball.

In the American League, the New York Yankees and the Chicago White Sox had fought a tough, seven game series. The White Sox finally prevailed, and the World Series drew closer for two teams of players who had spent their whole lives working for it.

Johnny LePlant began to write articles about baseball again. All of his columns on the subject were national stories devoted to the White Sox, who boasted one of the best pitching staffs in baseball and arguably the best player in the game: first baseman, Freddy Tuggs. Though his writing was good, even Johnny could not hide all his feelings between the lines. He hinted at a scandal, but failed to produce any evidence. If anyone asked him about it, he said nothing. It only hyped the expectations further.

In his mind, he saw the clues he needed. The most important dealt with the non-appearance of a certain someone in the family seats reserved for each game. Each time the television cut to a shot of the wives and kids celebrating the exploits of the Washington Memorials, Johnny LePlant knew it built up to his crowning moment. He could barely wait.

"Are we still not going?" Becky looked up from the TV after game seven of the White Sox/Yankees series.

Emily stood in the kitchen of her Minnesota home and worked on a potted plant. She had politely refused to join her daughter in watching the baseball game. As far as Emily was concerned, baseball could go to Hell.

"Mom?" The plaintive voice sounded again.

"You've got school," Emily answered patiently.

"It's the World Series, Mom."

"So what?" Emily's voice bit sharply into the air. "So it's the stupid World Series. You know, plenty of people don't even watch the World Series! It's a stupid game for stupid people!" Emily caught herself as her child's eyes opened wide in bewilderment.

"Are you okay?" Becky asked.

Emily took off her garden mitts and rubbed her hands until she regained her composure. "I'm fine," she finally answered.

"I don't think baseball is stupid," Becky said softly. "I'm sorry that you do."

Emily bit her bottom lip. "I'm just having a bad day, honey. Baseball isn't stupid."

"Then can we go?" Becky's eyebrows raised a bit.

Emily sighed. She knew it wasn't fair to deny Becky at least some part of Dean's big moment. "I'll tell you what. If it goes to a game seven, then we'll take a trip and see the game."

Becky smiled widely, and Emily forgot for a moment that her life was falling apart.

Chapter 50

Bernie took the mound in Chicago for game one of the World Series with renewed confidence in herself. She'd spent the last three days mulling over her two games against Atlanta. She hadn't been perfect, but she'd still won both. Tonight she looked sharp.

The knuckler teased the White Sox hitters for six innings. The batters felt the ball begging to be crushed to the deepest part of center field. But it always slipped away, just out of their reach.

The Memorials managed to put three on the board, all courtesy of a Da Bull slam in the fourth. Moss sat back on the bench, prepared to watch Bernie cruise through the last three innings like she had so often during the year. Unfortunately for Moss, it was a short cruise.

The White Sox opened the seventh with two quick outs, then back-to-back homers. Each measured more than four hundred and fifty feet. The knuckleball had stopped dancing and batting practice had begun.

"Time!" Moss called from the dugout and trotted slowly to the mound as relievers warmed quickly in the bullpen. Dean joined him there with Bernie. "You all right?"

"It didn't break," Bernie offered.

"Any thoughts?" Moss turned to Dean.

"It's been flattening out the last inning and a half."

"I'm throwing it right. I'm not trying to place it," Bernie replied earnestly.

"All right, all right." Moss lowered his voice to a soothing tone, which seemed out of place in the raucous environment of a baseball stadium. "We're still up one, so just relax and remember they are the ones who are behind."

Dean returned to home plate. Moss trotted back to the dugout. He tried to exude confidence in his decision to leave Bernie in the game.

The following batter slammed Bernie's next pitch into the gap for a double, and Moss came quickly to the mound. There was little discussion, and a relief pitcher entered the game. He ended the rally, and the Memorials went on to win game one.

Games two and three didn't go so well. Chicago rebounded from the loss to take the next two by the scores of six to four and eight to five. As she had all year, Bernie got the call in game four to stop the bleeding.

Her outing lasted five and two-thirds innings. As in the last game, she started strong. She faced fourteen batters in four innings. She even struck out two. Her team surged to five early runs, but in the bottom of the sixth, the knuckleball flattened again. The White Sox hitters began to tee off on her pitches. Four runners crossed the plate before a reliever was summoned to end the White Sox outburst.

Mad Max took the hill to save the win in the ninth. Bernie got the win and the series was tied again. In game five, Jose Martinez threw his best outing of the year for a complete game victory. Both teams then boarded chartered jets and headed back to Chicago for game six, a game the Memorials promptly lost.

The next night, Dean sat alone in his hotel room worrying about game seven. The Memorials would face Jackie Hardcastle, Chicago's best pitcher. He also knew that Bernie would be the pitcher of record. He had confidence in Bernie, but he also knew she had struggled lately. A struggling knuckleballer was a very bad thing. The phone rang in his room and brought him back to the here and now. He waited until the fourth ring to pick it up.

"Hello?"

"It's Amy. I just put my story to bed, and I — I wanted to see if you're all right."

"There's always tomorrow."

"I know. Look, if you're just going to sit there and brood — I'm not saying you are — but there are a couple of good old movies on TV." She swallowed. "It's better than having nightmares of facing Hardcastle in your underwear in front of thousands of people."

Dean almost laughed, except he'd had that dream. "I don't

know."

"It's up to you."

Dean looked around his room and studied the stark and sterile surroundings. "Where are you?"

"Room 1618," she replied calmly.

Dean turned numb as he pulled his sneakers on his tired feet. He threw on a t-shirt and walked quickly out the door into the hallway.

"Northwest Airlines is pleased to announce the arrival of flight 614, service from Minneapolis, Minnesota," the voice blared into the terminal at Chicago's O-Hare International Airport. Passengers waiting for the flight grumbled. It was over three hours late due to an earlier snafu in Detroit.

Becky Larson emerged into the terminal and ran to the nearest TV she could find. Emily, tired and haggard, followed her daughter.

"The game, the game. Who won the game?" Becky asked the bartender behind the cocktail lounge.

"Are you old enough to be in here?" the old man asked, almost amused at her overwhelming desire to know the score.

"No, I don't think I'm old enough to be in here, but I need to know the score." Her eyes wrinkled with worry.

The old man shrugged and winked at her. "The Memorials lost by one run."

"Yes!" she screamed.

"Are you a White Sox fan?"

"No, I'm for the Memorials." Becky called back and sprinted back to Emily. The old man shook his head and went back to wiping glasses.

"They lost," Becky said. "Now we get to see the game tomorrow, right?"

"Yeah, we do."

"Can we go see Daddy?"

Emily hesitated. She hadn't told Dean they were coming. She thought it would just distract him, and she hadn't relished another phone conversation ending in an argument. She was glad there was a game seven. Emily had given in to her daughter's desire after game five and booked the flight just in case the series was over in six. This was important to Dean, and therefore important to his child. She pondered just showing up at the hotel, unannounced. She wasn't normally a person who believed in a lot of surprises, but maybe a little surprise was just what their marriage needed. It couldn't hurt to try.

"Yes, we can go see Daddy." Emily patted Becky on the back.

Chapter 51

Link hurried back into the locker room. He'd forgotten his watch when he'd dressed to leave. He found it quickly, as well as a gym bag in the middle of the floor. Practice clothes tumbled from it, littering the place. The bag shouldn't have been there — not after the managers had been through to pick up.

Link walked down an inner corridor under the stands. He picked his way carefully and listened for the sounds of an unwanted intruder. His ears finally caught something, but it wasn't out of place. It was the sound of a baseball hitting a leather mitt. Link followed the sound to a indoor batting cage. Crouched behind the plate was Boney, wearing a catcher's mitt. A little more than sixty feet away, Bernie wound up and threw again.

Link almost called out to stop them. He wanted to know why they were out here late, the night before game seven. Bernie let a knuckleball fly, and all questions were answered. The ball didn't dance. It barely deviated from its long, slow arc to the plate.

"What's going on?" Link asked, startling the pair.

Bernie jerked to look at him. Her eyes were large and desperate. "Nothing."

"Nothing. That's quite a way to describe the first time Boney's crouched down like that in ten years," Link answered smoothly.

"I've lost it, Link," she said suddenly, as if saying it fast made it hurt less, much like ripping a band aid off the skin instead of pulling it slowly. "I lost my knuckler."

"I told you to stop staying that," Boney commanded as he struggled to his feet. "You can't lose a pitch, not at your age."

"We've been here for an hour, Boney, have you seen it?" Bernie's voice quavered. "You know what they call a knuckleball that doesn't dance? Batting practice. I'm going to pitch batting practice for game seven of the World Series."

"That's crap." Link grumbled and walked into the cage. He strode up to Bernie and snatched the bucket of balls next to her. "No more throwing tonight."

"I've got to find it."

"Link's right, Bernie. You got to save something for tomorrow," Boney added, thankful he didn't have to squat again.

"You aren't listening," Bernie yelled.

"You aren't hearing." Link faced the nun. "You think you're going to find what you're looking for in a batting cage? When you go out there every morning at five with the guys, do you think about baseball?"

"No," Bernie answered quietly. "Except lately."

"I don't know much about pitching, and even less about coaching. But I do know that you can get to that zone where you are unhittable. Now, it's not brain surgery to figure what's changed. Maybe all you need to do is listen to yourself." Link kept the bucket of balls and walked to the exit of the batting cage.

"What if I've changed?" Bernie asked.

"Then I hope who you've become can pitch as well as who you used to be," Link answered matter-of-factly. He waited and walked the nun back to the hotel. Boney watched them go and then looked up to the second story of the batting cage. A large black window hung there, and Boney waited for the man behind it to come down and stand beside him.

"What's the matter?" Moss asked his pitching coach seconds later.

"I don't know."

"You're the pitching coach, Boney." Moss rubbed his tired eyes.

"Why does the knuckleball work? I can give you physics, but that's only half the story," Boney scratched his bald head. "Whatever it is, I can't fix it. Maybe she shouldn't start tomorrow."

"I don't think that's a such good idea," Moss sighed.

"Why?" Boney asked.

"If we pull her start, her confidence is gone. We might as well dress up a mannequin instead. She's got to pitch. She got us this far, and I don't know if we can go the rest of the way by ourselves."

Moss's stomach began a deep ache and his temples began to throb.

Emily pounded on the door of room 1245 of the downtown hotel
for the third time. It was late, their plane flight had been delayed,
and she was tired. She needed Dean to open the door so she could
collapse on a bed.

"Where's Daddy?" Becky yawned.

"I don't know. Maybe they gave us the wrong room number."
Emily grabbed her suitcase and her daughter's hand and trudged
back down to the front desk.

In room 1618, Amy guided Dean to an overstuffed chair. The
catcher sat down stiffly.

"How are your shoulders?" she asked.

"A little stiff."

She reached down and grabbed the bottom hem of his T-shirt,
then slowly pulled it over his head. Dean trembled a little, as Amy
began to work his neck with her soft fingers.

"I'm his wife!" Emily started the explanation a second time to
the young gentleman standing behind the check-in desk at the hotel.
"He didn't know we were coming. That's why he didn't leave a
message for you to give us the key to his room."

"I'm sorry, but our policy is that we just can't give out keys,"
the slender guy offered.

"Emily?" The voice traveled the length of the lobby. Bernie
walked quickly from the front door to the side of mother and child.

"Bernie!" Becky shouted and ran to give the nun a hug.

"I thought Dean said you guys weren't coming."

"It's a once-in-a-lifetime experience, especially for her," Emily
answered.

"Have you seen Dean yet?" Bernie asked.

"He's not in his room, and this gentleman doesn't believe I'm
married to him." Emily pointed to the tall man.

Bernie leaned over the desk. "You know who I am, don't you?"

"Yeah. You're that nun who pitches for the Memorials."

"As a member of this team, I can personally vouch for these two
people. They are Dean Larson's wife and child. Do you really want
to keep them waiting out here?" Her eyes opened wide and the clerk

couldn't help himself. He gave Emily an extra key to the room.

The door to Dean's room opened slowly, and Emily, Bernie and Becky all walked into an empty space. Dean was not there.

"He normally likes to spend the night before a big game quietly, in his room. Where do you think he's gone?" Emily wondered out loud.

"I don't know," Bernie answered. She hadn't planned on Dean not being there. She figured he was asleep and didn't hear the first knocks.

"Becky, why don't you brush your teeth," Emily gently commanded. Once the girl was safely in the bathroom, Emily turned to the nun and said, "If he's with somebody else, you can tell me."

"Emily, I don't know where he is." Bernie remembered the conversation at the Pancake house. She prayed Dean had kept his promise to wait. "But it doesn't do any good to get upset over might be's, okay?"

Emily moved a few steps to the door. "I suppose I'll just have to go out and find him."

"No, you've had a long flight. Let me go," Bernie answered.

"You've got game seven tomorrow."

"Yeah, but I'm supposed to see Dean tonight about strategy anyway." Bernie wasn't entirely truthful, but she knew that at that moment she did have to talk to Dean Larson. "I'll bring him here just as soon as I catch up with him. He's probably just hanging with some of the guys." Bernie slipped out the door. She knew she needed some help finding him, and so she decided to turn to the one person she figured could find a lost ball player quicker than anyone else.

In room 1618, Amy finished the back rub she had started more than a week ago. "Feel better?" She wore a pair of loose shorts and a tank top.

"Much."

With her hands still on his shoulders, she leaned closer to his ear. "I'm going to order a little something to eat." She popped up and went to the phone. "Do you want something?"

"Sure." Dean's voice was slow and comfortable. He was settling in.

Amy knew exactly what she wanted, fresh strawberries and

seltzer. Wine wasn't good for Dean before game seven of a World Series. When she'd finished ordering, she looked at Dean again. They both knew how the evening would end. She knew also that it was her pace to set. She had waited a long time for this night, and rushing it was the last thing on her mind.

In the kitchen below, a tray of strawberries waited to go up. A room service waiter stood next to it and counted the five twenties carefully as Johnny LePlant looked on. The waiter nodded his head and heaved the shiny silver tray on his shoulder. He walked away, and Johnny got that warm feeling of triumph again.

Soon after, there was a short, quick knock on the door of room 1618. Amy swept to the door. Her eyes, however, never left Dean. She grabbed the door and flung it open.

"Just put it over there." Amy said casually, then froze as she saw the look of absolute horror on Dean's face. She turned back and found Bernie, standing rigid in the doorway. "I —," Amy stammered.

"You and Dean?" The nun spoke numbly.

"It's not what you think. You know me." Amy backed into the room looking for support. "And don't just stand there. Get in here."

Bernie stepped warily into the room and let the door close.

"I wanted to tell you. I even tried once," Amy rambled, but Bernie said nothing.

Dean grew hot and uncomfortable. He wished he wasn't there. He wanted to explain what he needed from Amy to Bernie over a long cup of coffee, not after midnight in some hotel room.

"Say something," Amy pleaded.

"I don't understand." Bernie's eyes were wide with shock. Her gaze fell on Dean and stayed there.

"Don't look at me, okay?" Dean ordered. "Just don't. You don't know what's it's been like."

"I don't want to believe it." Bernie's eyes got moist, but she refused to cry.

"Please, just go. We'll talk about it all later," Amy pleaded.

"No, we have to talk about it now," Bernie assured the pair.

Dean stood and ushered her to the door. "No, we aren't going to talk about it now."

"Dean," Bernie cautioned, "there's something you've got to

know."

"No, Bernie, there's nothing I have to know, except that you've ruined everything about tonight. And don't stand and judge me. After all, it was you who asked me about a divorce from the church!" Dean slammed out into the hallway and was gone.

"This is just great!" Amy seethed. That's when the second knock on the door came. She crossed quickly and threw it open. "Look, I know—," she stopped.

The waiter looked like a deer caught in the headlights of a car. Instead of the man he was expecting to see, there was a woman. This confused him greatly.

"Take it back. I don't want it." Amy slammed the door.

Bernie turned slowly to face Bernie. "You never mentioned you were thinking of sinning with Dean Larson."

"Well, I am so sorry. Would you have preferred somebody else on the team? Name the guy, and I'll see if I can accommodate you!"

"That's not what I meant."

"It doesn't matter what you meant. Is it less of a sin if you don't happen to know the guy?"

"I'm not in the wrong here."

"Not in the wrong? You just screwed everything up!"

Bernie's eyes narrowed.

Amy folded her arms and her voice rose, "What? Can't take it? Well, damn you. Yeah, damn you for spoiling my evening!"

"Do you even understand what you were going to do?"

"Yeah, I understand that I spend my weekends alone. I come home to an empty house. I get that my dates are a choice from a pool of lousy and lousier. By the time they get to be my age, the best ones have been picked through. But then one time, one time in the last two decades I have a chance at someone real and special. One chance in twenty years, and you had to get in the way. Do you hate me so much that you can't stand to see me happy for just one little insignificant night?!?"

Sister Mary Bernadette gathered herself together and walked slowly to the door.

"So you're just going to leave?"

"I have to fix a problem," Bernie called back over her shoulder.

"I'm dying here because of you, and you have to go fix a

problem?"

"I left Dean's wife downstairs in his room. I figure he's discovered her by now." The nun then left the reporter alone.

Bernie found the door to room 1245 slightly ajar and slipped into Dean's room almost unnoticed due to the eerie, unnatural silence that hung there. Dean stood in a corner without his shirt. Emily repacked a suitcase. Becky stood near the door, fighting tears.

"You have nothing more to say?" Emily's lips quivered at the words.

"No." Dean looked out the window.

"Emily, I think we should all talk." Sister Mary spoke from the doorway.

"Why's that, Sister? I think he's said everything he has to say to me." Emily walked to the door.

"Please don't leave," the nun pleaded.

Emily faced Dean one last time. "Maybe later you can stop by and explain this to Becky. How's that sound?" Emily reached out and took Becky's hand. "You know," she said without looking back, "we used to be the most important things in your life. Someday, I want to know when that changed." Emily disappeared, dragging Becky behind her.

Bernie let the door close.

"Don't start with me, Bernie," Dean said. "I'm not the only one in this room considering leaving a relationship."

"I thought you were going to wait until after the season."

"Season's only one more game. The situation got out of hand, so why wait?" Dean looked out the window.

"Because it's bad timing," Sister Mary said flatly from across the room.

"It's a little late for that. You heard her. I said all I had to say."

"Dean, this is your marriage and your child. Don't you think it requires a little more time?"

"I've got game seven to think about."

"You're just giving it away?"

"She walked. I didn't. Maybe it's like I said, people just change."

"So was it just because you were bored or was it because Emily wanted you to give up baseball?"

"You're not my shrink."

"You're just giving up, aren't you?"

"You can fight for some things too hard." Dean turned back to Sister Mary. "Just in case you're wondering what it's like to break it off, it's easier than I thought it'd be. All it takes is a few words."

Sister Mary thought about that. "Maybe you're right, Dean. Maybe this is for the best. Maybe I should take your example and follow it, but I just want you to ask yourself one question. When you sat out there on all those mornings before games thinking about what was most important in your life, what were you thinking about?"

Chapter 52

As usual, the team gathered on the field at five in the morning, and immediately their nerves started to fray. Bernie and Dean were not there. Vitamin called the hotel, but Dean wasn't in his hotel room. No one knew where he was. Bernie had gone to a local church and prayed for guidance from two in the morning until sometime after six, but the team would not find this out until much later.

The game itself was slated for that evening, but much would happen before then. It began with Dean Larson's second visit to Amy Springer's hotel room.

"I didn't expect to see you today," Amy said, almost guarded.

"I didn't figure I'd come." Dean stepped in and let the door close behind him. "I'm sorry about last night."

"Are you really sorry?" Amy asked. "Because I know Emily was downstairs, and you never came back. And you never called."

"Look, you are amazing. You understand the game and what it means to me. That's special. But you know how I go out on that field every morning at five and sort of think about what's important? Well, I think of Becky. She's the most important person in my life."

"I'm not asking to for you not to love your daughter."

"I know. It's just that Emily was a big part of making Becky a reality. And I feel I owe it to her to double check her importance in my life before I just walk away."

"Is this when I say thank you for flirting and almost sleeping with me? I think this is a big mistake. I think we could have been good together, and I think you know that."

"I — I should be going."

"Yes, you should."

It wasn't until the door closed completely, and she knew that the catcher was far away, that Amy Springer flung herself on the bed and sobbed. After thirty minutes, she put herself back together and prepared to do her job, which is all she felt she had left.

It was four o'clock in the afternoon before Dean finally had the nerve to knock on the door of Emily's hotel room. He thought it was better to have this conversation this way. He only had a few hours until game time, so there was a limited amount of talking they could do. He knocked and Emily answered.

"Can I come in?"

Emily stepped back to let the him in.

At the ballpark, the hours ticked by. Most of the team got there early, except for Bernie and Dean. At six o'clock, the nun walked through the hallway to the locker room. From out of the shadows stepped Johnny LePlant.

"Excuse me, Sister," the reporter oozed, oil in his voice.

"I don't want to talk with you."

"I didn't think you did, but I believe I can change your mind," Johnny answered.

"I seriously doubt it."

"I wanted to ask you if you knew anything about a possible affair between Dean Larson and Amy Springer?" Johnny waited for the bomb to drop.

Bernie paused. She almost forgot to breathe. She was a nun, and therefore lost in situations when a lie was what a person really wanted to say. "What are you talking about?"

"I'm talking about adultery. I'm talking about a young nun who knew and possibly helped cover it up. I'm talking about front page, lead story, headline material."

"Then you're talking to the wrong person." Bernie pushed on.

"You can't run from this. This kind of mess doesn't go away." Johnny smiled as the pitcher disappeared into the locker room.

Had Johnny not been so smug, and had Bernie not been so shocked, they might have noticed the figure hidden in the shadows. But neither did, although in retrospect, both would have dearly wished they had.

"Where is Dean?" Moss asked Bernie as she walked by the

coach. Boney stood there as well.

"I don't know," Bernie mumbled.

"What do you mean, you don't know?" Moss almost yelled.

"I haven't seen him today," Bernie said.

"I want to put this in perspective for you. Game seven of the World Series is about to start and we don't know where our captain is? I think you might come up with some ideas," Moss's voice trembled.

Bernie thought a moment. "He might be in his wife's hotel room."

Boney and Moss looked at each other, then scrambled for the phone.

"Was I that awful?" Emily yelled at Dean in the hotel room. They were alone. Becky was at a movie with some of the other team families. From there, they would go onto the game.

"No, you weren't," Dean said.

"Then what was this all about?"

"Well, you keep dogging me about baseball. About how you want me to quit 'cause we don't spend time together."

"Am I wrong?" Emily shouted.

"No, but you knew when we got married that I was a ballplayer. A ballplayer!"

"And for eighteen years I have respected that. During that time, I have spent six months each year as a baseball widow. I've given years to the game. I just thought you might want to give us some of your time."

The phone rang, and Emily snatched up the receiver. "Hello... it's for you." She handed the phone to Dean.

"Hi, coach... I'm aware of what time it is... yes, I'm on my way." Dean put the phone down. "I've got to go."

"Really, I thought you'd already gone." Emily turned away and marched into the bedroom.

Chapter 53

The team paced nervously in the dugout, already upset that their morning ritual had been blown by its two leaders. The game was about to start.

"In all my years of baseball, I've never seen anything like this before." Moss fought the urge to pace and lost. "I've had guys miss planes, guys miss buses, but never a guy miss game seven of the World Series!" Moss glared down his bench and saw the uncertainty in their eyes. He turned to Boney. "Where's Bernie? She should be warming up."

Boney abruptly stood and went back into the locker room.

Bernie knelt behind the curtain that cut her off from the rest of the team. She prayed for guidance and for her friends. There were no easy solutions there. Finally, she asked for forgiveness for herself. She knew she had been less than honest about her intentions the last few months of the season. She'd felt the pull of the game, and it was strong. She'd asked for some sign, some reason to help her decide and give her strength.

"Bernie!" Boney called out into the locker room.

"I'm over here," she answered.

"Well get your butt out there. The game ain't going to wait for you."

Bernie quickly stood and reached for a baseball mitt, one of the four she had been given by the team. She couldn't find them. She frantically searched her area. All four were missing, or at least hidden from her view.

"Bernie, let's go!" Boney commanded.

Bernie dove into her sports bag and ripped through tubes of sports cream and practice clothes and finally, finally found a mitt. It wasn't the one she'd expected to be there. Sister Mary Bernadette stood up and considered the piece of shabby leather in her hands. It was the baseball glove her little league team had sacrificed and saved for. It was their gift to her. She slid it onto her hand, and for the first time in a month felt comfortable.

"What is taking you so long?" Boney asked, as Sister Mary emerged from behind her curtain.

"Just getting some things in order," she answered.

"Good." Boney led his pitcher out to the dugout. "Uh — how do you feel about the knuckleball today?"

"Inspired," she said and walked on ahead.

"I hope so," Boney muttered under his breath, "because I'd hate to give those White Sox boys batting practice."

As Bernie went to throw a few warm-up tosses in the bullpen, Moss approached Boney, who was watching his prized pitcher throw.

"Is she any better than last night?" Moss asked.

"I don't know if she's any better, but she sure is different." Boney scratched his head.

"Bernie." Moss walked over to his pitcher. "How are you doing today?"

"Good. Really good."

"Regardless of what I may have said or thought earlier, you should know that you belong out here on this field. Now I want you to go out today and give those batters a taste of some fire and brimstone. Okay?"

Sister Mary nodded, a little perplexed as to exactly how to react to a pep talk. Moss returned to the dugout and his search for the missing catcher.

"Play ball!" The umpire called from behind home plate.

Becky Larson was the first person in the stands to see that Dean's number, 32, wasn't on the batting order that flashed up on the big screen in the outfield. She had no idea what the problem was, but she knew it must be bad for her father to miss this game. She quickly returned her attention to the game as Hardcastle, the White Sox starter, had already finished off the top of the first.

Andejar Morales started at catcher for Dean. Sister Mary gave him five warm-up pitches then called him out to the mound.

"I want you to do me a favor," she said.

"What?" Andejar asked.

"All we're doing is throwing knuckleballs today, all right?"

"But the coach said —"

"Trust me." Her presence overwhelmed him, and he nodded. Andejar ran back to the catcher's spot and knelt, as the first batter came up to the plate.

Sister Mary Bernadette crossed herself and looked skyward. She whispered something and returned to the game. She had no idea history was in the making as she came set and launched her first knuckleball of the evening. It danced right to left, then up and down. Andejar swallowed hard as the fear of trying to corral a pitch with this much movement jarred him. The batter swung and missed, strike one.

Andejar snapped the ball back to the pitcher. He shared a look with the batter and the umpire. All three had never seen a knuckler dance that much. Unfortunately for the White Sox, the movement continued throughout the rest of the game. Fortunately for the White Sox, their pitcher matched Sister Mary's effort.

Over the first eight innings, the game was a pitcher's duel. Hardcastle gave up two hits, one of which he erased with a double play in the top of the fifth. Sister Mary issued a walk in the bottom of the third. That was it. Through eight innings, Sister Mary had thrown no-hit ball.

In the press box as the ninth inning approached, Johnny LePlant sidled up to Amy Springer.

"Got a hot story for tomorrow, want to hear?" Johnny asked.

"Something must be wrong. You never share." Amy countered.

"This is something special. I'm going to break it at the press conference after the game."

"You want to tell me, tell me. If not, get out of my face."

"It's the sad, unfortunate tale of adultery between a major league player and a member of the press. Sleeping his way into headlines, how does that sound?"

Amy didn't answer.

Johnny continued. "And the twist, well you probably aren't going to believe it, but a nun may be implicated in a cover up."

Amy walked off to another section of the press box and never looked back at Johnny. She was ruined. Johnny would bury her on national TV after the game. Her options were to walk now and delay the inevitable, or have it land in her lap immediately. She watched Hardcastle warm up. She loved baseball. She loved being a reporter. There was no use delaying the truth, and maybe, just maybe, it would be lost in the glory of crowning a new champ. That's what she told herself, but she didn't believe it. Juicy stories always trump actual sports triumphs.

In the top of the ninth, Hardcastle got two quick outs. He bore down on the scowling third baseman, Link Molansky. On a two-one count, Hardcastle left a curveball over the middle of the plate. Link deposited the pitch over the left field wall. The Memorials led one to nothing, going into the bottom of the ninth with Bernie still in control, the no-hitter still intact. That's when Dean Larson showed up.

"Where have you been?" Moss yelled at his catcher.

"I had to take care of — of my marriage," Dean stammered.

"That's fine, just great. This is game seven of the World Series. Do you realize that?"

"Yes, I do."

"He's gone insane, completely nuts." Moss turned his back.

"I want to play the ninth." Dean asked.

"You don't show up. You don't leave word, and now you just want to walk onto the field and play?" Moss threw his hands up. "I don't think so."

"Please, coach. This last inning is important." Dean's voice was low.

Moss looked at his catcher. Bernie approached from the far end and whispered something into the manager's ear. Moss stroked his chin several times.

"Moss, we got to put some players on the field." Boney called.

"All right, but you better not mess this up." Moss barked.

Dean Larson took the field with everybody else. Somewhere in the stands up above, Becky Larson sat and beamed. She didn't have to worry about her father not being there any more. Farther up, Emily stood with tears in her eyes.

Derrick Johnson of the White Sox stepped into the box as the first batter of the inning. With fans screaming their heads off, Bernie and Johnson fought a battle of foul balls and just misses to a full count. Johnson then fouled two more pitches off, before Bernie missed outside. Johnson trotted to first base with a walk.

Bernie took a moment to herself on the mound. She crossed herself. At the same time, Moss crossed himself in the dugout. She stepped onto the rubber to face Joey Carmona, the second baseman. She nodded at Dean and threw the knuckleball.

Everyone in the park expected it, including Link Molansky who stood on the infield grass and sprinted off toward the plate the minute Carmona squared to bunt. Johnson tore off toward second on contact.

The ball rolled off to the first base side, so Link was neutralized. It was, in fact, Dean Larson who sprinted out from behind the plate. He barehanded the ball and looked at second base, no chance. Dean took the out at first.

Robin Brooks, the third baseman, took his stance and eyed the knuckleballer. Bernie's first pitch hung out like a ball on a tee for a second, just off the inside part of the plate. Brooks jumped all over it and pulled the pitch. A screaming ground ball jumped out to the gap between second and first. The crowd began to yell.

Tommy Chang flew into the hole out of nowhere. His body extended in a full dive, as his glove reached out and stabbed at the ball. He quickly slid up to his knees and flipped a throw to Vitamin. They beat Brooks by half a step. The no-hitter remained, but Derrick Johnson now stood on third. Time was called, and Moss made the slow walk to the mound.

"How are you doing?" Moss asked.

"I'm fine," Bernie responded.

"You know who's due up?"

"Yeah," Bernie and Dean responded together.

"I realize you got the no-hitter here, but one mistake costs us the game." Moss looked into Bernie's eyes.

"I will end this game," Bernie stated.

"But will you win it?" Moss asked.

"Let her pitch, Moss," Dean said.

"You saw the last hitter. This is Freddy Tuggs, the best hitter in baseball." Moss looked at his catcher.

"I trust her." Dean's voice was so sure that Moss stepped back.

The only other time Moss had stood in the ninth inning of a
World Series about to win, he had to watch it snatched away. He
looked into Bernie's face and remembered all she had meant to this
team. He knew the smart thing was to pull her, but today Moss was
about to find out what happens when you give the ball to your
number one pitcher and let her decide the outcome.

"All right, she stays." Moss walked away. He stood on the top
step on the dugout and emptied a bottle of antacids into his mouth
and chewed. He knew he had gambled the fortunes of twenty-five
players on his own past, but that's why they called him coach.

Bernie walked around the back of the mound as Tuggs
approached the plate. She paused and stood absolutely still for at
least five seconds. After that, she motioned for Dean to come to the
mound.

Dean jogged out to the mound and took off his catcher's mask.
"You want to go through the signs again?"

"No," Bernie said confidently. "You might say I already got the
call."

"I haven't called for anything yet."

"I know," Bernie said, a little less confident this time. "But I
didn't want you to be surprised."

"Bernie," Dean asked cautiously. "What are you going to
throw?"

Bernie looked up at the catcher and smiled, "The screwball."

Dean almost fell over. "The screwball? You haven't thrown a
screwball all year."

"He's not going to expect it."

"No, he's not, and you're not going to throw it."

"Yes, I am."

"No, you are not!" Dean was not going to let her make this
mistake.

"Do you remember in spring training when you asked me to
throw a curve, even when I thought it was the worst move in the
world?"

"Yeah," Dean answered.

"I'm asking for the same right now."

Dean waited on the mound. She was right about having faith in
teammates, but this was almost too much. He couldn't let this
happen, could he?

"Okay, Bernie, give me your best screwball," Dean said as he turned and trotted back toward home.

Bernie set herself on the rubber and stared in at Dean. She kicked and threw. It was not the regular short step, but a full windup with a whip-like arm motion. The entire stadium froze as the ball spun first one way and then back the other. The biggest problem was the ball was going too far back the other way. It slid off and just out of a diving Dean Larson's reach. As the ball rolled to the backstop, the electricity leaped as Derrick Johnson broke from third.

Dean dug his cleats into the grass as the ball stopped ten feet back and off to the left. Bernie bolted for home out of instinct.

Dean slid as he reached the ball. He snatched it with his bare hand and snapped the throw off in one motion. Derrick Johnson was five feet away from tying the game and was closing fast. Bernie reached the plate.

The ball, the runner and the pitcher met at the same moment on the third base side of home. Johnson never saw Bernie standing before him as a nun. Instead, she was the difference between him and a World Series ring. Bernie even said later that it was a legal play, even though she didn't really remember it.

The collision between ball, Johnson and Bernie sent the pitcher flying five feet back. For her, the game went black. The umpire quickly ran to the nun after Johnson stepped on home plate. He scanned the mitt carefully and found what he was looking for.

"Out!!!" The call echoed throughout the stadium. The fans went silent, as the Memorials leapt onto the field and gathered around Bernie, the proud owner of a no-hitter in World Series play. Somewhere in Moss Thompson's stomach, an antacid finally hit the right spot and for the first time in ten years, his stomach didn't ache.

The trainers from both teams quickly rushed to Bernie's side. They called for a gurney. The entire crowd waited as minute after minute passed. Finally, down on the field, Sister Mary Bernadette's hand begin to move. Soon she was sitting, still woozy but fully aware of the miracle that had just happened.

In the press box, Amy Springer never looked back at Johnny as the crew descended to the room for the press conference. The "no press in the locker rule" was still in effect, so everybody would have to wait. Johnny enjoyed that. He would have a captive audience for his breaking story.

Chapter 54

In the locker room, everyone congratulated everyone. Champagne flowed, and it was announced that Bernie was the Series MVP. Through all the partying, no one could find the offensive hero of the day. Where was Link Molansky?

In a dark hallway near the press conference room, Johnny LePlant walked alone. He practiced all the different ways to ask his question. How should he say it?

"Isn't it true, Sister Mary Bernadette, that you had full knowledge of an affair between Amy Springer and Dean Larson?" He smirked. That's when the hand grabbed his shirt collar and slapped his back up against the wall. In the dim light, he could see the stone cold face of one Link Molansky.

"Hello, Johnny," Link whispered fiercely.

"What are you doing? Let me go!" Johnny commanded.

"I don't think so, tough guy. You see, you plan on going in there and destroying one of the best moments anybody could ever have, and that ticks me off."

Johnny struggled against the grip. "Tell your friends to watch themselves then."

"I don't think anything happened."

"How would you know?"

"I have a friend at a certain hotel who knows a room service waiter. Seems some sleazeball paid this waiter off to get the goods. I did some checking this afternoon. I don't think you've got a story outside of innuendo."

"That's enough," Johnny spit back.

"Maybe it is. Then again, maybe it might not be worth it to you." Link strengthened his grip.

"What do you mean?"

"I might be forced to tell everyone about my personal dealings with you." Link's stare never varied. "How would the world like to know about the beginning of the year? Do you think the boys would get a kick out of how you used to bring me quotes that you wrote for me to say that blasted the nun? Or how about if I tell them that you asked me for the keys to that Winnebago, so you could sneak in and surprise the nun in her dressing room?"

"That would ruin you."

"Yeah, it would. But trust me, I'll do it."

"I don't believe you." Johnny glared back.

"It's your call. But if I were you, I'd ask myself one question. Do I look like a man who bluffs?" Link dropped the reporter and walked off.

"Why do you care about any of this?" LePlant called out.

Link stopped and turned around. "The nun is my teammate and — my friend. I don't have a lot of those. Most people end up being fake, like you, but whatever she is, she is no phony." With that, Link disappeared and Johnny was left to his decision.

The press conference started soon after with a few perfunctory questions. The entire team stood in the room and faced the army of reporters. Amy eyed Johnny, who was standing near the front, sweating. Finally, he couldn't take it anymore.

"Dean! Dean!!" Johnny called. The room fell quiet. Link eyed the reporter. Amy closed her notebook and prepared for the worst. Dean Larson put his hand to his ear to listen.

"Where were you —" Johnny stopped and cleared his throat. "Where were you during innings one through eight?"

"I was putting the finishing touches on this," Dean cleared his throat. "I am announcing my retirement from baseball. I realized today I have some pressing demands on my time that need to be met. Most notably, my daughter, Becky."

Johnny started to put up his hand again, but then caught the cold hard stare of Link Molansky. Johnny decided not to ask his question and said nothing for the rest of the press conference.

Dean's retirement was the biggest scoop of the night. While there were many other story lines, from Moss and Boney finally getting a championship to Link's series heroics, Sister Mary

Bernadette was perhaps the only person in the room that saw another significant event. Amy Springer, beat reporter for the Memorials, left the celebration early. Sister Mary understood.

Chapter 55

Soon after the game, Moss learned that his pitching ace wasn't returning to the team for the next year. Apparently, in the moments of her blackout after being leveled at home, she'd had another vision. It only added to the assurance she'd felt when she put her old mitt on again. She had a new mission from the Virgin Mary, and that meant going back to the little parish in Wanuga, Nebraska. Buddy, Boney and Moss tried for weeks to talk her out of it, but they failed. Bernie tried to reach Amy before she left, but the reporter was unavailable.

Dean moved back to Minnesota, where he got a job coaching a small Lutheran college team near his home. Emily and Dean worked very hard at things and saved a marriage and a family.

Johnny LePlant never did tell anybody what he knew. He changed to basketball for the next year as his sole sport to cover. He wanted to put baseball behind him, especially after he checked out what Bernie was doing on those secret trips to North Carolina. A utility infielder named Toby Haynes played triple A ball there, and Bernie had spent some time teaching him the knuckleball. The very next season, Toby Haynes returned to the big leagues as the fifth starter for the Washington Memorials.

Judge Vincent Black's ruling on press in the locker room was reversed the following winter. The reporters all lauded the new ruling and immediately began planning what they would do with access again.

The repairs to St. Francis Catholic Church in Wanuga, Nebraska, were finished in the late fall. It was a glorious rebirth for the building and a source of great pride in the community. The repairs also included a tall net to catch many of the foul balls resulting from

Sister Mary's new endeavor.

The vision that had Bernie received took shape the following March. It was a co-ed baseball camp. Among the instructors who stopped by to visit that dusty diamond next to the St. Francis Church in Wanuga, Nebraska, were Moss, Link and Boney. Bernie was the main draw, however. She was the first woman to win the Cy Young award, the first to win rookie of the year and the first to get World Series MVP. Her first camper was Becky Larson, who spent several hours learning to throw the knuckleball.

Bernie's camp closed on a Wednesday. On Thursday, Sister Mary Bernadette returned to her duties as a nun. These included boiler maintenance in the basement, teaching Sunday School and coaching the Wanuga Little League team, the only club she liked more than the Washington Memorials.

On an early summer evening, Sister Mary called practice and sent her little league team home. She watched as the kids packed all the equipment into two large bags. After they were gone, she raked the infield. When she got to the pitcher's mound, she paused. Sister Mary Bernadette toed the rubber and closed her eyes. She heard the crowd roar and the sound of a baseball hitting leather. Then she felt a baseball roll up and hit her ankle.

"What?" Sister Mary opened her eyes. She reached down and picked up the ball.

"I suppose a game of catch is totally out of the question," Amy Springer called out from near first base. She wore blue jeans, tennis shoes and a baseball mitt.

Bernie turned the ball over in her hands. "Not necessarily." She quickly ran to the dugout and produced her tattered mitt, now of World Series fame.

The two women moved deeper into the infield and began to toss the ball back and forth.

"How are you?" Sister Mary asked.

"I still get out of bed every day and read what I wrote about the previous night's game."

"That's good."

"Johnny never pursued the whole Dean fiasco. How did you manage that?"

"I really don't know, but the Lord does work in mysterious

ways," Bernie offered.

"I guess I should thank Him for that."

"Couldn't hurt."

"You couldn't have let anything happen between Dean and me, could you?" Amy asked.

Bernie paused as she received the toss. "No, I don't think I could've, at least, not without trying to stop it." She threw the ball back.

"I'm still mad about that." While Amy's words may have been hard, her tone was that of a person who had had come to accept recent history.

"I know."

"I bet you're still mad at me for wanting it to happen?"

"I was never mad at you, Amy. No one is perfect."

"Even if I told you that I still wish it had worked out?"

"You're my friend," Sister Mary smiled. "Nothing can change that."

"I realize it's over. Dean and I haven't spoken since game seven, and I don't think we ever will again. I would have had the affair, you know."

"Maybe that's why you met me." Sister Mary's voice was comforting.

Amy shook her head. "It's very difficult to hate you. Believe me, I've tried."

Sister Mary laughed. "It's my cross to bear."

"No, I think it's mine."

"You're pretty likable yourself," Sister Mary laughed.

"So interesting you should mention that. You see, I have a favor to ask you."

"Name it," Sister Mary replied.

"I've got a publisher who wants me to do a book on last year's rookie of the year."

Sister Mary chuckled to herself. "I think it's a pretty boring idea for a book."

"So do I." Amy grinned. "But a book deal is a book deal."

Sister Mary caught the next toss from Amy and held the ball. She surveyed her friend in the fading light of the early evening. A breeze swept across the field and filled the nun with joy. "All right, let's do a book."

"Now, who do we have here?" The voice crackled from the visitor's dugout. Father Michael stood next to the players' bench and eyed the two women playing catch.

"Father Michael, this is my friend, Amy Springer."

"Pleased to meet you," Father Michael smiled said as he tottered up to shake hands.

"It's lucky you should come out right now, Father." Sister Mary went on. "Amy wants to write a book about me."

"Oh really?" Father Michael's eyes lit up jovially.

"And you are just the person she needs to talk with."

Amy caught the ball and held it. "And why is that?" She threw the ball back to Sister Mary.

"If you want the whole story, you've got to start at the beginning." Sister Mary led Amy over to Father Michael.

Father Michael cleared his voice as Amy Springer took a tape recorder from a pocket and turned it on. "This is very important to remember young lady," Father Michael began. "Sometimes a miracle begins with a mistake."

Mary Theobald

David Hanson lives in Shawnee, Kansas, with his wife, two children and pet goat named Reckless. He is the author of several theater works, a few screenplays and the sports humor book, *101 Reasons to Hate Dennis Rodman*. *The Spring Habit* is his first novel.

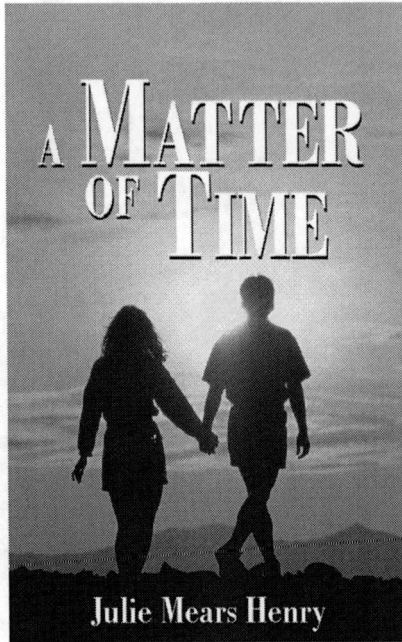

Enjoy these books available from Ad Lib Books, LLC

Fiction Books	Price	Quantity ordered	Total
A Matter of Time *by Julie Mears Henry*	$10.99		
The Spring Habit *by David Hanson*	$11.99		
Poetry Books			
The Longest Breath *by Greg Field* published by The Mid-America Press	$10.00		
From Ink and Sandalwood *by Cecile Franking* published by The Mid-America Press	$10.00		
Telling of Bees and Other Poems *by Ronald W. McReynolds* published by The Mid-America Press	$10.00		
Dreaming the Bronze Girl *by Serena Hearne* published by The Mid-America Press	$10.00		
Red Silk *by Maryfrances Wagner* published by The Mid-America Press	$10.00		
Promises in the Dust *by Bill Bauer* published by BkMk Press	$10.00		

SHIPPING

Number of Books	S&H
One Book	$2.00 USD
Two Books	$3.00 USD
Three Books	$3.50 USD
Four Books	$4.00 USD
More than Four Books add $.50 for each additional book	

Subtotal:_____

Shipping: _____

Missouri residents add .077250

Sales Tax _____

Total:_____

Your shipping information:

Name:_____

Address:_____

City:_____ State:_____ Zip:_____

Make checks payable to Ad Lib Books.
Return this order form with payment to:
Order Department, Ad Lib Books, LLC,
217 E. Foxwood Dr., Raymore, MO 64083